COFFEE IN CASTILLO

Shona Silverman

Coffee In Castillo

Cover artwork by Xael A Mottier

ISBN 979-863628347-8

Prologue

She reached the door and hesitated, one hand outstretched. The black heat washed around her body, its streamers licked over her skin and enveloped her in the velvet caress of a Mediterranean night. She felt the button under her finger tip, heard the muffled chime of a distant bell. In a bright rectangle of light the door opened. He was there, right in front of her, staring. She watched, faintly satisfied to see his eyes sweep down. That much had not changed, then. She found herself staring back. Cool air sneaked out through the doorway, chilling the bareness of her legs before slipping away and losing itself amongst the sleeping trees. He had been taking care of himself, still firm with masculinity that towered confidently upon muscled thighs. Would he still want her? She straightened up, remembering what her friend had said about posture. Shoulders back, chest out.

'So can I come in?' she asked. Her voice cracked, betraying her with a nervous squeak that interrupted the battle between the muggy night outside and the coolness of his home beyond that doorway.

He seemed surprised, guilty as he tore his eyes from her body and looked up at her face. 'Yes... yes, of course,' he replied.

The door closed again, cutting off the rasping overtures of the cicadas. The air conditioning rushed, its chill slipping over their bodies as she reached to kiss him.

Chapter One

Abbey parked the little white hire car on the boulevard. It was spring, before the crowds of summer families filled Castillo, and there was still plenty of space. Across the road, a row of shops and cafés faced the sea. Abbey crossed and walked a little way along. Café tables, round, simple and encircled with empty chairs, sprinkled the pavement. Abbey entered the first café that she reached.

'Hay servicios?' she asked the waiter. Her Spanish was terrible, she had just memorised a few words and phrases really. Still, it was enough to ask crudely for the bathroom. When she came back out into the sunlight she was feeling considerably less hurried. Impulsively, she decided to have coffee. It was a very small café, with maybe half a dozen tables set out under colourful umbrellas that flapped and fussed in the warm breeze. She sat down at one of the empty tables and ordered her drink. She smiled to herself when the waiter brought it to her, satisfied that she had achieved at least that much with her embarrassingly stilted attempts to speak the language. It was late in the afternoon and around her the other tables were empty, except for one man. She was sure that he hadn't been there when she hurried in. She sat back a little and tried to watch him without being noticed. He lifted a cup to drink, turning slightly towards her. Had he seen her? She could not turn away now, that would be too obvious. Abbey's eyes drifted down to his hands. In one he held an open book. A trickle of blue smoke rose from a slim cigar in the other. Abbey strained to see what he was reading.

'Hello!'

Abbey gasped when he spoke, at once embarrassed that she had been caught staring yet relieved to hear an English voice so far from home. He turned to face her, removing his sunglasses. He had intelligent eyes set confidently in a well-tanned, rather angular face. Perhaps his short, dark hair was just starting to get a little thin on top. It didn't matter. He was compelling, his symmetrical face finishing in the squareness of a neat jawline.

'Hello. I, um, I was just...' Abbey struggled to find something to say. Should she apologise for staring? That did not seem right. He was English, yet still she was struggling to speak to him. His eyes twinkled green as he watched her fumbling. He seemed to be waiting for her response. '...I was just wondering what you are reading,' she managed to say at last.

'Oh, this! It's nothing really.' The man closed his book, laid it down on the table and pushed it away as if to emphasise his point. He waved his hand at the chair next to him. 'Why don't you come and sit here? It will be much easier to talk.'

Abbey hesitated, then picked up her coffee and did as he suggested.

'So, what are you doing here then?' He turned to face her directly as he spoke.

'I'm here for Infotext.'

'Infotext? Is that a fiesta?'

'No, of course it's not,' she snorted, then immediately realised that she had fallen for his little joke. An explanation barely seemed necessary but she gave it all the same. 'We have an office in Castillo.'

'I know, opposite the station.' A wisp of smoke accompanied his words. He spoke softly, confidently.

'So, you live here then?' Abbey decided it was her turn to ask questions. She watched as he slipped his sunglasses back on.

'Yes, I suppose I do now. It's a long time since I went back. I have an apartment here.' His hand gestured again, vaguely suggesting that his home lay somewhere along the beach-front road. 'You'll have to come for a look, it's nice. Small, but nice.'

Come for a look? She didn't even know his name. 'I go back to England soon. Maybe if I visit Castillo again.'

Abbey's caution got the better of her.

He laughed, and his laugh was soft like his voice, gentle and reassuring. He turned towards the open door of the café behind him. 'Juan!'

The waiter appeared alongside them. He stared at the English woman, taking in the pale skin and blue eyes. She stared back, surprised by his rudeness. He was overweight, brown and faintly sweaty. A voice interrupted.

'Dos cafés, por favor.' Two coffees, please.

'Sí, Señor Lewis.' The waiter turned and slipped away.

'Oh, sorry, I should have introduced myself.' Lewis offered his hand to Abbey. She took it, but it was not the firm, businesslike handshake that she was accustomed to at Infotext. Sensitive, effortless, she felt his fingertips brush across the hollow of her palm as their hands separated.

'I'm Abbey,' she announced breathlessly.

'Pleased to meet you.' Both of them spoke at once, and they laughed together.

'So, what do you do at Infotext then?' enquired Lewis.

Abbey wondered how to make her answer sound at least a little glamorous. She hated being defined by what she did. It was boring, tedious, a job that sounded great but failed to deliver.

'I'm a business analyst.' Abbey blurted out the words, as if admitting to some kind of minor atrocity.

'Hey, that sounds fun.'

He could not possibly be serious, but Lewis looked like he believed his words. A disarming smile played around his lips. Abbey found herself wondering what it would be like to be kissed by them, to feel the softness of his lips against her skin as he made his way down her neck. Was that his leg touching hers under the table? The brief sensation brought her back to the present. 'No, it's very dull really,' she admitted. 'I prefer painting... when I get the chance.'

'Oh, an artist!'

'Hardly!' Abbey laughed. 'I just paint for fun. It's a

4

hobby, that's all.'

'I am a writer,' Lewis offered.

Abbey nodded, waiting for him to fill in the details.

Lewis lit another cigar and spent a couple of minutes watching people passing. It was getting busy and the sun was casting longer shadows. 'Do you like people-watching?' he asked casually.

Abbey nodded emphatically. 'Yes, I love it. I could do it for hours.' All those people, every one of them unique, each with their own story. A man in blue overalls passed by, carrying a little step-ladder. A young woman went the other way, carrying herself lightly. Everything she wore looked expensive, from the sunglasses on her face to the shoes that clicked as she skipped. She looked so carefree, like nothing in the world mattered.

'Jackie!' Lewis called out to her as she passed. Jackie spun round and danced across. She arrived at the table in a couple of strides and her eyes were laughing. Lewis addressed her as he waved his hand. 'This is Abbey. She's an artist.'

Abbey made to interrupt him, then changed her mind. He was talking to Jackie in English and it was obvious that they were long-standing friends.

'Join us. We're going to have cakes.' Lewis was standing. He drew up a chair for Jackie. She ignored it, her eyes sweeping over Abbey as she weighed up Lewis' new friend. Jackie's thick, sweet perfume filled the air.

'I'd love to, you know that. I have to get home. Maybe tomorrow?' Jackie's voice rose in pitch, turning the statement into a question.

'Ok, tomorrow then,' Lewis laughed, reflecting Jackie's easy optimism.

Jackie tossed a parting smile at Abbey and Lewis as she skipped away. They turned back to their coffee. A plate of assorted cakes had appeared on the table. Juan must have brought them out unnoticed.

'Oh, I can't,' protested Abbey.

'Why ever not?' Lewis challenged.

'Because... because...' Abbey glanced down at her belly and Lewis followed her gaze. She wore business trousers, grey and cream. Her work blouse, off-white and tight over the two rounds of her breasts, hid the rest. 'Because I'll get fat!'

'Fat? You?' Lewis spat out his coffee. 'You don't need to worry just yet!'

Abbey began to relax a little, allowing the inner tension to subside. She chose a cake and looked up into those green eyes again. She could feel his gaze drawing her, pulling her in. The sun was so low that its evening caress licked his face. She dreamed of doing the same, imagined him taking her in his strong arms. The orange rays warmed their skin as their faces moved closer together. Perhaps it had been worth coming to Spain on business after all. Now she could smell the spice of his aftershave. Infotext could wait.

'Oh my God!' shrieked Abbey, leaping up. 'I have to meet my boss at seven. It's already half-past!'

'It's ok, Abbey. You're in Spain now. Half an hour is nothing,' said Lewis calmly.

'No, Lewis. You don't know Vanessa. She'll be so angry... again.' Abbey pictured Vanessa's face, narrow and pale with those horrible skinny lips pursed and her cheeks sucked in. 'I have to go. I'm sorry.'

She took a few steps away, then glanced back for a second. The tables were filling up with evening diners and Juan was bustling about taking orders. Lewis was already picking up his book again. Above the café entrance, the blue awning was lettered in white. Cafetería de la Luz. The café of light.

The day dragged. It was Friday and everything had to be settled, put to bed. It was chilly in Infotext's Castillo offices and Abbey shivered. The meeting went on and on. Papers rustled on the big round table as the conference closed at last. Abbey burst out of the building into the warmth of the evening air. The sun was already nestling in the hills behind Castillo, throwing up golden rays that decorated the mountain's crown of clouds. She glanced at her watch as she crossed the road to her car. Ten to eight. Her heart sank as she climbed in and started the engine. Surely he'd be gone by now, even if he had been there at all. She turned the car around and was soon back on the coast road again, heading to Cafetería de la Luz. It was busy on the road, and it took until nearly eight thirty to get there. The shops and cafés were buzzing with life. Spaniards thronged the pavement and a constant stream of cars was passing. Her heart was pounding as she parked the tiny car. She got out. The shadows cast by the buildings stretched across the road and reached her side. She crossed over, already searching the faces at the tables. It was so busy that there was barely an empty seat. She got closer, pressing through the bustle. A woman bumped her shoulder.

'Abbey! Hola!' Hello. The woman slipped her sunglasses off, revealing her identity. It was Jackie, casually dressed in impossibly new looking jeans. The women paused briefly, each assessing the other. Jackie broke the awkward impasse. 'Lovely to see you again, Abbey. I wondered if you'd be back.' She spoke easily, with no trace of guile.

'I was looking for somewhere to eat,' explained Abbey.

'Well, here you are. La Luz is the best. Anyway, must rush!' Jackie threw the last few words over her shoulder as she left.

Abbey approached the café with unexpected nerves fluttering inside. If Jackie was around then Lewis might be close by too. There he was, seated at the same table.

'Abbey, come on, I was waiting for you.' Lewis smiled, his head haloed by the amber rays of the setting sun. He pulled out a chair for her. She sat down in a heated fog of childish excitement, momentarily embarrassed that she had allowed herself to get so carried away. 'Would you like coffee?' Lewis was asking her, leaning towards her slightly so that his soft voice could be heard above the café's background babble.

'Yes, Lewis. Thank you,' Abbey replied automatically. Empties from at least a couple of rounds of coffee already lay cold in front of them on the table. 'What's this?' Abbey picked up a magazine that lay alongside the cups.

'That's for you,' stated Lewis rather matter-of-factly. 'I thought that you might like to read it.'

Abbey picked up the magazine and flicked it open. Incredibly thin fashion models with fantastic tans stared back at her. *It's all in Spanish*, she thought. 'No-.' Abbey just managed to pinch back the words before she pronounced her dismissive thoughts aloud. Politeness was probably best. 'Thank you, Lewis, I'll read it later.'

Abbey watched Lewis's face, where mischief played and twinkled in his eyes. Realisation dawned upon her. 'Lewis, how did you know?' she ventured.

'Know what? That you would come here again?'

'Yes. You were waiting for me, weren't you? How did you know I would come back again today?'

'I just knew you'd come back,' he said simply. 'Juan?' Lewis was already looking around, searching for the waiter. An arm reached around, clearing the table then placing fresh coffee and a large plate in front of them. 'Gracias, Juan.' Thank you.

'Tapas?' Abbey looked at Lewis, questioning the plate of marvellously colourful and varied treats.

He nodded, amused at her naivety. He softened again quickly. 'Yes, Abbey. This is tapas. Welcome to Spain.'

The aeroplane gained height, climbing quickly away from the twinkling lights of Castillo. Soon they were left behind and Abbey sat in a little bubble of thought with the roar of the engines and the fidgeting of other passengers for company. It had not been a successful business trip.

They had failed to get the agreements that they needed and the post mortem with the directors on Monday was going to be horrible. Abbey was preoccupied, not with the meeting but with Lewis. His face seemed to be etched into her vision. Wherever she looked she saw those emerald eyes in that tanned, friendly face. Idly she wondered what would happen next. That was when it hit her. Apart from his first name, she knew nothing about him. Nothing. The captain's tinny voice filled the cabin. Slow, authoritative and utterly without emotion, he described the weather forecast for their destination. England was rainy, cloudy and cold. Abbey shivered. It would be a miserable journey home.

'I said, is it ready yet?'
An insistent voice brought Abbey back to the reality of her office with a jolt. Instinctively, she looked to see where the question came from. She swept back her long brown hair, stunned with surprise and shame.
'What? Oh, the report. Yes, Vanessa. It's ready.' Abbey could feel herself blushing as she spoke. It always gave the game away. Of course the report wasn't ready, she'd been daydreaming again, her mind drifting off to somewhere better. She had to admit the truth. 'Well, it's nearly ready, Vanessa.'
Vanessa did not answer. Thin, stick-like, she stamped away. Abbey stared at the screen, her blue eyes stinging with tears. She hoped that no-one would notice behind her glasses. Abbey didn't wear much make-up, just lipstick and a touch of perfume. She didn't mind wearing the glasses when she was working. People told her that her round face looked better with them than without, and it was probably true. She sighed unhappily. There was always so much to do, it was never ending. And it was so dull. Outside, the rain of the late English spring lashed down from a low grey sky. Abbey's mind was already drifting again, back to Spain, the sun and the blue sky. *What is he doing now?* she

wondered.

Freshened from its passage over the sea, a warm breeze played through the terrace of Lewis' apartment. He was sitting in the shade, a computer propped on his knees. He typed words rapidly on the keyboard, watching them appear on the screen, flowing and melding at his behest. A squawking sound interrupted his thoughts. Tanned face uplifted, his eyes followed a small flock of bright green parrots as they settled in the top of a palm tree. Absent-mindedly, he drew on a little cigar. Its smoke joined the wind, thinning and dispersing as it was carried away towards the hills that lay behind Castillo.

'Día!'

Lewis' housekeeper greeted him as she breezed in with a warm smile and a new mop. Short in height and broad in waist, she never said more than was necessary. Even her greeting was the shortest possible way of saying good day. She brushed past him, then turned and came back.

'What is wrong, señor?' She had noticed something about him, something sad and distant in those intelligent green eyes. Gabriela was a proper Spanish woman, motherly and direct. Her black, wiry hair was filling with grey and her face was dark and lined with the years of care. Her onyx eyes scrutinised Lewis, searching for an answer. 'You are thinking about her again, aren't you, Lewis?'

'Sí. Yes. I am thinking about her. I was wondering...' He answered her in fluent Spanish, only his accent betraying his English roots. 'I was wondering what she is doing now.'

'Maybe you will see her again. I can feel it... quizás.' Perhaps. Gabriela's voice tailed off as she spoke. She picked up her mop and left Lewis alone on the terrace with just his thoughts, the warm breeze and a little cigar for company. He turned back to his computer.

Every day was duller than the last. Abbey used to love her job, but now she could barely face each new morning. Nothing had been right since the divorce. Her beautiful house was gone. She rented someone else's sorry semi-detached house and drove a tatty, ageing car. It was already rusting and it only had two doors. Just two doors! Small things mattered to Abbey. A lot of these irritations seemed to come from her boss. Vanessa was always sniffing and making those silly tum-tee-tum noises. She interrupted Abbey all the time, checking on progress God knows how many times every day. Sometimes, Vanessa came over to Abbey to discuss a piece of work, but it was just an excuse to check up on her yet again, to see that she was working instead of daydreaming.

Perhaps Vanessa had a point there. Abbey was always daydreaming. Her mind left the office and slipped away from the grey English skies. It escaped to hot, sunny places where palm trees grew and there were no folders full of papers to analyse. She used to paint beach scenes when she was younger, fantasy-like sunsets reflected in gentle seas whose waves kissed the golden sand. *Relax, you're in Spain now. Half an hour is nothing.* Abbey remembered Lewis' words. Ah, Lewis. She had thought of little else since she got back to England. Imprinted upon her vision, his face haunted her. Like the fragrance of his drifting cigar smoke he was always there, following her, teasing her. Yet she knew so little about him. Abbey sighed. She had not had the presence of mind even to find out his surname, even less his telephone number or address. He was gone now, a lost dream.

Chapter Two

'Mum! I'm hungry!' The walls were thin and Luke's voice passed straight through them.

'Alright, in a minute!' Abbey shouted back, trying to disguise her frustration. *It's no good. This just isn't working.* She gave up, tossing her brushes into the dubious care of an old, stained pot. Washing up could wait. She stepped back from the easel and bumped against the wall. The smallest bedroom in Abbey's house was unworthy of its name. If you put a bed in there then you would not be able to close the door, let alone move around. As an artist's studio it was hopelessly cramped, but better than nothing. To paint, she needed to have her heart in it, to be fully engaged with her creative sensations, connected with feelings that were hard to find in the airless confines of the little room. Her heart lay elsewhere and she knew it.

'When you get a minute, can you take a look at these?' The scene was Infotext's London office, the voice was owned by Vanessa and the words that she spoke formed more of an instruction than a request.

'Yes, of course I will. No problem,' replied Abbey. That was a lie. She was tired, she already had plenty of work to do and she knew that she would not get a minute to look at yet more of it. She was not sleeping well at night and by day it was hard to keep focussed on sales figures, statements and reports.

'Thank you, Abbey.' It was Vanessa's turn to lie. She was in charge and deception was just part of the job. The office full of workers was there to serve her, to carry out her instructions and deliver results. For her, truth and honesty were irrelevant.

Vanessa was a terrible nuisance even on a good day. She took a devilish delight in her role as manager. It was not just Abbey that suffered as a result, everyone in the office fell victim to Vanessa's morale-crushing control. Her all-seeing radar left no-one in peace for a minute. As a result, they had all become quite adept at looking busy. If any slacking showed through, even for a moment, Vanessa would be right there in an instant. It was a well-rehearsed show. She stood by the victim, swept back her ridiculously dyed blonde hair to reveal her pinched face, then launched her attack. She always wore far too much make-up for work. The smell of it went ahead of her, advance warning that she was approaching to discharge another pile of folders and unload more work onto some unlucky wretch.

'Thank you, Vanessa,' Abbey said slowly and deliberately, taking another fat green folder of paperwork from her. 'I'll get on to it as soon as the Germany figures are done.' Abbey was lying again. She did not want any more work, she had too much already. Today, Abbey seemed to be catching more than her fair share of Vanessa's attention. She took a great deal of care to keep staring at the screen, doing lots of needless tapping and typing. Still, Vanessa seemed to be visiting her desk hourly.

'Abbey,' cautioned Vanessa, 'I'm waiting for the Spanish report too.'

Abbey just nodded and turned back to her screen. Report this, report that, report the other. It passed the time and paid the bills, that's all. She huffed, stood up and shouldered her bag. It was time to meet Debbie for lunch.

'Hey, Abbey, shall we sit outside today?' Debbie was cheerful and red-cheeked as she greeted Abbey. 'It should be warm enough if we keep out of the wind.'

'Here?' suggested Abbey as they rounded the corner. Behind the building, the ground sloped upwards forming a sheltered, grassy embankment.

'Yes.' Debbie was already sitting on the grass and unwrapping a triangular pack of sandwiches. 'I've got cheese today.'

'You always have cheese.'

'No, I don't.'

'Alright, nearly always then.'

'Well, it's easier to make cheese sandwiches. You just butter the bread, grate some cheese and shove it in. Done!' Debbie explained with a laugh.

'What is it like in Accounts?' asked Abbey, moving on to a new and more important subject.

'In what way?'

'Well, is everyone happy? Do you like it there?'

'Yes, I suppose so. What about you?'

'I hate it,' said Abbey sullenly. 'Every minute of it. Vanessa keeps giving me more stuff to do. She wants the Spanish report.' Abbey took a bite of her bread roll. 'She's right, though.'

'Who's right? Why?' Debbie was finding it difficult to follow Abbey's rambling.

'Vanessa. I should have finished the Spanish report for her a week ago.'

'And?'

'And nothing. It doesn't matter anyway. The figures are going to be terrible.' Abbey checked her watch. Half an hour was far too short a break. 'You know, they take two hours for lunch in Spain,' she observed.

'Two hours?' Debbie was impressed. 'But how do they get anything done?'

'Well, when I was at the Infotext office in Castillo, we stayed until seven each night.'

'That's late. No, I wouldn't like that. I mean, I'd get hungry,' frowned Debbie. Her light brown hair, cut tidily into a bob, was tucked behind her ears so that it would not annoy her by falling across the plumpness of her amiable face.

'It seemed better when they did it that way. The afternoons went faster there. Less of a drag. I don't know why really.' Pensively, Abbey munched her way through the last of her meal. Maybe it was the friendliness of the people or the welcoming brightness of the Spanish town that made the difference. The memories all mixed together into a hazy blend of chilled, modern offices and warm, busy streets. 'They were nice people,' she added, 'and I met a man.'

'A man? At Infotext?'

'No, in a café. He was from England, but he lives in Spain now. I think he's a writer.'

'Ooh,' grinned Debbie, 'that sounds exciting. What are you going to do?'

'I don't know, Debbie. I don't think I'm good enough for him.'

'What? Of course you are. You're good enough for any man!' Debbie was outraged. 'If you act good then you'll feel good. Chin up, shoulders back, chest out.' Debbie demonstrated her suggestion and her ample bosom bounced enviably.

Abbey tried it, holding her breath and thrusting her chest out in an exaggerated pose. 'Phaw!' she snorted as they both collapsed in fits of giggles.

'Well, it's a start,' laughed Debbie. She stood up and brushed the crumbs off. 'Come on or we'll be late back.'

Everyone looked up as Graham entered the office, letting the door slam behind him.

'Lovely day, isn't it?'

'Yes, glorious, great.' Everyone chorused their agreement obediently. Graham was Vanessa's boss. Bolshy, big and bald-headed, he commanded respect. Abbey felt a twinge of shame as she found herself fawning too, agreeing with his breezy, throw-away greeting just like all the others. Yes, the weather was good today - a proper English spring day with clear, pale-blue skies and fresh leaves on the trees. So Graham was correct, obviously, but it was just a greeting, a trivial everyday thing that really didn't matter. Abbey was jaded and tired of it all and she saw things differently. She took a mental step back and watched everyone, herself included. 'Yes, Graham. No,

15

Graham. Ha ha ha.' They gave him the answers that he wanted to hear and laughed politely at his recycled jokes.

'Vanessa, we need to talk,' Graham boomed. He had the kind of voice that was always set to maximum volume.

'Yes, Graham.' Vanessa's voice was smarmy. She smiled up at him, the thin lips false in their tight-pressed curve. Perhaps she was flattered to be called into a meeting with Graham. Everyone else was watching, none of them were envious. Fat and thin, the two managers left the room together and the door slammed shut behind them. Each and every one of those remaining in the office, from lowly administrator right up to international business analyst, had stopped what they were doing. They looked at each other questioningly. Something was afoot and it was soon revealed. 'Abbey?' Vanessa was already back, summoning Abbey to join the secretive meeting.

Abbey stared at the ceiling of her bedroom, wondering what terrible things were going to happen next. It had been a bad day, but she had been brave in the meeting with Graham and Vanessa. She had managed to stay calm, to avoid crying, even to be businesslike and polite. It was only her first warning and there had to be three of them before she could be dismissed. But what if it happened? Then how would she manage? How would she pay the rent and all the other bills, and feed herself and Luke? Eventually Abbey got bored with agonising about work. The same old worries just went round and round, like vultures circling a wounded animal. Her thoughts turned to love, a little trick that they always did to her sooner or later. She felt that hollow aching, saw the loneliness that stretched ever longer in her life. It was late and her room was dimly lit by a bedside lamp. She needed a distraction, something to take her mind off things.

I'll read for a while. Abbey reached under the lamp, into the little cavity of the bedside table where she pushed her books. Amongst them her fingers discovered the thin

16

limpness of a magazine. She pulled it out and slipped it into the pool of light under the lamp. It was the Spanish magazine that Lewis had given her at the café. What use was it to her? It was all written in Spanish and she had only taken it to avoid offending him. Someone had been scribbling inside the front cover. She thumbed through the pages, then opened them out at random. Apart from the unintelligible text, the pages looked much like those in any English magazine. The article staring at her seemed to be a book review, a wordy critique topped with a picture of the book's front cover. Abbey idly examined the faintly familiar image, adorned in large letters with the author's name. It was a book by Lewis Coleman.

'Lewis Coleman!' Abbey sat bolt upright in bed, panting with excitement. Could it be? She tore at the pages of the magazine, hunting for the scribbled biro. There it was, hurriedly scrawled yet perfectly legible. Lewis Coleman, a phone number, an exclamation mark. She read it again and again, making sure that it really was true. Then she closed the magazine and lay back, pressing it flat against her chest, daring to dream again.

Jackie lazed in a pleasant pool of shade under the café umbrella, relaxing in the breeze that slipped and flicked around her. Summer was coming and it could get quite hot by midday. She lit another cigarette as she watched Lewis read. It was puzzling just how many times he could do it, reading and re-reading his own work, checking for mistakes.

'How do you do it?' she enquired, raising a pair of perfectly shaped black eyebrows above the top of her sunglasses.

'Do what?' More information was needed if Jackie expected an answer.

'How do you have the willpower to keep going through it?'

'I just do it. Like you do shopping,' stated Lewis

daringly.

'You cheeky bastard! I don't 'do' shopping. And I only buy things I need.' The corners of her mouth turned up, revealing her playfulness even as she spoke. The cigarette smoke poured out with the words, softening and cloaking them. It was only social swearing and Lewis just smiled as he listened to his friend. Of course he knew that she was lying - she loved shopping and bought whatever she wanted.

'Go on then. What did you buy this morning, Jackie?'

'I bought a handbag,' she started. She stubbed out her cigarette, folding it in half in the glass ashtray. Broken, spent and discarded, it lay there amongst maybe half a dozen others.

'And...?' prompted Lewis, lifting his face and connecting directly with her.

'And a shawl. To match the handbag.'

Lewis kept silent, waiting to see if Jackie was going to add anything else to the list. He drained the last of his coffee.

'It's purple,' she said eventually. Jackie knew that purple was Lewis' favourite colour. This somehow made her shopping trip a little easier to admit to. She reached for another cigarette.

'You smoke too much,' accused Lewis.

'I do as I like,' retorted Jackie. 'You smoke cigars, so what's the problem?'

'But that is the problem,' he explained. 'You make me want to smoke more.'

Juan brought more drinks. Lighters clicked, smoke billowed, a silent truce descended. Across the boulevard, little white-tipped waves whispered as they visited the yellow sand.

'Lewis?' It was Jackie who eventually spoke first.

'Uhuh?' Lewis sipped his coffee and examined Jackie's face over the top of his cup. They always used plain white cups at Cafetería de la Luz. Juan said it was because they were cheap and Lewis kept breaking them. That was not true. Well, he had broken one cup. Jackie's face peered back at him, brown, sweet and friendly just like the coffee. 'Yes, Jackie? What's up?' he prompted again.

'I just remembered that girl.' Jackie's London accent made her comment sound somehow cheap, like one of those blue plastic disposable forks that they give away in chip shops back in England. It was an Essex accent really, but Lewis was from the Midlands. To him, every Southern accent sounded pretty much alike.

'Abbey. Yes, that's her name. Did you like her?' Jackie continued, probing a little.

'Well...' Lewis sat back and pondered. He and Jackie had known each other for a couple of years now and they had an easy friendship.

'I mean, what did you think of her hair?' The Essex twang continued, following Jackie's restless mind as it jiggled about, darting between each and any thought that happened to occur to her. 'And those eyes. Yes, I liked her eyes.' She gave her own opinion without waiting to hear his.

'Yes, I liked her eyes too,' joined Lewis, 'I noticed them straight away. So blue.'

'Anyway, she was fat,' stated Jackie flatly and quite unexpectedly.

'No she wasn't!' Lewis snorted. The insult was surprising even when it came from Jackie. She was a lovely person and she was fortunate enough to sport an enviable shape, but that did not give her any excuse to be so rude about other people. 'I didn't think she was fat at all,' challenged Lewis. 'Anyway, it was hard to tell.'

'I could tell,' insisted Jackie. 'Straight away.'

'Personally, I thought she was lovely.' Lewis spoke as if he might be revealing a special, carefully-guarded secret. His friend was quick to exploit the opportunity.

'Ha! So you do want her then!'

'I didn't say that.'

'That's what you meant.'

'No I didn't.'

'Did.'

'Did not. Juan! La cuenta?' Lewis put an end to the childish conversation by asking for the bill. The deep pool of his shadow fell across Jackie as he stood up.

'Jackie, I'm sorry, I'll have to go. I've got a lot to finish this afternoon.'

'Ok. Same time tomorrow?'

'Of course. See you.' A quick peck of a kiss on each cheek brought another lazy lunch, languid under the shade of a colourful umbrella, to a close.

Jackie turned back to her smoke-riddled pondering. Her eyes alighted on the table as she knocked off the cigarette ash. One end wedged securely under the heavy ashtray, their bill for two lunches and countless coffees fluttered expectantly.

'You bastard, Lewis,' she muttered as she dived into her new purple handbag.

'I still can't see why you want to go.' Rita was strutting about and trying to be bossy. It didn't work any more. Sensing her failure, she tried another tack. 'Why do you want to go all that way just to see a stranger?'

'He's not a stranger, Mum.' Abbey tried to discharge the energy that drove her mother's argument.

'Yes, he is.' Rita was adamant.

'No, he isn't!' Abbey sighed sadly. She didn't want to argue with her mother. At eighty two, Rita was frail and her voice kept breaking up into pathetic lumps of sound. 'Mum, take you hands off your hips and sit down,' she ordered. 'You can sit here, I've cleaned under it already.'

Rita sat down heavily in the arm chair and brushed over her lilac-tinted white hair with a skinny, blue-veined hand. 'Abbey, I'm just saying. I don't want you to get hurt.' Her eyes were distant. 'It's a long way from home, Abbey.'

Where is home? Abbey wondered. For her mother it

20

was simple. Rita lived in her flat in Calborough and that was her home. She owned it, Abbey cleaned it. Calborough was a nice village, even a bit posh. There was no litter or dog mess, and people spoke to you on the street. Abbey lived in a smelly rented house in Bullwood, a post-war urban estate. It was horrible. Abbey shivered in disgust. The contrast with Calborough could hardly be more stark and the urge to run away, regardless of whether that would be sensible or foolish, was quite compelling.

'Mum, I've told you. He's really nice. He's completely genuine and I want to see him again.' Abbey turned on the vacuum cleaner and fussed about the maroon carpet with it so that the noise drowned out her mother. Eventually she stopped and straightened up. *Why does she still treat me like a little girl?* 'Mum, I'm nearly forty!'

'Yes, Abbey, I know.'

'So why-' Abbey changed her mind and stopped. There was no point. 'Look. I'll ring you when I get there so you know I'm ok,' she suggested as she coiled up the cable and packed away the cleaner.

'Yes, love.' Rita seemed to give up the fight. 'Thank you.'

There was plenty of room to park on the road in Bullwood. The only other people on the estate that owned cars were the small-time drug-dealers who plied their shady trade in broad daylight. There was nothing to stop them, the police seemed powerless. Abbey slammed her car door and stepped over a squashed beer can on the pavement. She reached for it, then changed her mind. What was the point in picking up their litter? It would just be replaced with something else soon, dropped by mindless hands. She went inside and shut out the street. She paused at the top of the stairs, then bravely pushed the bedroom door open. She looked in across a sea of discarded pizza boxes, crumpled pop cans and God knows what else. The bed was at the end of the room farthest

21

from the door.

'Luke,' she started. There was no response. Luke, skinny and long, was folded untidily on his bed. He wore headphones that completely covered his ears. 'Luke! Stop playing that game and listen, will you?'

'Oh, it's you.' Abbey's son connected with her at last. He did something with his game controller to pause the action. The shooting and screaming noises stopped and life-like figures that were killing each other on the screen halted. The mayhem was at least temporarily suspended. 'What do you want?'

'What?' Abbey was stunned. From time to time Luke just blurted out the most thoughtlessly offensive comebacks.

'I said, what is it?' Luke looked inquiringly at her over the crumpled bed-clothes and plates of dried-up, half-eaten food. He ran his fingers through the length of his straight brown hair, crudely combing the worst of it back from his face. 'Sorry Mum, I didn't hear you come in.' He swung his legs over the edge of the bed and stood up. In a couple of steps he was alongside his mother, towering thinly over her.

'Luke, I'm going to Spain again,' she announced simply. She decided not to tell him that this time the trip was not for business. It would only complicate matters.

'Spain? What about me?'

'I'm just going for the weekend. Well, for four or five days really.'

'When?'

'Tomorrow.'

'Tomorrow!' Fear swept over Luke's face. He was twenty, but that was just a number. Luke had somehow failed to keep up with the years. 'But what will happen to me? What will I eat?'

Abbey surveyed Luke's filthy bedroom, scattered with remnants and rubbish. From the various remains, it looked like he never managed to eat more than half of each meal anyway. 'You'll have to stay with Nan. And when I get back you can tidy up this disgusting room. Honestly, it looks like a bomb-site.'

'Stay with Nan? Oh, Mum.' Luke slumped back onto his bed. He detested staying at his grandmother's. There was nothing to do, none of his things were there, it was a dead loss. And as for cleaning his room, well, that was simply unfair. 'Can't I stay here? There's nothing to do at Nan's. Do you have to go to Spain?'

'Yes, Luke. I've told you. You'll stay at Nan's, she'll look after you. And then...' she waved her hand at the dirty socks and screwed-up lottery tickets that littered the stained carpet. '...and then we'll clean your room.' She squeezed out and closed the bedroom door behind her, cutting off his protests.

The plane ticket was the cheapest that Abbey could find and of course this meant that it was for a flight which arrived at its destination at night. This time she was paying her own way and she was starting to see the cost of following her dream. *What if I get lost?* It was not just the money, thought Abbey. She had never been much good at finding her way around unfamiliar places and just thinking about the journey made her heart race with apprehension. She did not feel much happier once she arrived at the airport and actually started doing it. The place was enormous. She seemed to have walked for miles along identical corridors with endless glass walls and doors with No Entry signs on them.

'Passport please.' The young man was smooth-skinned and fresh-faced. Abbey thought that he could not be much older than Luke. He looked too youthful to be wearing that smart blue shirt and black airline tie.

'Yes, of course,' hurried Abbey, showing the airline official her document. 'I'm going to Castillo,' she added, in a nervous attempt to confirm that she really had managed to find the right boarding gate.

'Through here, Madam.'

Abbey glanced back through the glass door as she left the building. Courteous, efficient and fine-looking, the official was smiling and nodding as he waved through another gaggle of passengers. Abbey sighed. If only her life always flowed that easily. The sounds from outside faded as Abbey stepped into the plane and took her seat. It looked like a new aircraft. Everything was shiny and clean, but it had hard, thin seats that were set much too close together. *At least it's a short flight.* The doors were closed, the engines whined. Her journey back to Spain had really begun.

The sky over Castillo was inky black, pierced by stars. Although the sun had long set behind the mountain, the buildings were still alive. Their thick walls remained warm to the touch after spending another day basking. All low-rise, squat and whitewashed, the apartments lined up like huge square ghosts peering between the night trees. 46 Calle los Calamares. Number forty six, on the street of squids. *What a silly name for a road.* Abbey walked through the screen of palms and stood under the white arch that framed the doorway. Heart pounding, she pressed the door bell and waited.

Chapter Three

'I think I will try... this one.' Lewis spoke aloud as he picked the bottle up and checked the label. Vino Tinto de Castillo. Red wine, made locally from grapes grown in the vineyards that clustered along the lowest slopes of the mountain behind Castillo. He picked up two large wine glasses as he passed through the little kitchen, then stepped out into the brightness of the terrace.

'Blast.' Back into the kitchen again. A slim packet of cigarillos was still waiting patiently for him on the table. At the last moment he remembered to pick up his favourite lighter too. Fully equipped at last, he returned to the terrace and dragged two chairs into the soft rays of the late afternoon sun. He lit a cigar and poured some red wine, then settled back to wait.

'Debbie, why is Abbey away?'

Debbie looked up from her desk and a thin, puckered face stared back. *What is Vanessa doing in Accounts?*

'I don't know, Vanessa,' answered Debbie after a pause.

'Well, I'm not happy. There's a lot of overdue work and I've got no-one to do it. She should have cleared her time off with me first.'

Debbie stared at her. *Why should I tell her anything? Bitch.* 'I'm sorry, Vanessa. I don't know why she's away.' Two more words popped into Debbie's head. Together they formed a very simple way of telling the intruder to leave. It was tempting but she could not do it. 'Perhaps she arranged it with Graham,' she offered carefully. *Oh dear, that might have been the wrong thing to say.* Debbie wanted to get rid of Vanessa, but without saying anything about Abbey that would drop her in it. She smiled at her thoughts. *Drop her in it, what a strange expression.*

'Humph!' Vanessa spun round and marched out of the Accounts office, leaving a trail of bad perfume and lingering hostility behind her.

Darkness fell like a heavy cloak over Castillo. The doorbell chimed. Lewis placed his glass of wine on the terrace table and carefully balanced a half-smoked cigar on the lip of the ashtray. The bell rang again just as he got to the door. He opened it and there she was, nervously framed against the silent, darkened trees outside.

'Abbey, so good to see you again. You look great.' Lewis gushed, perfectly sincere in every word of it. He looked her up and down. She had taken the trouble to dress exactly right, not too formal yet spruce and smart enough to impress. Jackie was wrong and it only took a couple of seconds to see how unkind her comments had been. Abbey looked perfect. 'Don't stand there, come in,' beckoned Lewis.

Abbey made as if to kiss him on the lips.

'No, no, you do it like this!' exclaimed Lewis. He kissed her, quickly, on each cheek in succession. Left, right, left. 'We are friends, meeting again,' he explained as a puzzled smile lit Abbey's face. 'I know it's old-fashioned, but I like it,' Lewis continued. 'You'll get used to it. It's so... mmm... so Mediterranean.' His explanation was a little vague, but that was all he could think of. 'How was your flight?'

'Oh, it was ok. The plane was full.' Abbey stepped into Lewis' apartment. 'It was noisy for the whole flight. And the seats were uncomfortable.' Abbey regretted her words immediately. She did not want to sound like a complainer. 'But it was fine - it was nearly on time and it looked brand new.'

'That's good. You often get groups of lads on those cheap flights. It's more like a bus trip really.' Lewis reached to close the door behind her, shutting off the trees and the unseen cicadas that rasped and chirped in them all night.

'Come through to the terrace. I've opened a bottle.' He offered her one of the chairs and pushed a wine glass

26

towards her on the table.

'Oh, no. No thank you,' protested Abbey weakly.

'It's good wine. It will help you unwind a bit after your trip. I like flying, but it always wears me out. And you?'

'Yes, I suppose it tires me too.' Abbey thought for a minute, watching his face, following the leafy greenness of his lively eyes. 'But I don't like flying. I don't like it at all.' She was being perfectly honest, there was absolutely nothing about it that she liked. The airports, the queues, the cramped seats on board. She spoke her thoughts aloud. 'I hate it all.'

'Maybe you'll get used to it,' suggested Lewis. He picked up the bottle and made as if to pour from it into her glass.

'No, I... Oh, go on then, yes,' conceded Abbey. Perhaps the wine would help her to relax. She sat back a little, taking stock for a moment. Open apart from low walls on three sides, the terrace was spacious with terracotta tiles on the floor and a large roof that covered much of its area.

'It really is lovely to see you again.' Lewis broke the silence. He watched her over the rim of his wine glass, allowing his thoughts to roam. *I wonder...*

'It's very... tidy,' offered Abbey, trying to find something polite yet honest and complimentary to say.

'Oh yes. I had a quick clear up. And Gabriela always cleans on Fridays. She's my housekeeper.'

A housekeeper? Abbey felt a rush of envy flow through her. How wonderful to have a housekeeper. That must be why it was so tidy. 'I like your furniture, it's all very practical. Neat and clever.' She had been anticipating a crowded apartment, crammed with dark and ancient wooden furniture. Perhaps it might even be littered and unkempt, with dirty pots in the sink, the sort of place it would be if Luke owned it. But instead it was lovely and clean, devoid of clutter and set out with simple furniture. It was modern and functional, making the best use of the space. Considering that it was owned by a man, it seemed almost impossibly well organised.

'It's a shame that it's already dark,' said Lewis. 'If you had arrived earlier then you could have seen all of this properly in daylight.' Abbey joined Lewis as he stood at the dwarf wall along the end of the terrace. Under the night sky it was quite difficult to see what he was describing. 'The ground drops away quite quickly below here,' he explained.

'So, are there gardens here?' asked Abbey, waving her hand at the broad black band directly below. 'And then is that another row of apartments?' She could make out the squares of their flat roofs, set out along unseen roads marked by the points of yellow street lamps like a children's join-the-dots puzzle.

'Yes, that's right. But they are not like English gardens really. It's too dry in summer. Of course it can rain a lot here in winter, but we still like to have palm trees and agaves. I even have a bit of a cactus collection.' Lewis hesitated, wondering what other interests an artist and businesswoman might have. 'There are more apartments, then shops and things. There are a lot of older buildings lower down, nearer to the sea.' Lewis attempted to fill in some of the missing details and then left the rest for tomorrow.

Abbey looked out over the rooftops, taking in what she could of the view. In front, over the fairy-lights of Castillo's southern suburbs, lay the sea, a dark and silent secret. To the right, the lights petered out gradually, thinning into the night-time countryside. Looking the other way, the town's lights grew in strength and number. Bustling and busy, they rose upwards from the sea. Above them, the floodlit stone face of the castle stood proudly, admiring the town to which it gave its name.

'We could take a look around the area tomorrow if you like,' Lewis suggested. 'I'll show you everything, then you will recognise it the next time that you look from the terrace.'

'Yes, that sounds great,' Abbey replied. She looked straight at him and felt something odd inside her. What was it that drew her so powerfully to this man? She spent a few moments admiring his face. It was healthily tanned and well-proportioned. The light set into the terrace roof set shards of green fire blazing in his mischievous eyes. 'Will it be sunny tomorrow? What's the weather forecast?' Abbey asked absent-mindedly.

'Weather forecast?' Lewis laughed softly. 'Oh, we don't need to listen to the forecast. It's June now. It will be sunny every day until September.' He paused for a minute. He used to live in England too. 'Well, it will be like that nearly every day,' he admitted.

'It sounds just perfect.' Abbey's envy flickered again. 'You must love living here.'

'I like it in Spain. If I didn't then I would not have stayed. But I don't enjoy it when it's hot all the time. Luckily you sometimes get a few cloudy days.' His face brightened. 'Oh, and of course there are the storms too, especially towards the end of the summer.'

Lewis enjoyed the storms. Packed with emotion, they quietly waited on sultry afternoons, building and filling. Their towers grew, dark and foreboding, reaching above the mountains and finally descending, rushing down to lash Castillo. He liked the anticipation, then the release. In his books, he loved writing as if he were a storm, erecting a tower of emotion, decorating it with hope and charging it with jealousy. Then he would bring the tower crashing down, unleashing it, sweeping everything away in a tumultuous climax.

'Yes, I like the storms.' Lewis said quietly as he came back into the real world, to his terrace and the warm night and this beautiful woman. 'More wine?'

Abbey simply waited, her eyes following Lewis as he moved. For once she was just letting things happen to her.

'Here, let me fill your glass,' continued Lewis. He returned to the table and poured from the bottle into their glasses. Fragrance rose as the wine splashed, young and fruity.

'Thanks. No, that's enough. Too late. Oh well.' Abbey's limp protests seemed to fall upon deaf ears. Her glass was filled almost to the rim again and the bottle was empty. *Oh well, I suppose it will be alright.* 'This is good wine,' she agreed hazily, 'I like it.' She slurped at the glass noisily, but she was finding it harder and harder to care.

Lewis sipped and watched. There was no point pursuing serious conversation now. 'Is it ok if I smoke?' he asked, realising as he spoke that he may as well just get on with it. His lighter clicked, the blue smoke drifted from the terrace and lost itself in the sleepy gardens. He found himself in the store room again, bare feet cold on the hard tiles. He pulled out another bottle of the vino tinto and returned to the terrace. Abbey was still there, quiet, watching him through misty eyes. He poured and the red wine gurgled richly.

She asked about his writing, he asked about her painting. The polite carefulness of earlier faded, replaced by an easy openness as midnight came and went. He laughed as she told him about the scribbled writing in the magazine. She smiled as she recalled her nervous journey fuelled by restless energy. Its breathless promise was fulfilled. She was here now, sitting with Lewis, enjoying his effortless companionship.

'Let's look at the lights again,' Abbey suggested. She tried to stand up but something was wrong. The terrace seemed to be moving around, shifting under her feet. Beyond, the pretty street lights of Castillo danced. Lewis rose and joined her, wrapping a strong arm gently around her shoulders. He pulled her towards him and looked down into her eyes.

'I think we should go inside,' he said.

Abbey pulled at the blinds and threw open the window. The fresh coolness of the morning sea air washed over her. Everything was bright and quiet, the night buzzing of the cicadas was gone. The apartment was silent. She found Lewis sitting on the terrace.

'Would you like some breakfast?' Lewis' face was full of promise.

'Do you have some orange juice?' Abbey could not face eating just yet.

'Lewis?' Abbey looked puzzled when he got back with two large glasses of juice.

'Yes?'

'Have you ever actually seen one? You know, one of those crickets?'

'Cicadas? Yes, of course I have. There are so many of them. In the summer they go on all day. I don't notice them any more but the noise after dark used to really irritate me.'

'Did they get very loud last night?'

'I think so. It can be a right cacophony sometimes, but I never even hear it now. I don't think you were in a fit state to notice much at all last night!'

Abbey made a fuss of her orange juice, swirling it in the glass and sipping it carefully. Its chill sharpness was so refreshing. It tasted like it was straight from the fruit, not like the processed stuff that passed for orange juice in England. She needed to ask. 'What did you do last night? I mean, what did *we* do?' she ventured.

'Well, we drank some wine. Quite a lot of wine I suppose. I smoked some cigars. We talked.' Lewis laughed at the memory. 'Heh. You tried a cigar too,' he advised her, 'but you, um, you didn't like it!'

Abbey giggled, but the sound tailed off as she struggled to recall the night before. 'What happened after that? How did I get to bed?'

'I put you there. That's what happened.' Lewis took a moment to let it sink in, playing a little game. 'You were horribly drunk.' He smiled disarmingly as he connected with her eyes. 'It's ok. I just put you in the other bedroom and left you to sleep.'

The sun painted them with its sugary lemon yellow beams, sliding in low beneath the terrace roof. Lewis rested on the low wall facing her, haloed against the light. Abbey allowed her gaze to drink in the scene. Above smart grey jogging trousers, his white shirt billowed in the breeze that curled up over the gardens below. He caught her watching and raised his glass to her, offering a toast.

'To us!' he beamed.

'Yes, to us!' returned Abbey.

'Ah, so this is the next row of apartments.' Abbey stopped to take stock. So far all they had managed to do was to get through the gardens that brushed the terrace at the back of Lewis' apartment. Skipping and giggling, she had played along with him, teasing and hiding amongst the bushes and trees. Her new shoes, soft easy white trainers, were already coated with dust. She did not care. It felt like she was a teenager again. 'Do we go through here?'

'Yes, it's the shortest way to the shops.' Lewis led her down some steps between the last of the apartments and she found herself on an old street, lined with ancient residences and little shops and boutiques. Old ladies carried their groceries in old-fashioned baskets. A few younger shoppers browsed. Lewis and Abbey joined them on the pavement.

'Hey, slow down. Take it easy. There's plenty of time,' Lewis drawled. Abbey was unaccustomed to the easy pace of the Mediterranean. Lewis took her hand and pulled her back towards him. With an arm around her waist, she had no choice but to amble along.

'Let's go in here. It smells lovely.' Abbey pulled him into the panadería and inhaled deeply. The fabulous aroma of baking bread filled the little bakery shop.

'Mmm. This one looks lovely,' Abbey exclaimed.

'Este dulce, por favor!' This sweet pastry, please. Lewis had ordered and bought it before Abbey could even begin to object.

'Thank you, Lewis. That's very kind.' They were out of the bakery and Abbey was leaving a trail of flaky crumbs behind her as she ate her breakfast.

They turned a corner and headed downhill again. The streets narrowed, funnelling into the heart of the old town which nestled comfortably in the castle's shadow. It was like stepping into another world, a half-forgotten place networked with cobbled streets that were little more than narrow passageways. The balconies of ancient whitewashed buildings crowded over café tables and racks of shoes.

'Ah, these are so cute,' exclaimed Abbey. Without stopping to think, she picked up a teddy bear from a boutique rack. 'Look, this one has green eyes!' she beamed.

Lewis turned to see why Abbey had stopped. The little girl inside her was standing there, weight on one hip, her eyes wide in hope and a furry grey teddy in her hand.

'Oh, I'm sorry, Lewis. I wasn't thinking.' Abbey started apologising, making as if to put the cuddly toy back with the others on the rack.

'Lewis! Cómo estás?' How are you? A Spanish voice, cracked with the ageing of years, interrupted. 'I haven't seen you for so long,' the old woman continued in Spanish. 'You want this one for the pretty lady? I'll put it in a bag for you.' To Abbey's eyes she looked rather comical, a fat old lady in a white headscarf and a long black dress that pulled too tight over her stomach. Of course the Spanish words were lost on Abbey, but the old woman's friendliness was easy to see.

'Sí, gracias Maribel.' Lewis thanked her, smiling broadly. An enduring friend, she was one of the first Spanish people he had ever spoken to and would always be special for that. He turned to Abbey, passing her the little bear. She looked radiant. 'Come on, there's more to see. Then we can go down to the sea. Adiós!' He turned back to shout a simple goodbye to Maribel as they left.

They sat on the wall that separated the sea-front boulevard from the yellow sand of the beach. Together they looked back over the town to where the apartment hid, high up somewhere amongst the jumble of ancient and modern buildings, the parks and palm trees and gardens. It had been a long morning for the explorers.

'It must be about time for lunch,' suggested Lewis.

'I was just thinking how lovely Castillo is. I'm not ready to go back to the apartment really.'

'Oh, we're not going home yet.'

It was the first time that Lewis had referred to this place as home in front of Abbey and she was surprised how much it shocked her. True, he could speak Spanish beautifully. It just flowed from him, so warm and natural, like the soft summer zephyrs that skipped through the streets of Castillo. But he was an Englishman, a foreigner. It was difficult to believe that Spain could feel like home to him. 'Shall we eat in the old town?' Abbey suggested bravely, throwing off her thoughts.

'I prefer to go to my usual café today,' Lewis replied gently. 'We'll eat in town tomorrow.'

Abbey tried to sort through the confusion of the morning's lightning tour. 'Where is it?' she asked.

Lewis turned to look quizzically at his companion. 'Where is what?'

'Your favourite café. Is it far?'

Abbey's child-like gaze was earnest. 'No, Abbey. I think you'll make it,' Lewis said, half-teasing. Casually, he pointed across the boulevard.

It was right there in front of them. 'Of course! Cafetería de la Luz!' Abbey laughed. She followed Lewis across the road and took her place next to him underneath the shade of a blue umbrella.

Abbey lay in bed as the English rain drummed on the

34

roof tiles. She barely noticed it. In her mind she was still in Castillo, reliving every detail again and again. Her thoughts always returned to the last evening when the sunset draped its ribbons of orange and red across the sky. The endless warm breeze washed through the palms and danced up onto the terrace to toss and tangle her hair. Abbey closed her eyes and remembered the elation when Lewis at last took her in his arms and pressed her close. The sensation of that first proper kiss still thrilled through her, electric, passionate. Abbey reached out and picked up her grey teddy bear. She tucked the furry softness under her chin and smiled.

Chapter Four

That's good. I like that. Abbey had chosen just orange, red and black. She blended and merged, spreading and shading. The brush seemed to move with a mind of its own over the roughness of the heavy paper. *Um, maybe some ochre.* She took the lid off the yellow-orange shade. Her brush picked up the paint and more streaks grew, melding with the red and black, coming to life. *Just need the details now.* Abbey dabbed, pointing in the street lights and rooftops. Finally she stood back as far as she could, her shoulders pressed against the wall.

'Yes, that's it.' Abbey spoke aloud in rare self-admiration. Her sunset was as warm as Spain, richly coloured, alive with hope and promise.

'I painted last night,' Abbey told Debbie as they ate their sandwiches.

'What did you paint?'

'I painted Spain.'

'Oh, that's nice, Abbey.' Debbie sounded disinterested. She imagined towering hotels crowding over a hopelessly overloaded strip of beach.

'I thought you would be interested,' Abbey complained. 'It's a really nice painting. I spent a long time on it.'

'I went to Spain last year. It was too hot and there were tourists everywhere. Everyone spoke English in the shops. I suppose it was ok.' Debbie tried hard to sound enthusiastic, but failed miserably.

'Oh, that's not the real Spain. That's what it's like in some places, on the popular parts of the coast. But most of it isn't like that at all. Castillo is different.'

'Why?'

'Well, there are no big hotels to start with. It's just more... um... more natural. Everyone speaks Spanish, they go to work like we do here, it's just a completely different feeling.'

'So did you have to speak Spanish then?'

'No, Lewis did it for me.' Abbey thought back to her long weekend. Lewis had done it all, guiding her through the town, speaking to the local people, buying things for her. 'I am going to learn Spanish, so I can do it myself.'

'Do what yourself?' Debbie was curious now. 'It sounds like you are planning something.'

'I'm not planning anything.' Abbey thought for a moment. She realised that she had been doing exactly that, scheming away. 'Well, it must be nice living there. In Castillo, I mean, not in one of those tourist resorts. It's lovely and warm, and it hardly ever rains.' The romance of it all started coming back to her. 'Lewis is so lucky. He just sits in the shade, writing his books. He even has a weekly cleaner for his apartment!'

'Would you move there?' asked Debbie.

'Yes, of course I would.' Abbey surprised herself at how quickly she answered and how resolute she sounded.

'Abbey, be realistic. It wouldn't work for you.' Debbie was eating an apple, crunching and biting. She considered things for a while, watching the thickening clouds. She turned to face Abbey. 'It looks a bit black over there.'

'Yes, it might rain soon,' agreed Abbey, sounding resigned.' It always rained in England.

'You have your job here, your family, your roots.' Debbie's advice flowed now. She always spoke her mind.

'Uhuh.' Abbey acknowledged her friend's observations. Debbie was honest and direct. That was one of the reasons that Abbey liked her so much. If Debbie said something then it was usually worth listening to, unless it was about television of course. Debbie watched television for hours every evening. In contrast, Abbey detested all that shallow, repetitive rubbish that passed as entertainment.

'What would you do there?' questioned Debbie. 'It would not be like being on holiday. You would have to work and buy food and pay bills. Anyway, where would you live?'

'Well, I'd live with Lewis, obviously. I mean, that's why I'd be there, isn't it? As well as for the sunshine, of course.'

'Ok. But what if you fell out? Look what happened with Peter.'

'Debbie, that's got nothing to do with it.' Peter was Abbey's ex and she didn't like to talk about him. He was a Professor of Philosophy. Light-haired, with ageing freckles, he wore thick glasses and spoke with arrogance and self-importance. She had spent the last two years trying to put him behind her and she wanted to look forward now, to build a new life. 'Lewis is different. He is kind and sensitive.'

'A sensitive man? Ha ha.' Debbie tossed her apple core into the bushes.

Abbey turned away. Lewis was different. You could see it in his eyes, feel it in the lightness of his touch.

Debbie broke the silence. 'Oh, I'm sorry Abbey. I didn't mean it to sound like that. But you know how I feel about men.'

'It's alright, Debbie. I didn't take it personally.' Abbey turned back and flashed a reconciliatory smile. 'I'm a bit defensive about Lewis,' she explained, 'and I need to have my dream. It was all so lovely. We ate at his favourite place again and we drank red wine.'

'You never drink wine!' challenged Debbie.

'I tried to say no, but I gave in. It was nice to start with. Then I got drunk and we talked a lot. And then...'

'Yes? Did you...? I mean...' For once, Debbie was lost for the right words.

'Did he take advantage of me?' Abbey spoke Debbie's question for her. 'No. Like I said, Lewis is different.'

The rain started and work beckoned, unappealing and unavoidable. The two friends drifted back to their offices. Abbey sat down and rolled her chair up to the desk, reluctant to begin the afternoon's work. The screen stared back at her, waiting. Debbie was a good friend but she had a straightforward approach to relationships with men. It could hardly be simpler, she just avoided them altogether. Abbey could never do that. Her life was empty without the companionship of someone that she could trust, someone who cared. He had to be strong, someone to lean on. She wanted to feel the heat of passion and the closeness of their bodies, that much was natural. But there was so much more to it than that. He must let her reach his heart. Could Lewis be all this? Would she ever hear him say the words that she wanted to hear?

Infotext was quite a new company. Its London offices were open plan and filled with large, light-brown desks. Everyone sat on black, faux-leather swivel chairs. Abbey sat at her desk and pretended to be working. She stared at the screen, but she did not see anything that it had to offer. Instead, she saw Lewis. *It's all his fault.* It was his fault that the Spanish project failed. He had distracted her, wasting her time. It was because of him that she had been reprimanded at work and that she now spent nearly all of her time dreaming and scheming. Her mind was hundreds of miles away instead of here where it should be, grinding through her duties in the office.

'Hello. Abigail Houndslow speaking.' Abbey instantly regretted answering the telephone. If she had known that it was her mother calling then she would have just let it keep on ringing. 'Oh, hello Mum,' sighed Abbey. She was feeling miserable enough already.

'Abbey.' Rita launched straight into things, with no niceties. 'I'm not well again.'

Abbey groaned. She had heard this one too many times already. Rita always started this caper when she wanted some attention. 'What's wrong this time, Mum?' asked Abbey, though she already knew what it would be.

'Well, you know. The same as last time. I'm very poorly, have been for two days now.' Rita spoke slowly and quietly to demonstrate just how ill she was. 'Can you come and see me?' Her voice was like cracked old paving stones, crumbling and rough.

'Yes, Mother. Tonight. I'll come to see you tonight.' Abbey slumped down unhappily in her chair. It would have to be done.

'Tonight? I'll look out for you coming. And Abbey?' Rita's flaky voice continued.

'Yes, Mum?' *Oh no, now what?*

'There's a package waiting here for you. It came this morning.'

'Ah, thanks Mum.' Abbey brightened a little. It would be her language course. 'That was very quick, I wasn't expecting it yet.' Abbey was trying to picture the package in her mind. She loved getting new things. Just occasional little treats, something for herself. 'I only ordered it yesterday. Does it look all right?'

'How should I know? I can't see inside it, can I?' The speed and strength of Rita's voice had both made a very quick recovery.

'I was only asking if the package looked all right, Mum. It doesn't matter, I'll call in tonight and pick it up. Um, and see you too, of course.'

'Abbey, why do you keep sending your deliveries here? Why don't you give them your own address?'

'Mum, listen, I'll talk about it later,' Abbey hissed. She glanced around the big office to see if anyone was paying attention. Her colleagues were carefully ignoring her, protecting their own interests. Most of them had to deal with private matters on the telephone from time to time, it was just a matter of necessity for people who spent every working day trapped in there. But her boss might be a different matter. Vanessa could not be seen. Either she was doing something at the screens behind Abbey, or she wasn't in the office at all.

'What? Speak up Abbey, I can't hear you very well.' Rita was still there on the phone.

'Sorry Mum. I've told you dozens of times, I have to have them sent to you. I'm in here all day, at the office.

There's no-one to deal with it at home.'

'Yes there is. Luke can do it. What's wrong with him taking a parcel from the postman?'

'Oh Mum, you know he won't answer the door. He's up half the night playing games, then he sleeps all morning. Look, I have to go. I'll call in tonight, ok?'

'Yes, love. Bye.'

The wind was a bit of a nuisance. It tore at the edges of the tablecloths and earnestly tossed the umbrellas about. Napkins, stolen from the tables by the playful breeze, danced along the boulevard. Lewis got to the door of Cafetería de la Luz just as Juan was coming out.

'Ah, Lewis! Dentro.' Inside. Juan waved his arm towards the long, narrow room behind him. Lewis peered into the semi-darkness. On the left, rectangular tables were arranged in a neat line. Along the right side was the bar, made with heavy, dark wood. 'I'd better put those umbrellas down,' Juan commented, looking past Lewis.

'Can I sit anywhere?' Lewis called, wondering if any of the tables inside were reserved.

'Sí!' It did not matter where Lewis sat. 'But you might as well sit here, Lewis. This one is a bit larger.' Juan pointed to one of the tables. It was a little longer than the others and it was right at the front by the window so it was lighter there, at least in the daytime. The table was big enough to seat four people comfortably.

'I'm not expecting anyone else.' Lewis tried to explain to Juan that he would be dining alone. He had not arranged to meet anyone at the café for lunch, preferring a peaceful meal with time to ponder and think about things.

'Señor Lewis, you have the best table. I don't think it will be very busy today.'

'Gracias, Juan.' Lewis thanked him and sat down with his back to the rest of the room so that he could look out over the spotless white tablecloth and watch the weather outside. Leaves and little pieces of coloured litter blew past. It was unusual to see much of it in Castillo. Perhaps the wind was fierce enough to snatch it up from the bins.

'What would you like today?'

'Oh, Juan. Sí... yo quisiera...' Cafetería de la Luz was only a modest café and the menu was a short and simple one. It featured both traditional local dishes and modern additions. Regular customers soon discovered which their favourite ones were and Lewis, being at least as regular as any other now, was quick to decide what he would be having today. '...pescado frito, por favor.' I would like fried fish, please.

Something red flashed past the window and flew into the café, closing the door behind to shut out the wind.

'Hello everyone!' Jackie was wearing a red top and black trousers. She plopped down onto a chair opposite Lewis. 'What are you having?'

So much for the quiet lunch. 'I'm having fish. You're full of energy today, Jackie.' Lewis sat back rather defensively as her perfume slapped him in the face.

'Do you like it?' Jackie leaned forward.

'Do I like what?' asked Lewis. Was it Jackie's new perfume that she was referring to, or was he expected to comment on the generous cleavage that she was thrusting under his nose?

'It's French, of course. I only buy French perfume. No-one else knows how to make it, you know.' Her Essex influence surfaced through her cultured upper-class words. 'Do you like it?'

'Yes, Jackie. It's very... floral.' Lewis really did like it. Sometimes Jackie's taste in clothes was rather odd, but she knew how to choose a good fragrance. 'Have you had this one before?'

'No, it's a new one. They have just got it in at Sarita Suelo.'

Sarita Suelo was Jackie's favoured boutique. It was located in a street in the new town, the part of Castillo that had developed and grown in recent years. Sarita Suelo was always the first place to stock new things. 'I thought that was where it must be from,' Lewis observed. 'Did you get that top there too?' It was very revealing and Lewis felt compelled to stare.

'Yes, it was on offer. It was a hundred off! I thought you'd like it.' She watched Lewis trying unsuccessfully to drag his eyes away from her womanly display. Finally she leaned back, rather pleased with her success in making him pay some attention to her. She turned to the bar. The waiter was busy behind it, cleaning and rattling things. 'Juan, tortilla Española para mí, por favor.' Spanish omelette for me, please.

'Lo siento. I'm sorry, Jackie. You can't smoke in here. I've told you before.' Juan smiled disarmingly but purposefully at her as he came to the table. She reddened and put the cigarette packet back in her bag. She liked to do as she pleased but she knew that she was not really permitted to smoke inside. The ritual of smoking before a meal was simply automatic for her and Juan usually chose not to notice. His smile broadened in silent understanding. 'Gracias. Tortilla for you? I'll try to have it ready for you with the fish.' Jackie watched his receding back as he disappeared into the kitchen through the door at the rear.

'He loves his work, doesn't he?' she said, then continued without expecting Lewis to answer. 'He tries to get everything right and keep us happy.'

'Yes,' agreed Lewis. 'He's even going to try and bring our meals to us at the same time.'

'So, are you missing Abbey?' Jackie attempted to steer the conversation away from banal observations and towards something more important, something that was on her mind right now. 'I mean, she's gone back to England now. Do you miss her?'

'Well, it was good to see her again,' he confessed. Whatever happened between himself and Abbey, it would always be nice to have Jackie to talk to. There were not many English expats in Castillo, it was not that sort of town. Of the few that he had met, he liked Jackie the most. True, she was flamboyant and embarrassingly extrovert, but she was fun and honest and she was generally straightforward. But today, Lewis sensed an underlying agenda and was immediately on his guard.

'But did she give you what you needed?' Jackie leaned towards him, her assets heavy over her plate of omelette.

'What I needed? And do you know what that is?'

'Of course I do. I saw how you looked at her. Come on, Lewis, you know what I mean. Did she?'

'No, she didn't,' he admitted.

'Aha!' Jackie claimed triumphantly. She moved in for the kill. 'Well, you know you can always get it here.'

Lewis stared at the valley where Jackie's offerings met. Their junction narrowed and plunged down until it was lost in the expensive red fabric of her new top.

'Jackie, you know how I feel about you. How long have we known each other? It must be over three years now. You're a friend. A good friend. It wouldn't be right,' explained Lewis, attempting to see off the attack.

'But why not?'

Lewis tried to ignore the straining response that he felt in his trousers. Jackie was very attractive, she was single, she was fun and of course she was wealthy. But he was looking for more than obvious, simple things such as sex and money. There was a hollow in Lewis' life that needed filling, and this was not the way to do it. Jackie was tempting him with short term satisfaction and in the end he had to say no. 'Because it just isn't right. I'm sorry, Jackie.'

The wind was easing. Juan ventured out of his café and started opening up the umbrellas over the tables again. Through the big window he watched his customers as they finished their meals without speaking.

Not even a thank-you. Mother is so ungrateful. Abbey

banged the phone back down rather too heavily. The plastic clattered, drawing some low, disapproving looks. She chose to ignore them. In her mind she had already left, got out of this place and followed her heart. It was just a matter of time, she promised herself.

'Abbey.'

A thin voice, designed to wound, cut right into her. Her body jerked in surprise as she reacted to the shock. Almost in panic she swivelled round and found herself staring at Vanessa's skinny chest. 'Yes, what?' blurted Abbey. Said like that, it was rude and rather too loud, but she did not care any more as she stood up to face her boss. Abbey hated it here and she hated Vanessa. The chill of Vanessa's hard blue eyes stared back at her. Vanessa could never be attractive. She was much too thin, her cheeks hollow and pinched under the coating of her make-up. She pursed her lips, forming a horrible, acidic pout.

Vanessa spat out caustic words that burned. 'Abbey, you're on notice. You've got one month.'

Chapter Five

'Just a minute Mum. I'm having a conversation.'

Abbey waited impatiently. Luke was chatting with someone, another young male playing the same game. The players were connected together as they fought their battles, two people who were far apart yet united in their endeavour. 'Come on, Luke, I want to talk to you.' She didn't see why she should be kept waiting in favour of some remote adolescent who was no doubt pale, spotty and slouching in an equally filthy bedroom. Abbey regretted not dealing with Luke's messiness years ago. If she had nipped it in the bud then it might have been a great deal easier to handle. Anyway, it was too late for that now.

'Ok, Mum. What is it?' Luke put everything down and spun round so that his lanky legs dropped to the floor over the edge of his bed. He paused for a moment, then spoke again in a serious voice. 'You look worried.'

'I am worried, Luke,' she confirmed. 'Things have changed. I have to leave my job.' She could not bring herself to admit to her son that she had been forced out.

'Oh dear,' said Luke, starting to appreciate that this conversation was going to be important. It sounded bad. Perhaps it was even worth the interruption that it had caused to his game. 'So what's going to happen?' he enquired.

'Well,' started Abbey. There was no point putting it off. 'I think I'm going back to Spain. To live there.' She could see that Luke was getting ready to raise as many objections as he could think of. 'It's alright. You can come too,' she added hurriedly.

'To live there with you?'

'Yes. You can come too. You could still play and do the things you do here.' Abbey was thinking in a terrible rush. She had not planned any of this, events just seemed to be overtaking her. She could not leave Luke here in the house alone, he would never manage. Taking him with her looked like the only option, despite the fact that it would cost her a lot of freedom. Having Luke there would be quite a sacrifice on her part. His pale face watched her. A bit of sun might do him some good.

'But I want to stay here, with my friends and all my things,' said Luke plaintively.

Abbey thought his friends were mostly worthless game-soaked time wasters, but was careful not to say so. There was nothing to be gained by voicing her mind. Luke was entitled to make his own choices.

'You don't like my friends, do you?' Luke was challenging his mother. He had read her body language and seen her thoughts on her face.

'That's got nothing to do with it, Luke. Anyway, I finish at Infotext in July.' Abbey stopped to place a caring hand on his shoulder. 'Don't worry. I'll sort something out, it will be ok.' Abbey closed the bedroom door behind her. She had tried to sound reassuring, but inside she had no idea what she was going to do. It wasn't fair on Luke, he had not done anything wrong. The tears came as the weight of her guilt overwhelmed her.

'Oh, hello Abbey. How are you? Is it raining there?' Lewis joked over the line, his voice stripped and bodiless.

'Lewis, something's happened.' Abbey ignored Lewis' joking. She wanted to be light-hearted and respond with laughter, but she could not find the humour within her. Her hand gripped the telephone so tightly that her knuckles were white. 'I hope you don't mind me phoning.'

'No, of course I don't mind. What's happened?' His thin, metallic voice was measured and steady. Abbey found it reassuring to hear.

'I... I've lost my job,' she confessed. 'At Infotext. They don't want me any more.'

'They don't want you? Why ever not? I don't understand.' Lewis paused, giving Abbey the opportunity to fill in the gap with her explanation. She just waited, hoping that he would not press her for more information. 'So, what is going to happen?' he continued at last.

Abbey felt relief. She had rehearsed each step of this phone call, planning what she would say and how she would get through it. Now that she had got to this part she felt unexpectedly calm. 'Well, Lewis, I have one month left there. I have told my landlord that I will be leaving after that.' She was getting into her stride, ready to ask the big question.

'What about another job?' Lewis threw her right off course. The conversation was not supposed to go this way. 'Couldn't you just get another job and carry on as you are? You could stay in the same house. If you got a better job then maybe you could even move out of Bullwood,' he continued.

'Yes, I suppose so. That would be sensible. But...'

'There must be plenty of work available, Abbey. You are talented, you have a lot of experience. Surely your degree counts for something?'

'Yes, of course it does, Lewis.' Abbey paused, wondering how to phrase it. 'But I don't want to do any of that.' This summed it up as well as anything.

'Uhuh.' Lewis waited to hear more.

Abbey felt a flurry of agitation. 'I don't want another job like that,' she blurted. 'I hate it. Every minute of it. And I hate it all here. This house, everything.' Abbey remembered his little tease and finally acknowledged it. 'And you were right, it's mid-summer and it is raining.'

Lewis laughed over the phone, softly. 'I thought it might be. It's been a lovely day here. Maybe a little too hot, I had to stay in the shade all afternoon.'

'Lewis, you are so lucky,' said Abbey. 'Lewis?'

'Yes, Abbey?'

It's time to ask. She had to do it now, before the moment was lost. 'Lewis, I was wondering... well, what I would really like to do is...'

'Come and live here?' interjected Lewis.

48

'Oh! Yes, that is exactly what I was going to say.' In the end she had not even had to ask, Lewis had done it for her.

'I don't see why we can't try it, Abbey. Maybe for a month or two, to see how we get on. But you know what my apartment is like. It's big enough for two people, but that's about it.'

Abbey understood. There would be no Luke and none of her furniture either. Perhaps Rita could accommodate Luke in her spare room. That was yet another bridge to cross. She allowed herself a little smile all the same. A couple of months with Lewis was a good start and once she was there she could work on it.

'Bring your canvasses and paint, Abbey. You'll need something to occupy your time.'

'Yes, Lewis, of course. Thank you.' Her smile grew broader. Abbey had other ideas of how she would be passing her time with Lewis in Castillo.

Abbey carefully removed the heavy paper from her easel. She would wrap just this picture safely and take it with her. She could not take all of her equipment and materials, there was simply far too much of it. She was limited to the things that she used most. It was funny how easy it was to gather so much stuff over the years and then find that most of it was actually quite unnecessary.

'Mum, I've brought my paintings here. Will you look after them?' asked Abbey.

'Yes, of course, love. Why don't you hang some of them up? They would look nice on the wall and it would be such a shame to leave them packed away.'

Abbey was stunned. Her mother had never been complimentary about her painting. *She must be up to something.*

'Ok, Mum. I'll put some of them up. A lot of them still need framing. I'll buy some frames for them on Monday and do them next week.' Abbey liked framing her pictures.

It meant that they were much bulkier and difficult to store, but there was such a satisfying feeling of completion as she turned each one over and viewed her finished work from the front for the first time.

'Mum, shall I start cleaning in the kitchen first?'

'Yes, start in there. There isn't a lot to do, just the worktops and the cooker really.'

'Lewis has a cleaner coming in every week,' Abbey told Rita as she cleaned. 'Her name is Gabriela. We'll have to find someone to clean for you. I'll pay for it.'

'No, Abbey, I'll pay. Why should you pay for my cleaner?'

'Well, it's my fault, isn't it? If I wasn't going then you wouldn't need one.'

'Oh, don't worry. I can afford it.'

Really? Rita was always complaining that she had no money. 'Are you sure, Mum?'

'Yes, of course I am. You just find me someone, I'll pay for it. Anyway, I'm not worried about that.'

Abbey had cleaned the cooker and moved onto the worktops, clearing them and wiping them down. She let her mother continue talking, listening to her through the open door between them.

'You know how I feel about you going, leaving me on my own,' Rita said with increasing bitterness.

'But you won't be on your own, Mother. Luke will be here.'

'Well, what kind of company will that be?' Rita did not hold anything back, she was too old to worry about offending people any more. 'You know what he'll be doing. He'll just stay in that room, playing games.'

'Yes, Mum, I suppose so.' Her mother was perfectly correct, of course. Luke was not exactly a conversationalist.

'You never visited me much anyway,' Rita said.

The attack was building. This kind of conversation always escalated quickly and Abbey had to act now before her mother got out of hand. 'That's not true. I've visited every week and I came in to clean as well.'

'You've never bothered about me,' Rita continued, ignoring Abbey completely. 'You've always just got on with your own life. When have you ever gone out of your way for me?'

'But Mother, that's not true. You know...'

Abbey did not get a chance to finish her sentence before her mother interrupted. 'I've been alone for years. And now you're going off to live in another country. I bet you won't bother coming back to visit me.' Rita was launching into a full-scale tirade. 'You don't care. It's been like this ever since your father died.'

'No, it has not, Rita Houndslow,' stated Abbey emphatically. Some things could not be left unsaid. 'You had that man after Dad died, didn't you? Tom, wasn't it?' Abbey challenged her mother but there was no reply so she continued, though a little more gently. 'I thought you might marry him. He died when you were still at the old house, didn't he? I liked Tom, actually.' Abbey paused to draw breath, remembering the nice old gentleman who had brightened her mother's life.

'He never had children, you know,' stated Rita.

'Yes, Mother, you told me that dozens of times. And then after him there was another one as well. You know, the one you tried to keep a secret.'

'I didn't try to keep him secret. Why would I do that?' objected Rita, struggling to get to her feet.

'I don't know why, but you did. He lived here for years!'

Abbey could feel the tears coming. She stayed in the kitchen, exhausting herself cleaning by doing needless extra and unnecessary things. She loved her mother dearly, but wished that they could agree. Abbey hated conflict with anyone, even more so with the few surviving members of her family. They should work together, not fight.

'Alright, Abbey. You're right.' Rita sighed heavily and sat down again. The argument was over. 'I think you should go and check if Luke is ok.'

Abbey came out of the kitchen and crossed through the lounge without speaking. She would do as her mother suggested and look in on Luke. For some odd reason she felt obliged to knock on the door before she went in. Perhaps it was because she felt that she was not on home ground.

'Come in.'

'Hello Luke. I just came to see how you were getting on here.'

'I'm fine, Mum. No problem.'

To Abbey's surprise, Luke's bold words were completely justified. The little room was immaculate. Luke had set up a tiny table with his things on it, games, a clock, a few other articles. He sat up on the bed with his back propped against the wall, happily connected to the other players in his fantasy world.

'Mum, it's ok, you know.'

'What's ok?'

'It's ok if you go to Spain. I'll be fine here with Nan,' said Luke confidently. Abbey was lost for words. She sat down on the bed and put her arm around her son, a little boy hidden inside a pale, lanky adult. He spoke again. 'Just phone me a few times.' The little boy cried silently in his mother's arms.

The aeroplane lifted up through London's grey cloud blanket, emerging into bright sunlight that flooded the cabin. Abbey blinked in the sudden brightness. It was time to look forward now, to think of herself for once and try to make something of her life.

Wait at the airport, I'll come for you. Abbey replayed the sound of Lewis' voice in her head as she joined the shifting throng in the airport arrivals area. She stood still and let everyone flow past her as she strained to see over their heads. Strong arms wrapped around her shoulders and without warning Lewis was hugging her, pressing the length of his body against hers.

'Welcome to Spain, Abbey,' he spoke in her ear. He released his arms, unwrapping her. 'These cases look heavy. Let me help you.'

'Hello Lewis. Yes, thanks. They are heavy.' Abbey abandoned all the things that she had planned to say to him when she arrived. The trouble was, they were replies really. Lewis was supposed to tell her how he had missed her and how wonderful it was that she had come back. Then she was going to tell him how good it was to be back, yet none of that happened. For now, she would have to be satisfied with just his hug. There would be time for talking later.

'No, you are on the other side!' Lewis called out to Abbey as she reached to open the car door.

Abbey felt her face redden, then she made a deliberate effort to dispel her embarrassment. There should be no need to feel ashamed of a simple mistake like this. 'Ha! I thought I was still in England.'

'You'll soon get used to it,' said Lewis soothingly as he took hold of the open door and slid into the driver's seat.

Abbey joined him in the car, sitting on his right. She looked around her as they got under way. Everywhere looked so dry and the fields were much browner than on her last visit. The climate would be something else that she would have to get used to.

'We'll go straight to the apartment, Abbey. Then you can unwind a little.'

'That sounds lovely, Lewis.' *Why do I feel so nervous?* 'Were you waiting long for me?'

'At the airport? Oh, about an hour. It will take less than that to drive all the way home.' Lewis paused for a moment, then he continued. 'Of course I didn't mind waiting one more hour for you, Abbey. You were away for so long, I started to wonder if you really wanted to come back.' He glanced at her and she met his eyes. 'But I knew you would.'

As Abbey stepped out, Lewis was already at the back of the car, easing a large suitcase out. 'It looks like a big car from the outside,' he explained, 'but there's not much room inside it.'

'Oh, I like it. It's got character,' said Abbey positively. 'And the air conditioning still works. Phew, it's so hot out here!'

'Here, this might help.' Lewis passed Abbey a glass of chilled water as soon as the apartment door had closed behind them. 'Leave them for now,' he said, pointing at the collection of bags and cases. 'We can move those in a bit. It will be nice out on the terrace now.' He led her through to it and she skipped straight to the little wall at the far side.

'Ah, it's even lovelier than I remembered. The rooftops and the flowers. And the sea. I think I can hear it today.'

'Yes, you can hear it on the wind today,' said Lewis as he joined her. 'Softly.' His arms were around her, pulling her body close. She allowed herself to rest against him, feeling his hips against hers. She turned her face up and their lips met. As they parted again, she opened her eyes. His face was so close, the tanned skin laughing where it wrinkled a little as it reached the corners of his eyes. 'I'll show you your room,' said Lewis in a matter-of-fact tone.

'My room?' Abbey's heart sank. Just one kiss on the terrace and then it was back to practical matters. She sighed to herself and followed him back to the hallway to help him take her cases through. It was the same room that Lewis had put her in last time, when she got drunk. It was like the other rooms in the apartment, minimally furnished, clean, tidy and simple. It had white walls and pine furniture.

'The wardrobe and all of the drawers are empty. You can use whatever you like.'

'I didn't bring many clothes really,' started Abbey, 'I did not have enough space.' Unexpected sadness flooded through her as she remembered the things that she had left behind.

'Don't worry, you can bring more things soon. Would you like to help me cook?' suggested Lewis brightly. 'Something quite light today, I think. Light, but tasty. Come on, I'm hungry.'

Abbey followed Lewis into the kitchen.

'Heat some olive oil in this pan.'

'Ok. How much?' Abbey found herself responding easily to his instructions, as if being asked to do something by Lewis was natural and fair. Cooking with him was lovely, like joining a team in which she was a willing player. It was so different to being bossed around by Vanessa at Infotext.

'Is the oil really hot?' Lewis asked. 'I've chopped the garlic and chilli ready for you.' He passed her the ingredients. 'The flatbreads are in the oven already. Here, try this.' He dipped a finger into a pot and brought it out, drawing her close with his other arm around her waist.

Abbey closed her lips around his finger, keeping her eyes on his as she savoured the experience. 'Mmm. It's really good.'

'It's fresh houmous, from the market.' He released her as quickly as he had taken her and turned back to the table. In seconds he had spread a thick layer of the houmous over the hot flatbreads. 'The garlic, chillies and peppers go on top. There. These look great. Would you like a glass of wine?'

Abbey just nodded, allowing herself to be carried along without resisting. They ate on the terrace, watching the sky darken as evening came.

'More wine? They are smaller glasses this time.' Lewis struck a balance between temptation and reassurance.

Abbey read the label on the bottle as it hovered in Lewis' hand. She could see the part that said Vino Tinto, the same red wine as last time.

'No, I think I've already had enough,' Abbey replied cautiously.

'Maybe later, then.' Lewis put the bottle down again. 'There's a fiesta in Castillo tonight,' he announced.

'A fiesta?'

'Yes, they love them here. Street parades, dressing up, music. They know how to do it properly.' Lewis watched Abbey, sensing the conflict within. 'It's ok, we don't have to go anywhere tonight. We can join one another week.' He checked his watch. 'Five to ten. It's nearly time.'

'Time for what?' Abbey was puzzled. She followed Lewis to the edge of the terrace, to her favourite spot. The sky was deepest indigo blue, a velvet cloth pierced by the youngest evening stars. She felt his arms around her as the first fireworks burst over the town, scattering cascades of glittering flowers. His lips pressed against hers. Fireworks exploded red and green and gold, a cacophony of sound in a theatre of coloured light that rose to a climax as she melted in his embrace.

Chapter Six

'What was Juan saying to you?' Abbey's face turned enquiringly to Lewis as soon as the waiter was out of earshot. 'He was staring at me.'

'Well.' Lewis seemed to hesitate for a moment, as if he was considering how to phrase his reply. 'He was telling me that you look attractive.' That was true, although it was certainly not a precise translation.

'Yes? He seemed to say a lot.' Abbey prompted Lewis for more.

'And he said that he hoped you would be happy staying in Spain. He wants you to feel welcome here.'

'Really?' Abbey barely believed what she was hearing. Juan had been leering, scanning over her body without a hint of shame. 'That's very thoughtful of him.' She could lie quite politely when she really needed to.

Lewis did not feel entirely comfortable defending his friend in this way, it seemed a little unfair on Abbey. He decided to focus on the safer parts of the conversation. 'Juan asked if you liked the food. He was worried whether his café was good enough for you.'

'What?' Abbey sat back, laughing. 'Compared to the rubbish that they serve up in England, La Luz is heaven!'

'Yes, I suppose it is.' Lewis thought back through the years to another time. It was striking how quickly the memories faded, how half a lifetime was already little more than an ill-remembered dream. 'I must be getting used to it.'

'The coffee is much better here too,' added Abbey, positively.

'Shh.' Lewis motioned to Abbey, warning her that Juan was coming back.

'Aquí lo tienes, patatas bravas.' Here it is, Juan announced, placing Abbey's dish of spicy fried potatoes in front of her.

'Thank you,' responded Abbey in English.

Juan stared at her for a second, said something short to Lewis and bumbled away. The café was filling up and he was busy. Dark, round and perspiring, he rushed between the tables.

'Oh dear, Abbey.' Lewis tried not to sound too downbeat, but failed. 'You'll have to do better than that. What about that language course you bought?'

'I had a look at it.'

'Uhuh?'

'And it's hard. I haven't done much.' Abbey paused. 'Actually, I haven't really done any of it,' she admitted guiltily.

'You need to do something about it if you want to stay here. They don't speak much English in Castillo. How will you make friends?' Lewis' voice was becoming louder, more assertive.

I've only just arrived. Abbey's heart sank. For the first time, she wondered if Lewis was really right for her. If he was confident and assured then that was fine, but domineering?

Lewis continued in the same tone. 'They teach it at the college. You could try that.' He stopped talking when he saw Abbey's face change. 'Sorry. I didn't mean...'

Abbey ignored his apology and avoided meeting his eyes. Instead she turned her attention to her plate. The food really was surprisingly good at Cafetería de la Luz.

'Jackie, that was a bit close!' Abbey was nearly shouting. Although it was not a long way to go, Jackie had insisted on driving across Castillo to the new part of town. Her car was small, fast and open. None of the locals had cars like that, theirs were all rather practical and had proper roofs to keep the occupants shaded.

Jackie drove in a sporty, carefree style. It was not quite aggressive in the way that some of the young men drove around, just enthusiastic. 'This is the place,' she announced, braking suddenly and throwing the car into a tight turn across the road and into the car park entrance. Abbey stifled a gasp of horror. Jackie did not even seem to notice the other traffic at all. Couldn't she hear their horns blaring?

'Come on. We've got shopping to do,' announced Jackie as she yanked the handbrake on. She seemed to notice Abbey's pale, shaken appearance. 'It's ok, you're safe with me. I've never crashed.'

'This is a nice pair.' Jackie picked the shoes up off the shelf and slipped them on, then immediately took them off again. She loved handling things, testing how they felt. She passed one shoe across her face. 'Mmm, they even smell nice. What do you think, Abbey?'

'They're lovely. Um, yes. Stunning.' Abbey struggled to find the right words. They were an adorable pair of shoes, pretty, light and beautifully made from first class materials. 'They suit you well. How much are they?'

'Oh, I don't know.' Jackie fished around for the label and turned it over. 'Three hundred and ninety-five.'

'Three hundred and ninety-five?' squeaked Abbey. They were in Sarita Suelo, a boutique filled with desirable brands that had prices to match. There were only a few expensive shops like this in Castillo, all of them clustered on one street in the new town area.

'Yes. Good, isn't it? Sarita?' The boutique owner stopped tinkering with her jewellery display and was at Jackie's side in an instant. 'Have you got some red ones?' Jackie asked.

'Jackie! How are you?' Sarita sounded delighted. Abbey found herself riveted, her attention alternating between her new friend and Sarita Suelo's proprietor as a minor drama unfolded in front of her.

'I'm fine, Sarita.'

'You want red ones?'

'Yes, if you have them.'

'I don't think I do. They are all individually made.

Look.'

Sarita was showing Jackie how the artisan had constructed the shoes, turning one over and showing off the stitching along the sides. The conversation was in Spanish, but the gestures and faces told the story. The difference between Sarita's rapid-fire speech and Jackie's responses was obvious too. Sarita said something. Jackie listened, thought for a while and then replied carefully. She sounded like an English person speaking unfamiliar foreign words.

'I'll take these.' Jackie was nodding and smiling, Sarita was already wrapping up the purchase in bright tissue and slipping it into a smart bag with little rope handles.

'I could do with some new shoes too,' Abbey said as they stood outside the boutique. She glanced down wistfully at the bag in Jackie's hand.

'Let's go to the zapatería,' replied Jackie breezily.

'Zapatería?'

'It means shoe shop. I'll show you.'

Abbey followed Jackie through the maze of streets, struggling to keep up. Jackie bounded ahead, a fiery bundle of energy and enthusiasm.

'Here we are. Look, these are charming. Let's go in and try some.' There was no trace of mockery in Jackie's voice, not a hint of snobbery as she searched along the tightly-packed shelves of budget-priced footwear. 'What about these? Oh, and these are good too.'

'Yes, they look great.'

'Do they fit?'

'I haven't even got one on yet!'

'Alright. What about these then?' Another pair joined the jumble on the floor.

'These are comfortable. How do I look?' Abbey sauntered up and down the aisle.

'Perfect!'

Two happy women returned to the car park. It was another cloudless day and the leather seats were too hot to bear sitting on. The friends squirmed and giggled as Jackie launched her car onto the melting afternoon roads.

Alvaro climbed up through the gardens. The apartments were already in sight when he stopped to rest under the trees. A row of white blocks that peeped through the gaps, they looked down on him through a rippling haze of late afternoon heat. He dropped one end of his little folding step-ladder to the ground, resting its top against the blue overalls that shrouded him from neck to ankles. It was too hot to work in the afternoons and Alvaro was struggling to cope. Unable to refuse, he had taken on a lot of jobs this week. He was so busy that he was almost running between them, carrying his ladder under one arm and his tool bag with the other. The thing he disliked most, even more than the heat and the rushing about, was letting people down. He picked up his ladder and his tools and set off again.

'Keep still. Stop looking around.'

'Sorry. I'll try. It's difficult, you know.'

Alvaro could hear voices as he approached the terrace. A woman was asking someone to do something and a man was answering. Alvaro recognised Lewis' voice, carrying soft and deep through the trees on the humid summer air. He did not know the woman's voice at all.

'Come on, Lewis. I can't do it if you keep fidgeting.'

'Abbey, I'm doing my best.'

They were talking in a foreign language and all that Alvaro could pick out were their names. He was standing at the edge of the terrace now, yet neither of them seemed to have noticed him. Lewis was sitting stiffly upright in a chair, posed rather unnaturally. Opposite him sat the woman, pale and pretty with a fat pencil in her hand and an easel in front of her. Her long brown hair was brushed away from her face so that it cascaded over her back. Why did this woman seem familiar?

'Señor. Ahem.'

Lewis looked round when he heard the coughing. 'Ah, hello Alvaro. How are things?'

'Busy, señor. Very busy.' Alvaro stepped onto the terrace and waited politely.

'It's ok, Alvaro. Come on.' Lewis was on his feet, beckoning to Alvaro. 'This is Abbey. Abbey, this is Alvaro, our handyman.' The introductions were simple and brief, and Lewis switched between languages smoothly as he spoke.

'Hello Alvaro,' said Abbey brightly, slipping off her glasses. 'Pleased to meet you. But haven't we already...?'

Lewis watched as puzzlement shadowed their faces.

'I think we know each other,' said Alvaro shyly, his face reddening. He pulled on his moustache. 'I just can't remember where I've seen her. Did we meet in town?' He turned to Lewis, appealing to him for an explanation.

'I don't know, Alvaro.'

'It will come back to me.' Alvaro shrugged and turned, his eyes scanning the terrace canopy. 'So, where is the lamp?'

'It was at Cafetería de la Luz! You passed us at the café.'

Alvaro turned back to Lewis. 'Yes, of course. That's right. You had the lady with you, didn't you?'

'It was her first time in Spain,' explained Lewis. That was enough. Alvaro knew a lot of people in Castillo and passed gossip along like a bee carrying pollen from flower to flower. 'It's this one that is broken.' Lewis pointed to the lamp that needed fixing. Alvaro unfolded his ladder, opened his tool bag and got on with the job.

'Lewis, please. How can I draw you when you keep doing that?'

'Sorry Abbey. Was I fidgeting again?'

'No, you were watching Alvaro. I don't want you looking up there. Watch that tree outside, like I said before.'

'Oh, ok.' Lewis blocked a sigh. Having his portrait

painted was much less glamorous than he had imagined. In fact it was tedious. It seemed to be taking hours, time which might be better spent getting on with his writing instead. The manuscript was dragging its feet, taking much longer than expected. It was going to be late and his agent was already asking questions. He sat still and stared at the tree.

Lewis was cooking. He loved making meals now that there were two people to enjoy them. It made all the effort worthwhile and the whole activity was much more pleasurable. He did not much care for gardening, though he had a small garden under the shade of the arch and the tall palms that stood outside his front door. When he was a little boy he learned what a garden was, a place of endless wonder filled with leafy bushes, flowers and incredible insects that buzzed and crawled and flew. The lawn, that flat expanse of moist green, was an essential element. Every garden had a lawn. But here the long summer was too hot and dry for these things. Lewis' little kitchen garden was packed with cordylines and cacti, ice plants and agaves. He grew herbs and chillies in pots, harvesting them right through the season.

'Is there anything I can do?'

'Oh, Abbey!' She was back early and Lewis jumped when she pushed open the door. 'Not really, unless you want to chop some onions.' Lewis used a lot of onions. These, together with garlic and his home-grown chillies, seemed to be called for in nearly every recipe that appealed to him. He washed and dried his hands and turned to Abbey.

'Lewis,' she said simply as she fell into his arms, pulling him close and resting her head on his shoulder. 'I missed you.'

'But you were only gone for three hours,' he said, gently teasing.

'I was thinking of you all the time.' She looked up into

his eyes, her blue meeting his green. 'I couldn't concentrate at all.'

'Did you learn anything?'

'A few words. Hello, goodbye. How to tell people my name.'

'Oh.' Lewis was disappointed.

'I realised that I could already do most of it. And the tutor could barely understand our English. I don't know if it's worth carrying on.'

'You might be right. It's a shame but if that's how it is...'

'It was worth a try, Lewis.'

Lewis discovered that there were some spaces on the course after Alvaro told him that the couple in the end apartment were going back to England. Lewis didn't even know they were there. After that he stopped to talk to them a few times and they seemed nice enough people. Nice, but odd. They did not mix well with anyone. They never managed to gather friends amongst the expatriate residents and their Spanish was terrible. Perhaps that was why they had enrolled on the course. For whatever reason, they had given up completely now. 'It's a long way to travel,' observed Lewis.

'You mean to the college?'

Lewis nodded, disengaging from Abbey's embrace and picking up the first of the onions. He spoke as he chopped. 'Did you catch the bus ok?'

'Yes, I did. It was fine.' Abbey was quick to utter these words. She spoke rapidly, defensively. She did not like travelling on buses back at home, and disliked it even more here. She feared it all. Waiting at the right bus stop, getting on the correct bus, stating her destination, paying. Every step of it was loaded with risk and anxiety. Most of all, she dreaded the end of the journey. What if she got off too soon, or missed her stop and went too far? Despite it all and much to her surprise and relief, she got to the college and back without a hitch. 'The bus stopped right outside. It was cheap too.'

'Well, like I said it's a shame but if it's not worth the trouble then you might be better off learning like I did.'

'You must be talented. How did you learn?' Abbey enquired, dropping in a compliment at the same time.

'Well, I didn't do anything at all really.'

'You must have done something.'

'I suppose I just mixed with the locals and picked it up. Maribel started it off. You do remember Maribel, don't you? In the old town, with the shop that sells everything?'

'Of course I do.' A trace of irritation coloured Abbey's voice.

'Yes. Well, it happened naturally after that. I didn't have to think about it really.' Lewis picked up the long knife again, the onions trembled.

'Then that is what I'll do,' asserted Abbey emphatically. 'And pass me that knife. I'm chopping the onions.'

I've nearly run out. Abbey rummaged through a box of graphic pencils, turning over the stubby remains of what used to be a complete set. She picked a soft pencil out, sharpened it and turned back to her easel. Her hand flicked and fluttered, shading and filling the portrait. As she worked, she wondered how she would replenish her boxes. Although she needed nearly a full set of pencils, they were usually quite cheap. Pastels were inexpensive as well. But what about oils and acrylics? Where would she get them from? There might be somewhere in town that sold these things. 'Oh, I don't know.' Abbey sighed loudly.

'What's wrong, Abbey?' Lewis looked up from the computer.

'Oh, nothing.'

'That was a big sigh.'

Lewis was watching her, following her as she moved. He smiled gently, his eyes filled with compassion. Features softened by the falling dusk, he drew on a little cigar.

'Lewis, I just don't know how I'll do it.'

'Do what?' Lewis put the cigar down. Blue smoke trickled.

'Well, I need almost everything. Is there somewhere in Castillo that sells artists' things?'

'I don't know. I haven't noticed anywhere, but then I haven't been looking. Just a moment.' Lewis stood up and strode inside. There was a faint click and a wash of light flooded the terrace. 'Alvaro is good, isn't he?' Lewis did not expect an answer. He sat down next to Abbey and touched her shoulder. 'We'll find somewhere to get your things. I'll look it up or ask around.'

'Thank you, Lewis.' Abbey became silent again. She was worried. When she worked at Infotext she had been paid a modest salary. It was never going to make her rich, but it was enough to pay the bills. Working there made her unhappy, too. It was a miserable job. Now it was done and gone, and she would never want to return even if she could. 'It won't last long.'

'What won't last long?'

'My savings. I don't know what I'm going to do. You can't keep me and anyway that wouldn't be fair.' Abbey met Lewis' eyes. He was a good listener. 'I'll have to do something, but what?'

'You could sell these,' suggested Lewis. 'I mean, look at this. It's wonderful.' He picked up the portrait, still stretched over a board. 'This sort of thing would be fantastic in one of those boutiques in the new town.'

'But it's rubbish!' exclaimed Abbey. 'That's why I didn't bother showing it to you.'

'Well, I looked anyway. And it's very good. It makes me look younger.'

'Ah, Lewis. You are being too kind.'

'Not kind, just honest. I prefer it to a photograph. It still captures me, but it's not the same. Do you know what I mean? It's softer.'

'Yes, I suppose so,' Abbey agreed grudgingly. 'It's not

bad really. But I'm not good enough to sell my paintings. Really, Lewis, I'm not.' She slumped in her chair, defeated. A growing swarm of winged night insects encircled the lamp in the canopy, buzzing and clicking and banging their heads against its irresistible bright surface.

'Perhaps you could get a job.'

'No-one would want an English woman here,' retorted Abbey.

'Someone might...' ventured Lewis, becoming alarmed by her rising anger.

'I don't think so. Doing what, anyway? Cleaning? Waitressing?' Abbey stood up and stormed indoors, leaving Lewis alone with his cigar and the bickering moths.

Chapter Seven

'That one there.' Abbey pointed and the man looked.

'This?' He picked up a tube and offered it to her. It was not the one that she had pointed to.

'No, that one.'

'Which? This?' He picked out another one and looked inquiringly at Abbey.

Argh, it's so difficult. Abbey was buying paints and she was absolutely determined that she would do it all in Spanish. The man in the papelería knew no English anyway. It was a general stationery store, the shelves heavy with coloured paper, office equipment and writing materials. That it sold some artists' supplies was almost incredible, but it did and that was all that mattered. She pointed to a tube.

'This one. The yellow.'

'Ah, yellow. Here it is.'

Hey, he understood me! She put the tube of yellow paint down on the counter and carefully formed her next request in her mind before speaking it aloud.

'And I need orange.'

'Orange.'

'And red.'

'Red.'

Three tubes lined up on the counter. Abbey's shopping trip was going rather well.

'Do you have brushes?' she asked, framing each word separately as she spoke.

'Sí, por supuesto!' Yes, of course they had brushes.

Abbey was impressed. They had brushes, a range of them in popular sizes. Only one brand, but it looked good enough. 'Size two, please.'

'Dos.' The shopkeeper echoed her words and a size two brush appeared.

'And five and six.'

'Cinco y seis tambien.' Five and six too. 'Is that

everything?'

It was everything. Abbey paid and smiled sweetly at the patient man behind the counter. He had been very good, listening carefully to her as she struggled through her list and a queue built up behind her. She turned and walked past the ragged line. The sweaty, impatient customers shuffled forward, clutching their ballpoint pens and packs of printer paper.

'Café, señor!'

'Gracias, Juan.' Lewis took his coffee and thanked the waiter. It was still very early in the day and the café was empty. 'How are things?'

Juan pulled up a chair and joined Lewis at the round table on the pavement, allowing himself the rare luxury of a break. He got up again immediately, drew a second little cup of coffee from the machine and came back. Though he liked to pretend otherwise, he was much more than just a waiter. The café was his creation, his life. 'It's hectic, Lewis. The summer has been good. I expect it will be quieter soon. It always dies down in the autumn.'

'New car this year then?' Lewis teased.

'There's no chance of that. Not this year. She'll have to last a bit longer.' Juan was looking across the pavement to his old banger. It was red, terribly faded, and the doors and wings were marked with rusty streaks that recorded the driver's many motoring mistakes. 'It's getting hard to make a profit, to be honest.'

'Even on Saturdays?'

'On any day. I have costs, you know.' Juan grunted. 'And I need a new fryer. The old one really is finished now.'

Lewis nodded, commiserating silently.

'Anyway, what about you? Where's that girl? Has she left you yet?' The dark moon of Juan's face hovered, awaiting the reaction to his goading. Lewis picked up his cup and sipped the sweet, strong drink. Juan tried again. 'She's a fine-looking woman, you know. I bet she's good.

You don't want to miss an opportunity like that.'

'Well, I am not missing anything,' asserted Lewis. He pondered for a minute. 'It wasn't too good last night, though.'

'Oh? Why?' Juan could not hide his curiosity and he loved lewd gossip.

'We had an argument.'

'You? I don't believe it. You never argue with anyone. I don't know one person that's easier going than Lewis Coleman.'

'I do try to avoid things like that,' agreed Lewis, 'but she was complaining about money.'

'Ah, money. Always a problem. Just ask my wife!'

'Seriously though, Juan. She is worrying too much. She's talking about finding work or something. I tried to help but everything I said just made it worse.'

'So did she have a headache?'

'A headache?' Lewis erupted into laughter. It was a pithy way of describing rejection. 'Yes, I suppose she did. It took me about an hour to sort her out.'

'And then you...?' Juan's voice tailed off suggestively.

'Of course.' When men talk, some things can be left unsaid.

'There's no point. It's a waste of time.' Abbey was getting irritated again.

'No it's not,' argued Jackie, slipping off a flower-patterned kaftan and settling back onto her beach towel. 'You'll get a tan just like everyone else if you give it a chance.'

'No, I never tan.'

'Abbey, just relax and enjoy it. Do you want some help with that sun lotion?'

'No, I'll be fine.' Abbey shrugged off her clothes and smoothed the cream onto her pale limbs. She wondered if the black bikini was a good idea after all. Its shape was unflattering and the contrast of its dark colour only emphasised her whiteness.

'You'll need to be careful today,' cautioned Jackie. 'We won't stay too long.'

Abbey pulled a book out from her bag and opened it up. She peeped over the top of it, taking in the scene. The summer was nearly over and the bigger children were back at school. It was still pleasantly warm and the sand was dotted with people basking in the golden September sun. She tilted her head to one side. *It's not quite right.* Maybe the sun was still too high, or the expanse of sand too broad. Whatever it was, it simply would not make a good picture. Abbey resolved to come down again and look one evening instead.

'Why don't you take your top off?'

Abbey's musings were interrupted and she turned towards the voice. Jackie's melons hung down, oiled, bronzed and voluptuous. *How can I compete with those?*

'It's topless here,' continued Jackie, rather obviously. 'You can't do it up near town, but it's fine on this part of the beach.'

'I, um, I don't do that,' ventured Abbey.

'You'll get tan lines, they will look awful.'

'Tan lines don't look that bad. Anyway, what does it matter? Who is going to see them?'

'You will see them. And Lewis will.'

Abbey felt herself reddening.

'You do let him see you, don't you?' enquired Jackie, lifting up her sunglasses and resting them on the top of her head.

'Yes, of course.' Abbey wondered how much to say.

'What is it like?'

'What is what like?' That was a stupid question. It was perfectly obvious what Jackie was asking about. 'It's good,' she admitted.

'Only good? Is that all?'

'Ok, well, he is good, like I said. He takes his time and does the right things.' Abbey's blushing had faded. It was getting easier to talk to Jackie. 'He's very obliging. Do you know what I mean?'

'He does what you ask?'

'Yes, that's it. Except when he's dominating, of course.'

'Wow, it sounds like you've got it all, Abbey. You do realise how lucky you are, don't you?'

Abbey did not reply. Was that a flash of envy she saw in Jackie's face?

'It's alright, Abbey. Don't worry, he's not interested in me.'

If that was meant to be reassurance from Jackie then it was an odd way of putting it. She was still talking, chirping and cawing like a tropical bird.

'So, are you taking that top off then?' Jackie persisted.

'Not today. I might do if we come again.'

'Fair enough. What are you reading?'

'Oh, just some rubbish. A romance, with a bit of mystery in it. What do you read?'

'Not much,' admitted Jackie. 'I haven't got the patience for it. I close my eyes and think of things.'

'What do you think about? The past?'

'Oh, no. I try not to think about the past. I think about nice things. Food, what to buy, where to go. That sort of stuff.'

Abbey knew almost nothing about Jackie's history. Where she was from, how she acquired her wealth and came to live in Spain. Abbey sensed there was a story to be told, something that Jackie would prefer to keep hidden. Abbey tried to read her book but couldn't stop puzzling. She glanced sideways at Jackie, lying there sunbathing with her eyes closed. In the end Abbey had to ask.

'Jackie?'

'Mm?'

'I like your accent.'

'Thank you.'

Abbey was deliberately cautious. She wanted to learn about Jackie, but without risking their friendship. 'Where is it from?' she continued.

'It's from Harfield, in Essex. Do you know Harfield?'

'No. Well, I know roughly where it is, but I've never been there.'

'You haven't missed much.'

Abbey laughed. Harfield was created from virtually nothing after the war, a sprawl of new housing that trampled over picturesque villages and ancient farmland. It was soulless and no-one ever had anything favourable to say about it.

'We lived near the railway, 'cos the houses there were cheaper,' offered Jackie.

'Wasn't it noisy?'

'No. The London trains went past all day but you soon got used to it. I never even noticed them. Harfield was still horrible, though. After university I never went back.'

'University?' Abbey spoke the word out loud and immediately regretted it. Jackie was not the university sort. She was just not serious enough. Abbey could not imagine such a flighty, whimsical person getting down to work on anything even remotely academic. 'Sorry, I didn't meant to be rude.'

'You're not rude.' Jackie brushed the apology aside. 'I did ok with it, really.'

'What did you study?'

'Oh, sciencey stuff.'

'Sciencey? You mean like biology or chemistry?'

'Not really, no.'

'Engineering? Technology?' Abbey's suggestions were ignored. She tried something more adventurous. 'Quantum physics?'

Jackie laughed. 'You don't want to know about it.' She dismissed the questioning with a weak-wristed wave.

Abbey had pried enough for now and her curiosity would have to keep for another time. She turned back to her book. In seconds she was interrupted.

'No, I never went back.' Jackie sat up on her beach

73

towel as she repeated the words. Her straw-coloured hair flowed down her back.

Abbey watched as Jackie swept a hand around, caught up the yellow cascade and brought it forward over a shoulder. Her body looked fantastic, like someone half her age. It was a shame that she wore too much make-up even at the beach.

Jackie crouched forward and wrapped her arms around her knees. The laughter in her eyes had cooled. 'You'll get sunburnt if we stay any longer. Come on.'

Bullwood was baking. It roasted slowly in the hot wind. The weather man blamed the autumn heatwave on unusual conditions, hot air flooding in from across the English Channel. It was something that he called a continental plume. Things were the same a few miles away in Calborough, except that the streets there were littered with luxury cars instead of discarded beer cans and torn-up lottery tickets. Rita got up from in front of the television and walked about. She made small circles around her chair first, then larger ones right around the room. It was happening again and she did not understand it. How could she be hot and cold at the same time? Her face was fevered and damp and the air seemed too thick to breathe properly, yet her hands and feet were cold and numb. Walking was not helping. Perhaps some other activity would. She went into the kitchen. The flowers on the windowsill had already given up, turning their tired heads down to stare blindly at the floor. She started cleaning and moving things, lining them up on the worktops with obsessive precision. For a moment she paused, pressing her hands on the table for support, gasping for air. She reached to open the window and her elbow brushed against something. The vase fell, Rita watched it helplessly. It turned as it descended, flowers flicking and scattering. The oval glass seemed to flatten as it struck the floor, breaking into shards as water sprayed a starfish pattern on the tiles.

'Tom?'

Tom did not reply.

'Tom? I need some help in here,' Rita called again. The silence waited. She worked her way along the kitchen, holding onto the edge of the worktop and stepping gingerly around the broken flower stems and crystallised glass. She crossed the lounge and pushed open the door into the little bedroom. The room looked a lot more untidy than she remembered.

'Nan. What's up?'

'Oh. I was looking for Tom.'

'But Nan, Tom's dead,' stated Luke flatly.

Rita stared at him, her mouth hanging open. 'Dead?' There was a pause. 'Yes, of course he is. I forgot.'

'Nan? Are you ok?' Luke turned and stood up.

'Yes. No, something's wrong.' She offered a hand, yellow and limp, to Luke. He recoiled from the cold touch. 'What should I do, Luke?'

'I don't know, Nan.' Luke's brow knitted. He did not have a clue what was wrong with his grandmother, nor what to do about it. 'Ring Mum. She'll know.'

'She doesn't care about me,' spat Rita. 'She's hundreds of miles away, with that fancy man of hers. What's his name?'

'Lewis.'

'Yes, Lewis. Huh. He hasn't even got a proper job. I bet they just sit there all day, drinking wine and laughing.'

'Look, Nan, I don't want to argue. Just ring Mum, will you?'

Rita backed out of Luke's room and pulled the door closed. Her hand reached for the telephone. 'No,' she voiced to herself. 'No, I won't ring her. What can she do? Nothing. I'll feel better again soon. Like last time.'

Abbey squirmed and twisted in the wooden chair, battling unsuccessfully to find comfort. Her clothes felt like hairy sandpaper, itchy and abrasive. She wore a loose t-shirt, but even the slightest touch from it was unbearable.

Lewis looked up from his computer, his clattering fingertips fell quiet. 'Abbey? Are you ok?'

'Yes, Lewis. I'm fine.' She sent him a smile, forcing it out in an attempt to cover up. What he received was a pained grimace.

'I can see you shuffling about from here. You're worse than a cat on hot bricks.'

'It's my back.'

'Your back?'

'Yes. And my shoulders. They really hurt.'

'Let me take a look.'

Abbey did not protest, allowing Lewis to slip the shoulders of her t-shirt down. Underneath, her skin was bright red and hot to the touch. The sunburn covered her shoulders and the top of her back, and it looked nasty.

'It's badly burned, Abbey.'

'I know.'

Lewis became increasingly concerned as he looked over Abbey, taking in the extent of her problem. 'You should have said something earlier.'

'I didn't want to trouble you.'

'Trouble me? Oh come on, Abbey. Surely you know me better that that. How long have you lived here? It must be getting on for three months.'

'It's only two, even if you count my earlier visits.'

'Well, it seems longer.' He was standing in front of her now. He surprised her by placing a fingertip under her chin, tilting her head up. The power of his eyes drew her to him, a green magnetism that connected and engaged. 'I care about you, Abbey,' he said. 'I thought you would have realised by now.' He reached to wrap her in his arms.

'Yow!' shrieked Abbey as the burning pain shot across her shoulders.

Lewis released her instantly. 'Sorry. It's my fault. I just forgot.'

Abbey's breathing was slowing again as the discomfort faded. 'It's ok. Not to worry. It was only painful for a moment. Have you got anything for it?'

'There should be some lotion in the bathroom. It's from last year but it will still be fine. I never thought I'd need it again, to be honest.'

Abbey cast an envious look at Lewis' perfectly tanned brown, then darted inside. She was back in a few minutes, clutching the bottle. 'Lewis, I think you'll have to help. I can't reach.'

He took the bottle and stood behind Abbey. Once again he eased her shoulder straps down. 'You'll have to take this right off,' he observed.

Stripped to the waist, she presented her back to him. The outline of her bikini top was imprinted solidly in white against a red background. He tilted the bottle onto his fingers and dabbed at her experimentally with the creamy lotion.

'Ooh, it's cold!' Abbey jerked away from Lewis in shock.

'Come on, you'll have to let me do it.'

The lotion went on, smoothed gently and expertly over Abbey's shoulders, then down her back. Lewis stopped below the white band left by the bikini strap, then slipped his cool fingers past her neck and onto her chest. He poured more lotion and continued down, reaching to cup her pale, cool ovals. He was lifting and playing, massaging her gently. She closed her eyes and allowed it to happen, enjoying the sensation. Tingling and melting, she idly noticed how the umbrella fronds of the palm trees rippled and bowed in the breeze.

'Oh, Lewis. I want to be with you forever.'

He paused, his hands supporting her globes softly as she looked up at him through her eyelashes. 'Yes, Abbey.' His hands moved again.

'I love you, Lewis.'

Lewis slid his hands off her body and closed the bottle

without speaking. Abbey's euphoria melted away and she came back to reality. With it came the realisation that on the terrace they were in easy view of anyone who might pass through the gardens below or even a neighbour who might take the trouble to peek from another apartment.

'Pass me my shirt, would you?' she instructed Lewis curtly. *So, he cares about me but he doesn't love me.*

'No, you don't need it.' Lewis' voice was firm, his strong arms around her waist irresistible. She found the sweetness of his lips as he pressed his chest against her bare body. At last she broke away, breathless.

'Come on, let's go inside,' whispered Lewis.

Never releasing his hand, she followed him into the cool interior. Just caring would have to be enough for now.

Chapter Eight

'Lewis, that dog is barking again. I don't like it. The noise comes through the wall, you can hear it all over the apartment.' Abbey was grumbling. Sometimes a volcano rumbles like that, steaming and hissing, threatening to erupt. 'Next door is at least five meters away but I can still hear it in here. It's been on and off all morning.'

There was no reply. In between the barks, Abbey could hear tapping. Lewis was out on the terrace, seated at the table and working on that damned book of his. He hardly did anything else. Surely the noise bothered him too.

'Lewis, can't we do something about it? I could play some loud music, but I don't want to. I don't really like the tunes they play on the radio.'

'Why?' Lewis finally acknowledged that she was speaking to him.

'They are different to what I'm used to.'

'You are here now. Of course it's different. It's just part of the experience. You know, lots of things are different.' Lewis stopped as he lit a small cigar. 'The food, the people, the weather. And yes, the music that they play on the radio. Why don't you like it? It's got a lot of Latin influence in it, it's hot, full of passion. It matches the weather!'

'It distracts me, I don't want it so loud and anyway it's simply wrong. It doesn't actually deal with the problem. It just covers it up.'

Abbey was framed in the doorway, holding her little grey teddy bear against her left shoulder as if she were comforting a baby. In truth, the teddy was comforting her, its soft cuddly form tucked under her chin. 'Lewis, I've had enough now. Please do something about it.' She stood waiting, appealing to him.

Lewis put his cigar down on the edge of the ashtray, taking a few seconds to balance it carefully. 'I thought you like dogs. You always stop and stroke them. I have to wait while you make a fuss.'

'Yes, but that's different. Those are good dogs. Well, good owners anyway. Owners that train their pets and keep them under control. These people don't know how to look after a dog. They just leave it to do what it wants.' She indicated the neighbours by tilting her head accusingly in their direction.

'What can I do?' replied Lewis, exasperated. 'I can't tell them how to live their lives. They were here before me, Castillo is their home too.'

'You speak good Spanish, don't you?' Abbey the volcano was erupting. 'Listen, it's terrible. It's not fair. It's rude.' Her words were glowing red lava and billowing acid smoke. 'I'm going round there now.' She strode out onto the terrace, her face a mask of anger.

'No, Abbey, that's not the way to do it. I don't want to upset them.' Lewis was becoming quite alarmed. Abbey tried to push past but he blocked her route, preventing her stepping over the low terrace wall and storming upon the neighbours.

'You don't want to upset them? What about me?' she returned. 'This is my home now, I have to live here too.'

Lewis was taken aback. Was this her home now? It was his apartment, he had only invited her to stay for a while. He was doing her a favour, giving her a unique opportunity to sample another way of life. He never promised that it was forever.

The dog was still barking. 'Arf, arf, arf.' It made a lot of noise for a small animal.

'Alright, I'll go and have a word. Wait here,' Lewis instructed.

Abbey sat down in one of the slatted wooden chairs and stared coldly at the table. On the ashtray, Lewis' cigar had gone out. Tipped with dead black ash, it waited sullenly for its owner. Lewis took the trouble to leave his apartment through the front door and Abbey heard it close behind him. On the terrace, she searched for something to distract herself with, something to soften the anger that she felt. It had taken hold of her, hijacking her mind and directing her thoughts. Her eyes fell upon the computer screen and the words it displayed formed into sentences, drawing her in. In turn, the sentences grew into paragraphs, knitted sheets of words that drew scenes. People lived inside those scenes, participants talking, loving and laughing together in an imagined world.

'There.'

Lewis' announcement made Abbey jump. Engrossed in the pages on the screen, she was completely unaware of his return and his voice came as a complete surprise. She looked up guiltily, but Lewis just smiled in his special way. Unfathomable, his expression was both caring and cool at the same time. He seemed to be waiting for her to say or do something. On the trees that fringed the terrace, the season's old dry leaves chattered amongst themselves.

'Oh, It's stopped. The barking has stopped,' Abbey marvelled.

'Always I am asking him but he is not buying.'

'Pardon?'

'I am asking him for the flowers. He is saying no always.'

'Ah. Yes, now I understand.' Maribel leaned on the shop counter, squashing her ample folds against its time-worn wood. 'You could say it like this: I keep asking him for flowers but he won't buy me any.' She spoke slowly, then paused to let her suggestion sink in. 'Don't worry, lady. Um, what is you name?'

Lewis opened his mouth to speak, ready to take over.

'No, Lewis, I am doing it,' interrupted Abbey. 'Me llamo Abbey,' she announced. I'm called Abbey.

'Yes, Abbey. Don't worry, you are doing very well. You will soon speak Spanish as well as I do.'

'Thank you, Maribel.' Abbey doubted Maribel's optimistic confidence but did not wish to seem ungrateful.

'I need to buy some things,' she started and Maribel's face cracked into a smile of anticipation. 'I need... I don't know how to say it.' Abbey turned to Lewis. Now that she needed him, she regretted brushing him away earlier. 'Lewis, I need washing line and pegs.'

'Washing line and pegs? Whatever for?'

'Just ask her for them, please.' Abbey had a programme, a secret agenda. The humble washing line was part of the plan. It was time to start working her way into every aspect of Lewis' life, changing things. If she could become part of his everyday routine, essential and indispensable, he would have more reasons to value her. He would accept her companionship fully, take her into his heart, have her as part of his life for ever.

Maribel fetched the pegs and a bundle of line. 'How do you think Lewis learned to speak Spanish so well?' she challenged. 'Because I helped him, that's why. You should have heard his first attempts!' Maribel pursed her lips and drew in her breath, making a whistling sound that mocked Lewis' early efforts.

Abbey laughed, Lewis didn't.

'But he's a good man.' Maribel offered her opinion to Abbey as if Lewis was not even there. Then she turned to him and did the same about Abbey. 'She has everything, Lewis. Beautiful, intelligent. Are you going to marry her?'

Lewis was stunned. He was used to Maribel's directness, but this looked like a proper trap. Whatever he said could be dangerous. He glanced around the shop. Maribel and Abbey were both watching and waiting, each with her own reasons for wondering what his reply would be. A gaggle of other customers were waiting too.

'Quizás,' he said. Perhaps. That was a very useful word to know and one which seemed sufficient to satisfy Maribel's curiosity for now. He tried unsuccessfully to read Abbey's face to see if he had got away with it.

'Abbey, did you like your teddy bear?' Maribel rescued Lewis with her incidental question.

'Oh, yes, I love him.'

'Good. Lewis, listen to me.' She turned to him. 'You should buy her flowers to show her your love.'

'Yes, yes.'

To Maribel, this sounded more like 'No. Leave me alone.' Old, wrinkled and wise, she shuffled off down her shop to see if she could convert a clutch of browsers into buyers.

Black trousers, a white apron and a pot belly hurried into the kitchen. Above his stomach, Juan carried a new fryer. It was still in its enormous cardboard box and he struggled to slide it onto one of the work benches. All sorts of things that should not be there got in the way. Pans, bags of flour, a slotted wooden block filled with knives. Juan pushed them aside and lifted out his new acquisition. It was the first big purchase that he had made for a long time. Shiny steel, matt black handles, sparkling wire nets. It was a shame that there was no time to enjoy the novelty of its pristine perfection. Juan filled it with cooking oil and plugged it in. The oil gurgled and warmed, a nasty smell filled the café.

'Mujer!' Woman! Juan shouted for his wife. Surely she could hear him. He tried again, this time rather more politely. 'Mi querida!' My dear!

'Yes, Juan?'

'This place is a mess. How many times have I told the chef to put things away? Where is he, anyway? He should be here by now.'

'Oh, I was going to tell you. He's off today.'

'Off? Again? Now what's his excuse?'

'I think he's sick.'

'But it's Saturday. He knows how busy we are on Saturdays.' Juan wiped the sweat from his forehead.

'Is this the new fryer?'

'Yes, of course it is,' barked Juan.

'Don't talk to me like that. It's not my fault. He's let me

down as well, you know. It's not just your café, it's mine too.'

'Yes, Reina. Sorry.' Contrite, Juan hung his head.

Reina was the same age as Juan and equally overweight. Her hair was bundled up in a headscarf. Unlike Juan, she was endowed with a generous bosom and plenty of old-fashioned bossiness. 'It smells terrible,' she said pointedly. 'Is it burning?'

'I think it's just because it's new,' Juan suggested. 'It will be fine by tonight,' he added hopefully.

'Listen. I'll serve the tables today, you do the cooking,' said Reina firmly.

'Yes, dear.' He started clearing the worktops. It was going to be a long, hot and tiring day.

Luke's bedroom was getting worse. It was a slow decline, a battle between order and disorder that played out as the months passed. Disorder had gained the upper hand but Luke did not notice. He was at home in his room, a dishevelled young man whose crumpled shirt and torn jeans matched the chaos around him. The battle of the bedroom took second place to the one that played out daily on his screen.

'Go in. I'll cover you.' With headphones covering his ears and a microphone at his chin, Luke dispensed commands to his team.

'Into the hut?' came the response.

'Yes, in there.' Luke confirmed his instructions as he scanned the screen, checking how things were going. Ammunition, time left, the condition of each member of his team. He was an old hand and he took in the data instantly. The list of players on the screen changed, a new participant appeared. Years of game-play had made Luke indifferent. New people popped up all the time, initially as spectators. Sometimes they stayed around for a few days and occasionally one might join his team or become a regular opponent. Most of them disappeared without trace, never to be seen again. He casually looked over the information to see the new player's name. Sally.

'No.' Luke expressed his disbelief simply. Only males played. Why would one of them call himself Sally? It must be a prank, someone having a bit of fun.

'I'll have some fun as well,' he declared. The plan was simple. With the rest of his team listening in, he would engage the witless joker in conversation. It should only take a few seconds to reveal the frivolous attempt at deception and pour ridicule upon its perpetrator. Click. He was connected.

'Hello Sally.'

'Hi Luke. How are you doing?'

Her voice was sweet, almost spicy. Breathy, shockingly intimate in his headphones, it stunned him into silence. She was real! In his mind he pictured the girl behind the voice: slim, dark, long black hair, brown eyes.

'Luke?' Sally prompted him again.

Before he could think of anything to say to her, his ears were filled with gales of laughter. Everyone playing the game ripped into him, burying him under a deluge of humiliation. The list of names on the screen changed again and Sally was gone.

'Alvaro, what are you doing here?'

'Señor?' Alvaro's moustache twitched. He raised his black eyebrows in enquiry. 'The lady asked me to come. Has she changed her mind?'

'Changed her mind? About what?'

'About the hooks. She wants me to put hooks up,' explained Alvaro.

'Oh no. They'll be for the washing line.'

'Sí, for the washing line, señor.'

Lewis shook his head. He did not want a perpetual display of damp laundry decorating his terrace. 'Abbey!' he called.

'No need to shout.'

She must have been waiting just inside the apartment. 'Abbey, Alvaro is here to put up your washing line.'

'Great,' she said brightly. 'Alvaro, can you-'

'But you can't do it,' interrupted Lewis.

'Why?'

'Because it will look horrible. I don't want a washing line.'

'And I do.' Abbey stood her ground. Lewis faced her and the battle lines were drawn. Their second argument was about to flare up, a trivial dispute about two hooks and a length of clothes line.

Alvaro found himself witness to a tasty piece of gossip that was developing right before him, but at the same time he could feel the job slipping away. Little as it was, he needed the money. 'Señor, señorita, por favor.' Sir, miss, please.

Lewis glanced at the handyman, then turned back to Abbey. 'Where do you want it?'

'Across the terrace.' She pointed out its intended location along one side.

'Across the terrace? It will look dreadful with towels and shirts and underpants billowing all day.'

'No it won't. The wind is hot and dry. The clothes won't need to be out for long.'

'But Gabriela does the laundry,' Lewis pleaded. He was getting desperate for defensive ideas.

'She could be cleaning inside instead of running your clothes to the lavandería each week.' Abbey moved just a little closer to Lewis. Inhaling deeply, she thrust out her chest to maximise what modest assets she possessed. She looked up at him through her eyelashes.

Lewis' resistance crumbled. What did it matter? It was only a washing line. 'Alvaro is waiting. You'd better show him where you want the hooks.'

Jackie let herself in to Lewis' apartment and locked the door again behind her. It was dark inside, but the light in the terrace canopy was on. She waded through the long bright rectangles that it cast on the tiled floor of the apartment and pushed open the back door. Yes, Abbey was there. Alone on the terrace, she sat with her back to the door. Everything was bright against the dark evening beyond. 'Hiya!' called Jackie, flouncing out into the pool of lamplight.

'Jackie, what are you doing here?' Abbey looked perfectly surprised.

'Oh, I don't know,' returned Jackie casually. 'Where's Lewis?'

'He's gone to the bodega to get some wine. I didn't want to go.'

The bodega was a local shop that was open all evening and sold not just wine but all sorts of groceries and useful household supplies. Jackie plonked herself down on the chair next to Abbey. 'What's this?' she asked, pointing at a sheet of paper on the table. It was covered with figures and notes.

'Oh, it's nothing.' Abbey picked up the paper, folded it and slipped it into a pocket. 'I'm surprised at Lewis,' she said, pointedly changing the subject.

'Really? Why?'

'Well, he's usually very well organised, isn't he?'

'Uhuh,' agreed Jackie.

'But he ran out of wine. Completely. He's always telling me how fantastic he is at planning things.'

'Maybe he just forgot about the wine or something.'

'I suppose so. Did you let yourself in?' queried Abbey, still perplexed.

'Yes. Is there anything left to drink?' Jackie brushed Abbey's surprise aside and made an obvious display of looking around the terrace.

'There might be. I'll look in the store.'

'It's ok, I'll look.' Jackie sprang up and skipped towards the store before Abbey could argue about it.

'You know I was married, don't you?' asked Jackie through a beery haze.

'No. You never said. Hang on, I really have to go.' Abbey disappeared into the apartment.

'What was I saying?' prompted Jackie.

'Sorry, that beer goes straight through me,' Abbey explained, dropping back into her chair. 'I can't remember. Oh yes, you said that you got married.'

'Ah yes. Married.' Jackie picked up her glass, swallowed, then produced a short, squeaky belch.

'Jackie!'

'What? It's only a burp.'

They both giggled.

'He was a horrible man. Imagine someone that's the opposite of Lewis. You know what I mean? He was ugly and fat. And he was small.' Jackie carefully placed her beer glass on the table, then held up two fingers a few inches apart. 'This small!'

The laughter subsided and Jackie pressed her lips together tightly into a grim line, then spoke through her teeth. 'He never once asked me for sex. Never.'

'So why did you marry him?'

'Good question, Abbey.' Jackie shrugged. 'You were married too, weren't you? We all make mistakes. Anyway, it didn't last long.'

'So you divorced?'

'No. He died.'

'Oh, I'm sorry,' started Abbey.

'No, don't be sorry, Abbey. He was a lousy, selfish bastard. No-one will miss him. He died, he was buried, I transferred the money and came to Spain. That's all there is to it.' Jackie swallowed her beer noisily. 'What about you?'

'I lost everything in my divorce,' admitted Abbey. 'He took it all.'

'You did it wrong then,' stated Jackie flatly. The

alcohol was winning.

'What could I do? My solicitors let me down. I didn't know what should have been mine and they never told me. After the case it was too late.'

'Money isn't everything,' Jackie observed.

'Jackie, how can you say that? You came here and bought an apartment. You've got that car. And you shop at Sarita Suelo, for God's sake! Doesn't that make you happy?'

'I suppose it does. I can do anything I like now that he's gone.' Jackie laughed as she tossed back the yellow waterfall of her hair. 'Well, almost anything...'

Autumn swirled through the terrace, tugging at their clothes, reminding them that summer can't last forever even here. A light popped on inside the apartment.

'Hello!' Lewis strode onto the terrace. 'They didn't have Vino Tinto de Castillo so I had to go into the old town. Did you miss me?'

Both women looked blank. Hours had passed by unnoticed, made irrelevant by cold beer and easy conversation. Miss him? Neither of them had given Lewis' long absence a moment's thought.

'Perhaps I ought to think about going back now.' Jackie rose unsteadily.

'I'll see you out,' offered Lewis.

Lewis stood with Jackie under the arch at the front. 'Thanks for coming round,' he said. 'After the washing line thing, she went inside and hid,' he confided quietly. 'She was working out her finances. She wouldn't let me see them, but I don't think things are very good. She got quite upset about it and everything I said just made it worse. That's why I asked you.'

'It's fine, Lewis. No problem. I've enjoyed it... and the beer was super!' Jackie reached around Lewis and pressed a wet, drunken kiss onto his lips. Seeing an unmissable opportunity, she grabbed his bottom with both hands and pinched her fingers together.

'Hey!' exclaimed Lewis.

'See you tomorrow at La Luz?' Jackie did not wait for an answer. Tossing a triumphant laugh over her shoulder, she disappeared into the autumn night.

Chapter Nine

Lewis looked at himself in the mirror. He did not feel very good, but it was difficult to say just what was wrong. There was an awareness of something amiss in his stomach and a hint of a headache that eluded his attention each time he tried to find it. There seemed to be something odd about his limbs too. Again it was hard to be sure why, but the weakness was so bad that he was almost stumbling. An unfamiliar heaviness dragged down on him. He looked back through the door into the bedroom. Abbey was still asleep, sprawled across the bed with sheets over her hips. The smooth bareness of her back moved gently as she breathed. It was only a few hours since he had been caressing those curves, sliding his hands over her back and down to her hips. Remembering, Lewis chuckled at his unshaven reflection. The evening of beer and gossip that Abbey enjoyed with Jackie did not render her outright drunk, rather she appeared dreamlike and just slightly disconnected. Uninhibited, they explored and experimented. Most of it had been good, and some of it delightful. Kneeling behind her, his climax came suddenly and he shouted out, his head tilted back in ecstasy. But that was last night. Now it was light and it was morning and he had to get on with things. There was writing to finish. Abbey's companionship, as well as her passion, were welcome new things in his life. But he had not anticipated the other things, all the distractions and diversions that stole his time.

'Jackie!' Abbey stumbled out onto the terrace and into the cool brightness of morning. Lewis and Jackie sat at the table. Judging by the number of cigarette and cigar stubs in the ashtray, they had been enjoying each other's company for quite some time already.

'Ah, good morning Abbey,' said Lewis breezily.

Abbey eyed him coldly. She despised rudeness in

others, and always made an effort to avoid it herself. Despite the twinge of shame that this produced inside her, she just could not bring herself to greet him.

'Hi, Abbey.' Jackie was effervescent, full of energy. 'Is something wrong?' she added.

'I... I was just surprised to see you here so early.' Abbey darted a glance at Lewis and then turned her attention back to Jackie. *Well, they don't look guilty.* Lewis' eyes were smiling, as compassionate and easy as ever. Jackie wore red lipstick and too much foundation. Why did she remove her eyebrows and then draw them on again like that? It always made her appear just a little bit startled.

'Early? It's nearly twelve.' Jackie's eyebrows lifted even higher as she spoke. Abbey did not reply, so Jackie continued. 'We were waiting for you to get up but we didn't want to disturb you. We're going to La Luz.'

'Thank you.' Abbey acknowledged Jackie's explanation flatly, carefully hiding her own surprise that she had slept so late.

'That's ok,' chirped Jackie.

Abbey wanted to believe the simple explanation. The pieces of the jigsaw were falling together convincingly enough, disarming her suspicions.

'Come and sit down. We'll go to the café when you've had a bit more time to come round. Would you like some juice?' Lewis made to stand up but failed in his efforts. He sat down again heavily.

'Are you feeling alright?'

'Lewis, are you ok?'

Both women spoke at once.

'Yes, I'm fine.' Lewis screwed up his face and immediately changed his mind. 'No, I'm not.'

Abbey was by his side, a hand on his shoulder.

'I feel kind of... feeble,' admitted Lewis.

Abbey looked him over worriedly. This was not the rock that she had come to know. The sturdy muscled tower of confidence and potency was fatigued and haggard. She noticed his stubble for the first time. He had not shaved this morning.

Abbey was on the bus. She sat on the right, and this put her alongside the edge of the road so that she could watch the scenery as it slipped past. In England, she always sat on the left. It was an age-old habit that she simply could not shake off. Even when she was choosing her seat on an aeroplane, she still preferred the left hand side. Though it was surely unimportant when flying, the compulsion was irresistible. This journey was different, it was one that she had been thinking about for a few days and everything about it was carefully considered. She needed to buy autumn clothes and she wanted to do it alone. Taking the bus to Centro Nuevo gave her a chance to try out some more Spanish, expand her horizons and consolidate her sense of independence. Lewis was resting in bed. Jackie seemed much less concerned about him than Abbey was, dismissing it lightly. 'Oh, he's caught some kind of virus. It's nothing. He'll be fine again by tomorrow.' *How could she know?* She was probably sitting at Cafetería de la Luz now, drinking Juan's coffee and smoking.

Buildings flashed past, the last of Castillo petered out and was replaced by green-threaded brown fields watched over by crumbling farm houses. There were patches of rough land, stone-strewn and forgotten, that seemed to belong to no-one and be used for nothing. Then orange groves, planted with regimented rows of trees, filled the view. Lewis had mentioned them, telling her how the air hung heavy with the nectar of their blossom every spring. Behind the orange groves rose the mountains, distant slopes decorated with vineyards and crossed with the white lines of centuries-old cart tracks.

Silver and black monoliths appeared in the distance, ugly and incongruous. The low sun caught their surfaces and fractured into shards of light that could be seen for miles, an early warning of the architectural horrors to come. 'It's no wonder they call it an urbanisation,' Abbey muttered. At least the planners had hidden the factory units and warehouses at the back and constructed the most attractive buildings closest to the road. These were the offices, tall and businesslike with darkened glass windows. Abbey had been here before, but not by bus. On previous excursions to Centro Nuevo she drove there and parked her little white hire car behind the offices. Infotext rented space there, in the cheaper section overlooking the factories and car parks. Back then, Lewis was still a tantalising mystery. It had just been a chance encounter, the unexpected comfort of a soft English voice in a foreign place. Abbey smiled at the memory of their meeting, a place and time forever suffused with light and unfamiliar warmth, rich with the aromas of coffee and cigar smoke. The promise she saw in those compelling green eyes had not been an empty one. In strong arms he swept her away on heavenly waves. Almost every day they were connected by the pleasure that they shared, fervent, breathlessly releasing the desperate urgency of their bodies. Yet it was only physical, the fevered heat of passion that could never be mistaken for the flames of love. They lived together and lay together but Abbey felt unsatisfied, hollow. Something was missing.

Centro Nuevo, new centre, was the product of a local politician. It was an enormous complex of retail endeavour and political vanity. Four floors of shops, restaurants and more, each a web of promenades and plazas with marbled floors and chromed pillars. Abbey stood in one of the avenues. A jeweller's, a men's fashion shop, a tiny leather boutique with its windows full of straps and studs and indescribably cruel-looking things. Next to that, unlikely as it seemed, was a branch of a national bank. Abbey span round. A hairdresser's, a perfume shop, a silver and glass-fronted place called Cool. It seemed to sell gifts but she had lost interest. The envelope of sound folded in around her, slapping against her ears. There was shouting and shuffling. People were laughing, the din filled and boomed. Somewhere there was a baby crying pitifully and the noise was unbearable. The roof seemed to be getting lower, the shop-fronts pressed in on every side. It was sweltering now and so much busier than when she arrived. Abbey breathed quickly, the reluctant air caught in her throat. Her heart raced, her fingers tingled, she felt hot and cold at the same time. The noise built up to a high-pressure climax inside her head, melting and fusing together into a high-pitched buzz. *I have to get out of here.* Where was the exit? She pushed through the faceless people, hurrying between the shops. She reached the glass doors at one end. They had huge letters stuck on the glass. Supermercado. It was a supermarket, bright inside with fluorescent light, white shelves and endless rows of identical packages and tins. That was no good. Her panic increasing, she turned and retraced her steps. Back past the bank and the hairdresser's and the leather shop with its brash perversity of face-masks, whips and intimately shaped accessories. There was a shop that sold phones. She didn't remember seeing that before. Still, there were lots of phone shops in every shopping centre. It must have been there, she just hadn't noticed it.

'Which way is it?' Abbey could sense herself lifting up, breaking into a run and feeling momentarily embarrassed about it. Yet no-one seemed to notice. Perhaps they were too busy with their own lives, buying gifts and new phones that they didn't need. The concourse widened out, Abbey had to stop and rest. Her fingers found the cold steel of a metal railing for support. She leaned on the barrier and looked down. Three spans of escalator zig-zagged into infinity below, moving stairways that were speckled with shoppers flowing serenely from floor to floor. Nausea welled up inside her, she swallowed hard. The blindness closed in and then there was just greyness, the roaring in her ears and the cold metal in her hands.

Abbey felt a gentle hand on her shoulder. Through the din she could hear a woman's voice speaking to her.

'Abbey, it's ok. I'm here now.' The voice paused, then said more things. It seemed kind, though Abbey could not understand all of the words.

The terrible rushing noise in her ears eased and normal sounds started to replace it. Abbey could hear footsteps again, passing people were laughing and talking. As the light came back she saw shops and escalators and a worried face.

'It's alright,' repeated the worried face.

'I... I want to go home now.' Abbey heard her own voice, distant and child-like.

'Sí. I'll take you.'

'But you don't know where I live.'

'Of course I do. Venga conmigo!' Come with me.

Abbey was bewildered, frozen, a grey stone-sculpted statue cemented to the marble floor.

'Abbey, come with me. It's Gabriela.' Gabriela bent down and picked up the crumpled plastic shopping bags piled at Abbey's feet. Abbey looked unsteady and confused. Gabriela cupped a steadying hand under Abbey's elbow and watched as the life came back into her eyes. 'I'll take you home.'

Jackie opened Lewis' front door to see who was calling. 'Hi Abbey. Oh, hola Gabriela.' She looked them both up and down. Abbey was expected, Gabriela was not. 'You look tired, Abbey.' Jackie's voice rose in pitch as she spoke, turning her blunt observation into a question.

'Yes, I'm shattered.'

'Did you get everything that you wanted?'

'No.' Abbey looked forlorn. 'It was a disaster.'

'I found her on the top floor, opposite the phone shop,' explained Gabriela with needless detail. 'She was... um... I don't know. She was a little confused.' Gabriela was a simple woman, but she was polite too.

'I had a panic attack, Jackie,' stated Abbey directly.

'A panic attack?'

'Yes. I get them sometimes. Well, I used to. I thought they had stopped.'

'Disculpe...' Excuse me, Gabriela interrupted timidly. 'I have to go now. Will you be safe?'

Safe. What an odd way of asking. One simple word that suggested so much. 'Yes, Gabriela, I will be safe now,' Abbey confirmed. 'Thank you so much...'

'Sí, sí, it's no problem. Adiós.' Gabriela said goodbye and slipped out through the door, closing it quietly.

'What is it like then?'

'Well, everything closes in on you. You get hot, and you can't see properly any more.'

'You can't see properly?' It was a Jackie question, another statement that rose to a squeaky crescendo.

'I suppose it's like tunnel vision, but you can't understand what's in front of you either.' Abbey tried her best to explain, but it was difficult to convey the sensations to someone who had not had the misery of experiencing them.

'That sounds scary.' Jackie slipped another cigarette out of the packet and searched for her lighter.

'Yes, it is scary. Your heart goes bang-bang-bang.' Abbey patted her chest, showing how the pounding feels. 'You just want to run away, to get out.'

Click! A yellow flame leapt above Jackie's fingers and she sucked it into the white tube of her cigarette. 'I'm glad I don't get panic attacks,' she said with smoky breath and obvious feeling.

'I won't go there again,' asserted Abbey.

'Where? To Centro Nuevo? Course you will. You can't avoid a place forever just because you had one bad experience.'

'Yes I can. Like I said, I'll never go there again. Never.'

'You will,' Jackie persisted. 'I'll take you next time. Juan!' As far as she was concerned the subject was closed and there would be no more negotiation. The challenge of getting some service at Cafetería de la Luz took over. 'Where is he? We've been waiting ages.'

'Jackie! Lo siento!' Juan rolled up to the table, bringing his apologies with him. 'What would you like?'

Jackie placed her order and Juan departed.

'Hey, he didn't even ask me what I wanted to drink,' complained Abbey.

'You're right. He just ignored you. How rude. Juan!' Jackie's voice rang out again, booming across the café and overpowering the feeble chatter of the other patrons.

'Sí?' He was back at their table, addressing Jackie.

'You forgot Abbey.'

Juan looked surprised, but it was very badly faked. He pulled his mouth into a fatty smile, but his eyes were not laughing. 'What are you wanting?' he asked Abbey, using the kind of English that was usually dispensed to tourists.

Abbey remained composed. She placed her order in Spanish, with thickly accented but perfectly formed accuracy.

Juan's rubber smile sagged as he listened. 'Sí!'

'He doesn't like me, does he?' observed Abbey dryly after he had gone.

'I don't see why not. But I think you're probably right,' Jackie agreed. 'He was never like that with me, even when I first came to Castillo.' She drew on her cigarette, then crushed it in the ashtray. 'He always stared at my boobs. He still does. You'd think he'd be used to them by now.'

'Men always stare at boobs,' said Abbey in a matter of fact tone. 'It's normal.' She sat back so that Juan could lean over and deposit a large plate of tapas in front of them. 'These look good today,' she observed.

'Smashing. Absolutely wonderful!' piped Jackie rather pompously. She surveyed the array of little appetisers, made from cheese, tomatoes, olives, fish and more. Together the morsels made a satisfying meal, and were perfect for sharing between friends. There was no better format for combining good food with agreeable conversation. 'I wonder if Lewis has found himself something to eat.'

'I hope so.' Abbey realised that she had barely given him a single thought since leaving him alone again in his apartment. 'Jackie...'

'Yes?'

'Why were you at the apartment?'

'I was looking after Lewis.'

'That's my job!'

'You were busy shopping and having panic attacks,' returned Jackie.

'What?' Abbey exclaimed. She felt as if she had been punched in the face.

'Oh, don't be such a wimp. Honestly, you're so sensitive.'

'No I'm not.'

'You are,' stated Jackie. 'Anyway, it was his idea. He rang me after you'd gone off to Centro Nuevo and said he was still feeling lousy. It's his second day with it, you know.'

'I know. But you were there for a long time. And he is still in bed...'

'Look, Abbey.' Jackie was exasperated. 'We didn't do anything. He's not interested in me.' Abbey did not look like she was being persuaded by Jackie's argument. Jackie sighed and reached into her bag, seeking her elusive lighter once again. 'You really are over-sensitive, Abbey,' she muttered.

The clouds parted and drew back to the mountains. They revealed the cleanest black sky, washed, cooled, purified by the evening rain. The town of Castillo, a maze of contrast between deep shadow and bright electric light, stood crisply outlined. Everything was wet and fresh, renewed and reborn, ready to face the fair temper of the brief Spanish winter. The eaves dripped and splashed down into puddles. Rivulets trickled into drains, carrying away the dust of summer. A folded umbrella leaned against an artist's easel, together forming geometric triangles with feet set securely on the paving stones and tips pointing at the white pinpricks of stars above. Across the plaza, the rectangles of the store windows transformed late shoppers from coloured figures with faces and eyes into the blank forms of dark silhouettes as they passed. A night-time mirage of textured lights and distorted shapes was coarsely mirrored in the wet streets.

The artist worked, her companion waited. Both sat on little metal folding chairs with plastic seats. As she painted, he watched. Someone passing by might from time to time pause to look at this strange couple and peek furtively at the developing image on the canvas. The artist's brush picked up paint and moved, it stroked and layered. The scene was a square, the focal point of a town richly rendered in oils. She stopped painting to squeeze shamelessly brazen colours onto the palette. The brush moved again and flashed red, orange, yellow and green. The painting came to life as the occult mystery of its shadows was broken with rippled fissures of colour. Onlookers gathered, forming a loose semi-circle of silent admiration.

'There's a few people watching you now,' said Lewis quietly in English.

'Yes, I know,' replied Abbey, equally hushed.

Lewis reached into his shirt pocket and slipped out a slim packet. 'I've only got one cigar left,' he whispered. 'There's an estanco across there. Will you be ok if I nip over and get some more?'

'Yes, of course I will.'

Broad and dark in a knee-length coat, Lewis' shape crossed the square and made for the tobacconist's. Abbey picked up more paint on her brush. Behind her, the crowd of onlookers was thickening, pressing in more tightly around the back of the spindly folding chairs. Abbey glanced around at the circle of ghostly faces. The early sprinkling of appreciative onlookers had been rather flattering, a minor distraction that quietly complemented the creative process of capturing the feel of a city night. There were intrusive voices now, people pointing and arguing as the numbers swelled. Quarrelsome jostling broke out, someone nudged against Abbey's shoulder. She drew her brush away from the easel, her heart pounding.

'Quiero ver!' I want to see.

'Mi turno! A ver!' My turn, let me see.

Lewis' empty chair fell against Abbey's knee. A fat man squared up in front of the picture, perfectly ignorant of Abbey.

'Aquí, hermano!' Here, brother. His moustache wriggled with the words. He pulled on a jacketed elbow and his brother, bony faced and hollow eyed, joined him. With the men came a repulsive smell, a disgusting fusion of alcohol and stale urine. 'Es bueno.' It's good, announced the moustache loudly.

Abbey was not flattered. She was surrounded by them now, a wall of bodies. The air was heavy with unfamiliar accents and horrible odours. *Where's Lewis? I can't leave all this stuff here.* She felt sick, the fear gripped her inside. A thick voice, boorish and coarse, started right behind Abbey. It was offering her something in the most obscene terms possible.

'Señora. Quieres follar?' Lady, do you want to... *What?*

Chapter Ten

'Bugger off, will yah?' Someone at the back was shouting. No one seemed to take any notice. 'I said, bugger off! Now!' The voice, loud and gravelly, moved into the crowd. *What is she doing? They won't listen to her.* Abbey's thoughts raced. She did not dare intervene. The noisy woman found her target and jabbed her finger at his chest. 'Oy, you. What makes you so special? Pervert!' Her Essex accent, roughened by years of smoking, rose in pitch and lashed at its target. He flinched as each syllable whipped into him. 'Go on. Ask *me* if I want a shag!' she screamed at his face, her red lips framing the words with rage. She spoke in English but there was no need to understand the language, the meaning of her challenge was perfectly obvious.

Everyone was looking at the man now, waiting to see what he would do. It was like watching a pet goldfish in a glass bowl. His mouth opened and closed a few times, then like that fish he turned silently and swam away. The crowd loosened and frayed. Someone dropped a few coins into Abbey's tired old plastic box of brushes as he left.

'They have dirty old men in Spain too, you know,' a jubilant Jackie announced brightly.

'Jackie, I don't know how you dared to do that,' said Abbey. 'You don't know what might have happened.'

'Well, it could hardly have got much worse, could it? What are you doing here on your own?'

'I'm not on my own. Lewis is with me.'

'Really?' Jackie made a show of looking around, as if Lewis was hiding somewhere close by and she had simply overlooked him. 'I can't see him,' she finally announced.

'He was here, but he went to buy some cigars.'

'Uhuh. Anyway, are you ok?'

'Yes, I think so.' Abbey took a moment to check things over. Apart from one knocked-over chair, nothing was amiss. 'Everything seems to be here. Jackie?'

'Yes, Abbey?'

Under the electric street lights, Jackie's triumphant face looked gleeful. 'Jackie, thanks for saving me. It was getting a bit rough.'

'No problem. I was just passing by, you know. Thought I'd take a look,' said Jackie nonchalantly.

'You enjoyed shouting at him, didn't you?'

'Now that you mention it, I suppose I did.' Jackie was momentarily thoughtful. 'I didn't think it was much fun at the time, though. Are you done?'

'Done? Well, I'm not doing any more painting tonight, obviously.'

'I thought you might want to finish it. I'll stay and defend you against the locals if you like, until that big brave bodyguard of yours comes back. Just how long does it take to buy a few cigars? Sheesh!'

Abbey bristled, then saw that Jackie was laughing. 'It does seem to be taking an awfully long time. No, I think I'll pack away. I can complete the picture at home.'

'I'm back.' Lewis arrived with a sheepish grin and a bundle under his arm. 'Hey, that looks great.'

'No, it doesn't. It's not finished yet. We were just leaving.' Abbey was surprised at herself, at the bitterness that coloured her words as they tumbled out. 'I'm sorry, Lewis. It's just that you left me here on my own.'

'I asked you first. You said you would be alright.'

'I didn't know what to expect. The crowd got ridiculous.'

'Ridiculous? There's no-one here now.'

'Jackie sent them away,' explained Abbey. 'She shouted at them.'

Abbey watched as Lewis greeted Jackie, kissing her on alternate cheeks. Why did they linger as they touched? Why did their eyes connect for just a little too long?

'Abbey, these are for you.' Lewis whipped the bundle

out and thrust it into her face, a spray of flower buds and leaves that burst from a neatly wrapped cone.

'Oh. So it wasn't cigars that you were after,' said Abbey breathlessly.

Lewis passed her the bunch of flowers and reached into his pocket, feeling for something. 'Yes, it was.' He slipped the box out of his pocket and ran a finger over it. 'But I had some time to spare, so I went for those too.'

They were just an afterthought. Abbey was tired, her thoughts were chasing each other in circles. So what if the flowers were an afterthought. 'Thank you, Lewis. Here, can you carry the chairs?'

Abbey was singing as she cut a little off each stem. She always trimmed the cut flowers like this so that they lasted longer. Each one was laid out carefully on the kitchen sink drainer, forming a tidy queue of stalks and leaves, each crowned with a promising bud. 'Have you got a vase?' she called out.

'No. You'll have to use something else.' Lewis' voice resonated through the apartment.

'Ok.' Abbey decided on a thorough approach, opening each cupboard door in turn and checking the contents of the shelves within. She was surprised to discover things that she had never encountered before, despite living at the apartment for maybe half a year. An electric food mixer that looked like it had never been used, baking tins of various sizes that nestled within each other like Russian dolls, a box of plain white candles. The beginnings of a scheme began to form in her mind. 'Lewis, have you got anything planned for tomorrow evening?'

'Not really. Why?'

'Oh, nothing. Just don't arrange anything. I'll cook for us two.'

'That will be lovely,' echoed Lewis' voice.

Abbey wondered if he had got the hint clearly enough. 'Just me and you,' she added. She did not want Jackie popping up and spoiling things. She moved on to the next cupboard in the row, opened the door and saw it right away. 'Lewis...' started Abbey. She went through to the lounge to show him. 'You have got a vase.'

'Oh my God, Jackie, it's huge!' Abbey stood and stared. Jackie's lounge was bigger than the whole of Lewis' apartment. It was split over two levels. No, make that three – she could see that there was another step down to some kind of dining area with a table and some upright chairs. One wall was almost entirely filled with glass windows, looking out over the rooftops towards the distant azure sea.

'Are you impressed?' Jackie flopped down into one of two vast, soft sofas.

'Impressed? I am amazed. Why didn't you tell me that you lived in a palace?'

'You never asked. Come and sit down. You don't have to stand on ceremony, even if you do think it's a palace.' Jackie nodded her head towards the sofa opposite her.

Abbey descended a room-wide step and sank into the cushions. She leaned back, cosseted. It was almost like floating. 'Ooh!'

'When I took over this place it was like a cave. It even echoed. I just got a chaise longue to begin with, but it looked so lonely. So I got these. They're from Italy, you know.'

Stunned by the opulence of it all, Abbey nodded in silent acknowledgement. There was a sweetness in the air, almost like the scent of flowers but oddly artificial.

'Do you mind if I smoke?' Jackie already had a little white tube between her lips. It twitched comically as she spoke.

'Of course I don't mind.' Abbey could hardly say no. It was Jackie's home, she was free to do as she wished. She watched as Jackie rocked forward and busied herself with her lighter. It was only now that Abbey noticed the ashtrays. Unlike Lewis, it seemed that Jackie did not bother going outside to smoke. This explained the synthetic perfume, heroically exuded by air fresheners whose challenge it was to mask the tobacco smoke.

'Would you like a drink?' Without waiting for an answer, Jackie sprang up and bounced out of the room. She was soon back, bearing two stubby little glasses.

'Thanks!' Abbey lifted her glass to her lips and stopped. What on earth had Jackie brought? Alcoholic vapour assailed her nose, so irritating that she could barely stop herself sneezing. The shot of clear liquid in the glass smelled strong, with a distinctive, piercing flavour that Abbey struggled to identify. 'Err, what is it?' she asked timidly.

'Oh, you haven't tried orujo before? Well, there's always a first time,' smiled Jackie mischievously. 'It's made from grapeskins. They drink it a lot in the North, you don't see it very often down here.'

'Grapeskins?' It didn't sound very appealing.

'Yes. Go on, trust me.'

Abbey took a sip. 'Aniseed?'

'Yes.'

'It's quite nice...' said Abbey adventurously. Perhaps she had misjudged her new friend. Jackie had a special kind of appeal, boisterous and full of life. Inside her was a cheeky little girl that peeped out through the heavy make up and clouds of cigarette smoke.

The morning wore on. Jackie refilled the glasses of orujo and the women sank deeper into their squishy couches.

'I could have had someone else,' Abbey blurted.

'What do you mean?'

'Instead of Lewis. I could have had someone else and stayed in England.'

'So why didn't you do that then?'

'No-one asked me.'

'Then you could have asked them. It's not only men

that are allowed to take the lead.'

'Actually, there was no-one to ask,' admitted Abbey. 'No-one was interested in me. I'm not pretty enough. I'm too old. Too small.' She pointed at her modest peaks as she said the last two words.

'Don't be ludicrous. You're not ugly. And what has your bra size got to do with it? You could make more of your body, Abbey. You need to take pride in it, maximise your assets. You know, show them off a bit.' Jackie wriggled her shoulders in a little shimmy. Under her blouse, two globes of flesh bounced obligingly.

'It's all right for you, Jackie. You've got enough to show off. It doesn't apply to me. I can't do... that!'

'Like I said, you should use what you've got. Let me take you shopping, I'll find you some clothes that will help.'

'That's kind of you, but, um, I'd rather not.'

'So you're still off going to Centro Nuevo again?' enquired Jackie, raising her sculpted eyebrows in time with the rising pitch of her voice.

'I really don't want to go back there, Jackie.'

'I'll take you in the car. You'll be safe with me. Deal?'

'Ok. Deal.' The orujo was strong, deliciously intense. It was rather early in the day for it and Abbey could feel the alcohol taking effect. 'I didn't want to waste any more years alone,' she said, by way of reconnecting with her thoughts about men.

'It works for me.'

'I don't know how you do it. You're always happy, aren't you?' It was a rhetorical question which needed no answer. 'I couldn't do that, not even if I lived in an apartment like this. I need to share my thoughts, to be part of something more than just myself.' Abbey drained her glass. 'I've put a lot of effort into Lewis. I was lucky to meet him, but it just seems such hard work.'

Jackie waited to hear more, lifting just one eyebrow in inquiry.

'Yes, I've wasted enough years,' declared Abbey. 'Let's

go shopping tomorrow. Maybe we'll find something for me to wear that even Lewis can't resist!'

Jackie's kitchen was as impressive as her lounge. It was a huge square place, lined with pristine white wall cupboards, black granite worktops and an enormous steel cooking range. The floor was a sea of white alabaster, veined with waves of whiskery grey. In the centre of this translucent ocean sailed an island, a waist-high rectangle of granite with yet more cupboards beneath it.

'You've got a lovely kitchen,' exclaimed Abbey admiringly.

'I don't bother to cook much. It's so much trouble. Anyway, it's only for one. A girl doesn't want to do all that messing about, it's not worth it.'

'No, I suppose it's not.' Jackie's casual comments unexpectedly drove Abbey back in time, as if to an earlier life. Back then, her marriage was over and Peter had gone. Luke was still there in the house, but he just ate pizza. Abbey might as well have been alone, cooking just for one person every day. It was miserable.

'Here, take this.'

'What? Oh, sorry, Jackie. I was miles away.'

'I know you were,' laughed Jackie. 'If you carry those plates through then I'll bring the drinks.'

They sat around the dining table on the lowest level of Jackie's sprawling residence.

'The garage is under this part,' offered Jackie spuriously, speaking between mouthfuls. 'Is the food ok for you?' she enquired.

'Yes, it's fine.' Abbey was lying. It was tapas, but so disappointing. Almost unrecognisable, it was nothing like the freshly prepared selection that arrived on enormous plates at Cafetería de la Luz. Tapas at Jackie's was a thoroughly commercial affair, mass-produced, pre-packed and sold through the soulless shelves of giant supermercados.

'I need some warmer clothes. I've hardly got any.'

Abbey changed the subject, though for genuine reasons too. There were many things about Spain that she loved. The town was perfect and the people that she talked to in her fragmented Spanish made it a pleasure to be part of. But as the months passed she discovered more and more things that did not meet her expectations. Maybe it was because of the sepia-tinted memories of family holidays abroad, maybe it was the glamour that television travel shows bestowed upon every sun-drenched beach that they presented as if it were a paradise. Whatever it was, it had succeeded in building something unrealistic in her mind, a fusion of idealistic dreams of a perpetually hot place where money is unimportant, work unnecessary and where time is just a distant clock left behind in a cold country. But it was not like that. It was chilly enough for coats now and the town bristled with dripping umbrellas on rainy days. Abbey did have plenty of time, but even that was not working in her favour. All those hours she used to toil through every week at Infotext, now they were hers to do with as she wished. She did not miss the job itself even for a second, that was certain. Yet time exists to be filled and Abbey found herself ruminating, wondering about her mother and worrying about her son. She spoke to Rita on the phone from time to time, always receiving the same shallow reassurances that everything was perfectly wonderful. There was the money thing too. *How will I manage?* Abbey's dream was starting to crumble.

'Abbey, you're day-dreaming again!'

At the sound of Jackie's voice, Abbey resurfaced. She came back into reality, into the enormous plush lounge. *Lunch must be over.* This was confusing. 'Was I? Sorry. That's what artists do, you know. They have to daydream for inspiration.' Abbey could hardly believe that she was spouting such rubbish. 'It's a painter's privilege.'

Jackie just laughed and reached for another cigarette.

'Speaking of privilege, I'm doing a meal for me and Lewis this evening,' continued Abbey, moving back onto safer ground. 'Just for the two of us,' she tagged on, pleased with herself for cleverly hinting that this was going to be something private and special, an event that Jackie should not gatecrash with her characteristic thoughtlessness.

'Wayhay!' Jackie exclaimed enthusiastically. 'It's about time you did something romantic.'

'Yes, I thought so...' started Abbey.

'You can show him how you really feel, tell him how much you love him!' Jackie screwed her face up as she spoke. 'I can picture it now. Soft music, dim lights. And good food of course, as you're cooking...'

'What time is it, Jackie?'

Jackie looked at her watch. 'Four. Hey, do you like this one? I got it from Sarita's shop.'

'Four o'clock?' Although she intended to politely compliment Jackie's new timepiece, Abbey's surprise caused her to drop her thoughts. 'It can't be that late.'

'Well, it is,' stated Jackie.

'Oh Jackie, I'm so sorry. I have to get going. It's been lovely, thank you.'

They were at the door.

'You're more than welcome, Abbey. We should do it again soon,' smiled Jackie.

Outside, the wind played. It was harmless and mild, woven from a kinder yarn than that of any autumn back home. It moved along, dragging its softly gloved fingers over the walls and roofs and slipping the cloth of late seasons over Castillo.

It was about seven when Lewis was allowed back into his apartment. Although the locals ate their meals late in the evening, he had never managed to adopt their convention. By six o'clock or so, he was too hungry to wait any longer. And why bother? It didn't matter. He stubbed out his cigar, leaving its desolate brown remains to wilt damply in the ashtray on the terrace table.

'Are you ready to eat?' asked Abbey, her eyes twinkling innocently.

'Yes!' Lewis answered simply. Something smelled great, and the pangs in his belly were too much to ignore.

'That's good,' replied Abbey. She was standing between Lewis and the rest of the room and as he moved across to gain a view of the table that she had spent so long preparing, she mirrored his movement. 'What's the password?' she asked childishly.

'Um, I don't know.' Lewis played along, content enough to be part of the game for a short while.

'Yes you do!' Abbey turned her face up at him and puckered her lips.

Lewis placed his hands on each side of her waist, bent down a little and planted a kiss. It was a bullseye, the secret key that opened the way to the dining table. He sat down and faced Abbey. She had really made an effort, there was a damask table cloth, flowers, even some simple white candles that infused their little nest with mellow light. As he ate, he kept glancing at her. So pretty, her face marked with only the first caring lines that life's experiences confer. 'The wine is very nice.' Lewis took another sip and swirled it around his mouth before swallowing. 'Yes, it's really very good. It's not Vino Tinto de Castillo and I don't remember buying it.'

'That's because I chose it,' smiled Abbey. 'I called in at the bodega and asked the boy what he recommended with this.' She pointed at the plates, piled with yellow rice.

'Boy?'

'Yes. Well, he looked younger than Luke so that makes him a boy. Anyway, he knew a lot about wine.'

'Mmm, it certainly looks like he did.' Lewis was enjoying the wine, and it went perfectly with the paella.

'You made this yourself?'

'How dare you!' Abbey was being an actress, entertaining her one-man audience with mock indignation. She found it difficult to keep up the act for more than a few moments and her face quickly softened. 'Yes, I cooked it. It's turned out well, even if I say so myself!'

'Abbey, this is excellent. Absolutely wonderful.' Lewis interrupted his stream of praise to venture deeper into his meal. The rice was richly filled with seafood, shellfish and prawns. It was reinforced with chopped chorizo, the spicy sausage that was enjoyed throughout the country. Every forkful was a tasty surprise. 'I didn't think that there was such a thing as gourmet paella.' Both of them laughed at the suggestion.

'How did you get on at Jackie's?' asked Lewis, leaving his question as open as he could.

'I had a good time, thank you.'

Lewis stayed quiet, waiting to hear more.

'Her apartment is fantastic. Have you seen it?'

'Yes, I have been there once or twice,' admitted Lewis. 'She doesn't have visitors there very often. What did you talk about?'

'Women's things. Clothes and stuff. I won't bore you with the details. We're going to go shopping again.'

'Good idea, you should do that. Jackie is very good at buying things. Too good, in fact!' Lewis quipped.

'Big, isn't it?'

'What's big?' Lewis sighed inside, being careful not to reveal his frustration. Sometimes it was difficult to follow Abbey as her thoughts leapt from one thing to another and back.

'Jackie's apartment.'

'Oh. True, it's vast. That's one of the problems. It doesn't matter how much furniture she adds, it will never feel right.'

Abbey was puzzled. 'What do you mean?'

'Like I said, it will never feel right. It's all so open. I like light and space, but not that much.'

'Everyone's different, Lewis. It suits her.'

'Yes, I suppose so. She's big on everything. You're getting to know her quite well now, aren't you?'

'We're getting on ok. But it's difficult to be sure. She's great fun, always laughing. But I wonder what lies within. I think she has secrets, you know.'

'I wondered about that too. Underneath the front she puts on, there's another Jackie.' A frown passed across Lewis' face, quickly replaced by a disarming smile. 'The candles are a nice touch.' He was impressed with the amount of trouble that Abbey had taken. 'Did you get those from the bodega too?'

'No, I found them in your cupboard!' Abbey chuckled. She fell silent as their eyes connected.

Lewis offered Abbey his hand, she took it and together they rose to their feet. The candles flickered and watched politely as he unbuttoned her blouse and slipped it off her shoulders.

'Shall we take the motorway?' suggested Abbey. The new toll roads were unlike British motorways. Almost empty and impossibly smooth, they were even pretty with flowers growing in planters alongside them.

'No, it's farther that way,' objected Jackie. 'Let's use the coast road. It's more fun, anyway.' Jackie reversed the car up the slope from the garage. 'I don't like the look of those clouds.' She pressed a switch. A folded roof appeared magically from its cover behind them, then expanded and settled over the sports car. 'You had to get out and do it by hand with my old car,' tutted Jackie. 'It was such a bother.'

Abbey was still fiddling about, pulling her seatbelt on as they reversed onto the road.

'Ok?' asked Jackie.

'Yeah, fine,' replied Abbey, trying her best to sound blasé. Something was tightening deep within her, an inexplicable sense of fear that gripped and twisted.

The engine roared as Jackie catapulted them into their journey. The old coast road ran out of Castillo, past the Infotext office to Centro Nuevo. They were barely out of town before Jackie's amateur weather-forecasting proved correct and the rain started. The first of the olive groves appeared on the right, mysterious and misty behind sheets that fell from a menacing sky. Abbey turned her attention back to the front. Through the swishing wipers, something dark and bulky loomed and grew quickly.

'Jackie!' Abbey's hands were clenched, her body rigid with fear.

Jackie was not listening. She was busy thrusting her vehicle through a screen of road spray. She pulled on the steering wheel and the car glided across. 'Done it,' she smiled triumphantly. The plodding bus was behind them now.

'Jackie! There's another one!' Abbey's plaintive cry came again, but it was too late. The car was snaking about, obstinately ignoring Jackie's desperate attempts to control it. Then they were off the road, sliding sideways, backwards and sideways again, bumping over the rough ground. The tyres scraped and skipped over the rubble and scree. Abbey was numbed beyond thought with fear, helplessly waiting for the world to stop spinning. The windows filled with leaves and branches and the grinding noise stopped. Then there was nothing but stillness and the forlorn ticking of raindrops on the fabric roof.

Chapter Eleven

'Are there any onions, mi querida?'

Reina lifted an eyebrow in surprise. *My dear?* That was unusually polite for Juan. Her usual retort would have been a curt suggestion that Juan should look for the onions himself. On this occasion she thought better of it and went to check in the corridor behind the kitchen. A precarious blue tower greeted her, teetering threateningly. She reached up and took a couple of empty plastic crates from the top of the perilous stack. *Aha.* The third one down was still full.

'These are the last ones,' Reina advised her husband as she plonked her harvest down on the bench.

'There's enough for today,' said Juan. He scooped some out and set about them, expertly skinning, slicing and chopping. 'Did you phone that order through?'

'To the verdulería? Yes. But I can still add onions if we need them. How many?'

'Ten kilos. You can't run a café without onions.' Juan laughed roundly, stopping when he noticed that only he found the joke funny. 'No, five kilos will do this time. We're not so busy now. Jackie's gang won't be coming in for a while, either.'

'That's all you care about, isn't it? It's just the business and money and profit.'

'You know that's not true, my dear.' Reina's accusations had found their target, putting Juan on the defensive. 'I love my customers, all of them,' he said with inflated sincerity.

'Ha. Only when they are in here spending money. You should show a bit more compassion sometimes, Juan.' Reina turned her back and stamped off to telephone the grocer's.

Jacqueline Trayman-Smith, Habitación 5. Private room number five was a good one, endowed with a window that looked out towards the distant grey sea. There was a single bed, high with a tubular frame and a deep skirt which cleverly disguised the lifting mechanism beneath the mattress. In the corner stood a square table served by a cushioned chair. Along one wall was a hard two-seater sofa, upholstered in a needlessly garish mid-blue cloth. Like everything else in the room it was simple, functional and perfectly characterless. Jackie sat down on the sofa to survey the panorama of white, chrome and blue that would be her home for the rest of the week. They called this wing of the building The Hotel. She snorted, sounding a false laugh that summed up the place. It was a modest institution which held grand, as yet unfulfilled, aspirations. Even so, it was comfortable and quiet, the meals were pleasant and the medical care was the best available.

Jackie was supposed to drink a ridiculous quantity of water each day, a quite silly command from the doctor. She stood at the sink and filled a plastic cup under the tap. It was painful to place her lips around it as she drank. She looked into the mirror and a terrible mask stared back. The cuts were still fresh, their torn edges pinched together by the surgeon's stitches. She knew what it meant and she knew that it would be for a long time. The bruises that coloured her skin would fade, though it might take months. That was just where blood had been seeping inside. As time went by they would darken and change chameleon-like through shades of red and purple into blue and green. Yes, the bruising would go eventually, though it was going to be quite a challenge to hide that lot with make-up. It was the cuts that worried her. She turned her head from side to side, impressed in a gruesome kind of way at how they marched like battalions of purple armies that ripped across her left cheek, her forehead, her chin. The plastic band on her left wrist slipped out from under the sleeve of her gown. Even in The Hotel, all patients were compelled to wear these nasty identity bracelets. How demeaning it was to be labelled with your own name and room number like some pitiful, demented old person who went wandering through the corridors at night.

'Shall we go to see Jackie? I'm worried about her.' Abbey was sitting in the dining room in Lewis' apartment.

'No, I think she said she had another assessment this afternoon,' said Lewis. He was lying.

'But that won't take long, will it? I still haven't seen her since the accident. I just want to look in on her.'

'I don't think you should.' Lewis was scratching around for plausible objections, anything that he could say which would delay Abbey coming face to face with Jackie.

'Why not? Come on. I'm supposed to be moving around now. The doctor said I should rest for one day, then I have to be active so that my muscles don't stiffen up.'

'I just think... she needs a bit more time.' Lewis was losing his noble battle to keep the women apart. Jackie needed time to heal at least a little. Abbey needed protecting, shielding from the shock of her friend's injuries.

'More time? Don't be ridiculous,' snorted Abbey. 'How do you know that? Pass me the phone, I'll ring her now.'

'It's over there,' said Lewis, defeated. He nodded across the room. 'You can fetch it. Like you said, you're supposed to be active now.'

Jackie paused when the path reached the big tree again. She lifted a cigarette slowly to her lips, lit it and carefully drew in the smoke. The garden was a beautifully tended rectangle of shrubs, palms and lawns enclosed on three sides by the hospital buildings. She was beyond tears, hollow, lost. There was no going back, the damage was done. *It must be nearly time for my next dose.* Everything was hurting, her whole body was a bundle of misery after its traumatic contortions. For the hundredth time, she felt the impulse to feel her face. Her fingertips met the ridges and followed them across the devastated remains. Yes, this was what hurt the most. She pushed her cigarette packet back into the pocket of her white hospital robe and set off once more, wandering aimlessly around the same little circular route.

'Jackie!'

Jackie's hands flashed up to her face as she instinctively attempted to hide it.

'Jackie. I tried to ring you. How are you getting on?' Abbey raced up the path to greet her friend. 'Why are you hiding your face like that?'

'Oh, Abbey. It's terrible,' came the half-muffled reply. 'Didn't you see it when it happened?'

Jackie felt Abbey tug at her robe.

'Come on. Trust me. I'm going to see you sooner or later,' begged Abbey.

Jackie relented and dropped her arms. 'There. Now look. I'm ruined, aren't I?' She watched as Abbey scanned her face, eyes flicking this way and that. She waited for Abbey's expression to change, expecting it to reflect the hopeless anguish she herself felt. It didn't. 'Well, what do you think?' snapped Jackie, regretting her rudeness instantly. It was just a reflection of her bitterness, her shame. 'I'm sorry, Abbey.'

Abbey ignored both the testiness and the apology. 'I think you're a lot better than I expected.'

'What did you expect?'

'On Monday you told me your face was destroyed. It's not destroyed. It's not bad at all.'

'Not bad at all.' Without expression, Jackie repeated Abbey's words.

'Can I see your room?' Abbey asked.

'My room?' Jackie wondered why anyone would want to look at a hospital room.

'Is it a good one? I bet it's a lot nicer than the wards in England.'

'Ha ha ha!' Jackie was surprised to hear herself laugh. It hurt but it was a relief to realise that she could still do it at all. And Abbey was right, public hospitals in England could be a grim experience. 'I'll show you.'

Gabriela wielded her mop with majestic ease, swishing it across the apartment floors in great wet arcs. 'Where's Abbey?' she called out without stopping.

'She's at the hospital,' replied Lewis.

'I thought she didn't need to go to hospital.'

'She's visiting Jackie there.'

'Oh.' The swishing stopped and Gabriela looked up. 'That's who was driving, isn't it?' Her voice adopted a solemn tone. 'It was only a matter of time, Lewis.'

Lewis stopped trying to work at the computer and sat back, fully devoting his attention to his housekeeper.

'She nearly ran me over once. In the new town,' stated Gabriela. The old lady twisted her mop in the bucket to wring it out. As she did so, she warmed to her theme. 'I'm not criticising your friend, but she always drives like they do in films. Loca!' Mad, said Gabriela, neatly criticising Lewis' friend.

'She's never crashed before,' said Lewis defensively.

'Like I said, it was just a matter of time.' The swishing started again. 'Lift your feet, Lewis.'

Lewis did as he was commanded.

Gabriela busied herself cleaning under the desk. 'It could have been worse. Thank the Lord that they are both alive.' She stood and looked straight into Lewis' eyes, her face careworn and compassionate. 'I don't bear grudges, Lewis, you know that. You will tell them that I wish them well, won't you?'

'Yes, Gabriela. I will,' Lewis said firmly.

'I love the view,' said Abbey enthusiastically.

Jackie joined Abbey at the window of her hospital room. 'It's not bad.' Her voice was cheerless.

Abbey looked at the swollen face beside her. Physically, it really was not as bad as she had expected.

Yet everything that defined Jackie was missing. Where was she? Flat, disinterested, the fizz was gone. Was she still hiding inside, or was that gone too?

'I want to go home, but they won't let me,' announced Jackie.

'I expect they want to be sure you'll be alright,' Abbey suggested. She tried to sound neutral so that she would not reveal her fears. 'How do you feel?'

'Perfect.' Of course that was a lie. A big, shiny, bright red whopper of a lie.

'You've got a fantastic room, Jackie. Not what you're used to, of course, but as these things go it's great. Plenty of room for visitors, even a sofa for them.'

'I don't need it.'

'Don't need what?'

'The sofa. I don't need the sofa. No-one visits me. You're the only one that bothers.' Jackie sat down on the painfully blue cloth. 'I've got no-one, Abbey. No-one.' Tears slipped out and fell, tracing silver lines over her battered face.

'Hello Mum.'

'Abbey? Is that you?' Rita's voice croaked.

'Yes, of course it's me. I have something to tell you.'

'Why don't you ever ring me?' persisted Rita, completely ignoring Abbey. 'You never ring me.' The croaking fragmented more, it was pitiful by design. 'All you think about is that lazy man. Has he got a proper job yet?'

'I do ring you. I rang last week, didn't I?' Abbey let the other insults go unanswered. She was used to them.

'Yes, love. I think so,' Rita grudgingly admitted.

'Listen, Mum. I was in a car crash.'

'When are you coming back to see me?'

She doesn't listen at all. 'Mum, I said I was in a car crash,' repeated Abbey.

'Were you, love?' Rita sounded concerned but it only lasted for a couple of seconds. 'I bet Lewis was driving, wasn't he? I told you he's no good. He's only interested in you for one thing. What does he do all day? Watch girls, drink beer and get fat, I expect.'

When Abbey was married, her mother always praised Peter. Worthless, pompous, self-centred Peter. Lewis could not be more different, yet the old woman was constantly putting him down. In Rita's mind he was an overweight slacker, a hedonist without a care in the world. How typical of her. Despite the diatribe, Abbey seemed to have got her message through at last. 'Lewis wasn't even there. I was with Jackie. You know, my friend Jackie with all the clothes?'

'You told me about her.'

'The car crashed.' Abbey still could not bring herself to blame her friend. 'We skidded and went off the road.'

'You weren't hurt, were you? You don't sound hurt.'

Abbey wondered how her mother could make that judgement from her voice alone. 'No. I think my seatbelt saved me. Jackie is poorly though.'

'Ooh, I'm sorry to hear that.'

'She's smashed her face up a bit, but I think she'll be ok given time,' explained Abbey. It was funny how her mother seemed more concerned about someone that she had never even met. 'Is Luke there?' asked Abbey. He needed telling too.

'He's asleep, Abbey. He sleeps all day. Shall I wake him?'

'Oh, he's terrible. No, leave him. Just tell him that I rang and I'm fine, will you?'

'Yes, love. He spends all evening talking to that Sally girl on the computer. Then he plays his game all night. He did tell you about Sally, didn't he?'

'Sally? Who's she?' Abbey was caught between curiosity and indignation. Luke had not said a word to Abbey about this.

'Oh, did I let the cat out of the bag? He met her on that game. She's always there, chatting away with him. I can't hear what she says, though. He always wears headphones.' The disappointment in Rita's voice was obvious.

'It will just be another of his invisible friends, Mum,' said Abbey dismissively. 'I'll ring you again soon.'

'Yes, love. Bye.'

Abbey stared at the phone in her hand. Rita was ungrateful and her attitude to Lewis was unforgivable. But she was still Abbey's mother. Abbey felt guilty. It was a long time since she had been back to see her mother. *Why do I feel so homesick?* The flat in Calborough was a smashing little place but it was home to Rita and Luke, not Abbey. She would never be more than a visitor there. Someone else surely occupied that stinking rented house she used to endure in Bullwood. The same stale smell was tainting their curtains and clothes instead of hers now. Abbey had nothing of her own left in England other than memories and obligations.

'Abbey, what's wrong?' Lewis curled his fingers around her hair where its brown tresses cascaded to her shoulder, sweeping it back to reveal the sadness deep within the blue of her eyes.

'I don't belong anywhere,' she sniffed.

'Yes you do. You belong here with me,' said Lewis reassuringly.

'But it's not my home, is it? It's yours, I just live in it.'

'Well, technically, yes. I own it. But this is where you live now. So it is your home too.' He was adamant. Abbey lived with him now. 'Do you wish you were back in England?'

'No. Yes. Oh, I don't know.' Abbey broke down as the conflict inside her took over.

'What could you possibly miss about England? The rain?'

'Don't be stupid, Lewis. Of course I don't miss the rain.' She shot him a look through the tears, enough to tell him that he was being ridiculous. 'Anyway, it rains here too. Look at all those clouds. It's going to start any minute.'

'It doesn't rain nearly every day here, though, does it?' challenged Lewis. 'And it's not cold all the time. I only have to run the heating for a couple of weeks in the winter.' He sat down next to Abbey and hugged her.

Abbey rested her head on Lewis' shoulder. 'I just feel lost sometimes. I'm sorry.'

'Don't be sorry.'

'Lewis, why did you come to Spain?'

'Because I wanted somewhere quiet. I like the solitude here. The weather is much better, obviously. I love the long summers. And the food...'

It sounded like Lewis had plenty of perfectly sound reasons for moving here. 'Does it feel like home to you?' asked Abbey.

'It does now, yes. To start with it was difficult. I was a foreigner and I had to work hard at it before people accepted me.'

'Neighbours?'

'Everyone. Neighbours, Alvaro, Gabriela, even the local council. I had to go there so many times just to organise things and sort out the taxes that they even knew my name when I walked in. After that, things got a lot easier.' Lewis laughed wryly. 'They can be quite helpful if they want to.'

Abbey shifted in Lewis' arms, turning so that she could see his face. She spoke carefully and deliberately. 'Lewis, do you love me?'

He didn't answer. Though he pulled Abbey a little closer and hugged her just a tiny bit more tightly, his gaze still went past her, over her shoulder. Darkness was falling and soft Spanish rain blew across the terrace, misting over the wooden furniture.

There were garish blue chairs in the reception area, great rectangular blocks of stuffed cloth. They could not possibly be restful no matter how you sat. The seats were much too large, the slabs of their backs too distant. Like everything in The Hotel, reception could have been excellent but it was not. There were worthy intentions. It was supposed to be smart, comfortable and functional all at once. Despite the expense, it just had not worked out like that.

'Your taxi is here, señora.'

'Gracias.' Jackie thanked the girl behind the desk, leaned forward and parted with the gaudy wedge of her seat. The glass doors eased closed behind her and she stepped back into the real world. With its wipe-clean surfaces, sterile hospitality and tasteless furniture, the clinic was gone.

Juan was making a lot of noise, stacking up chairs and tables in the back corridor of Cafetería de la Luz. He loved his round tables, they were perfect for the job. Sturdy and easily cleaned, they still looked new after a full season on the pavement. Winter was in charge now and dining had moved indoors. The chairs and tables huddled together cosily, beginning their short hibernation. Juan would be back to wake them up when spring came. He washed his hands and waddled back into the kitchen.

'Reina?' Juan called out rather pointlessly. The premises were small and he could see instantly that his wife was not in the kitchen. She must be in the front then, serving customers.

'Juan!'

He heard her shouting for him before he even got to the swing door that led into the restaurant.

'Sí, mi querida?' Yes, dear?' Lunchtime was looking busy and Juan was feeling increasingly cheerful.

'Tres tortillas, Juan. Esta mesa.' Reina relayed the order from the table that she was standing at.

'Three tortillas for table one,' confirmed Juan, glancing at the group of diners that encircled the big table by the front window. He went back into the kitchen and started getting together all the ingredients that he needed for their dishes. He liked it when several people wanted the same thing, it was so much easier to turn it out quickly.

'Now then, eggs, potatoes, onions... maldición!' Juan swore as the realisation hit him. Someone must be to blame for this. 'Why didn't that woman order enough onions? I'm always telling her that you can't run a café without onions. She'll have to tell them that they can't have tortillas.' He stamped back into the restaurant. Reina turned to him from the bar where she was preparing another round of coffee.

'Reina, they can't have tortillas. I can't make them without onions. Why didn't you order enough? We always get ten kilos.'

'Go and tell them then. You can see I'm busy.'

Juan arrived at table one. 'Ah, my English friends,' he began with exaggerated feeling. It was the usual bunch. Lewis, tanned and confident, was almost like a local. Abbey sat next to him. Juan was not sure what to make of Lewis' girlfriend. So different to Lewis, she was still a proper foreigner. On the other hand, she was always eager to please, desperate to earn approval and find acceptance. She at least attempted to speak Spanish, even if it was sometimes impossible to understand what she was saying. Across from them sat Jackie. 'Mierda.' A particularly foul word slipped from Juan's mouth. Jackie was wearing sunglasses and a headscarf but a lot of her face was still exposed. Despite her make-up, the bruises looked awful. What distressed Juan the most was that hers would be the first face that customers saw when they came through his door. He looked around the table. His customers, both with and without sunglasses, all waited expectantly. 'Sorry, you can't have the tortillas,' announced Juan. 'We're, um, we're short of some ingredients today. Would you like to choose something else?'

The customers commenced conferring. 'I'll come back in a few minutes.' said Juan. He turned round and almost crashed into Reina. 'Have you seen her?' he hissed.

'Seen who?' Reina was impatient to deliver her tray of drinks. That greasy lump of a husband was blocking her way.

'Jackie. I mean, have you seen her face?'

'Jackie is fine,' Reina stated sternly. 'Have you got a problem with her?'

'She's right by the door. And she looks-'

'In the back! Now!'

Reina's hoarsely whispered command left Juan in no doubt that he had made a mistake. He followed her dutifully into the kitchen and steeled himself for what was surely to come.

'I don't want to hear what you think she looks like. You should treat the lady with respect,' Reina let loose with a stream of boiling words. 'Why will it put customers off? It doesn't look like it to me. Have you seen how busy it is, and you're wasting time in here grumbling about a little bruise? Do you think you're so pretty yourself?'

Juan shrank away, cowed by the onslaught.

'You need to think about other people, Juan. Think about how she must feel.'

'As you say, dear,' Juan meekly replied.

'Now you get right back out there and sort out table one's order.'

'Yes, dear.' Juan made to escape into the restaurant.

'And another thing, Juan.' Reina was not quite finished.

Juan paused, leaning against the swing door. His weight eased it open and he hovered on the threshold of liberty.

'Running out of onions was your fault, not mine.'

'Yes, dear.'

Chapter Twelve

Outlined in black, her eyes were crystals of blue ice. They were there all the time, watching him, missing nothing. She was wearing a black dress. It was old-fashioned, almost Victorian. The tops of her white breasts squeezed out above the tightly laced bodice. Her eyes caught him staring at the skin. She spoke to him, her voice low and husky. This was not the wispy thing that he had imagined, with black hair and easy brown eyes. She was nothing like that, nothing. Her bleached hair was barely blonde, her eyebrows pencilled. He wondered if she had noticed his trousers. Inside, something hot and long and fat was trying to escape. The rigid poker was pressing out against his clothes, straining at the cloth. Surely she must have noticed it by now. Her dress fell away, he stared at her unwrapped wonders. Her eyes gripped his and dragged him into her perfumed world. He fell inside, trapped by honeydew, intoxicated. His hands discovered the soft roundness of her burlesque bounty. He felt her hand cupping around the back of his head, pulling his face close. Her lips drew on his and at last she closed her eyes. Their compelling sapphire draw was cut off but she was still in charge, pressing him to her. Something gripped at him. Fingers wrapped around his shaft and massaged his iron mass. Of course she had noticed.

Sally pulled Luke close. There was so much of him. Everything that made Luke was long, spindly and slender. His dark brown hair was tied back neatly, the clean lines of his cheekbones angled down his narrow face. She closed her eyes and inhaled through her nose as their lips met. He smelled of nothing at all. For every move that she made, he hesitated and stumbled. It was clear that he had been truthful. For Luke it really was a new experience and Sally wanted to be sure that it would be unforgettable. He was clean, unspoilt, with so many discoveries to make. There was only one chance. This was a unique opportunity to introduce him into a new realm, a domain ruled by passion and pleasure. She pulled at the zip on his trousers, the garment parted and she reached inside to free the one part of Luke that was long yet not slender. Her body responded in anticipation. The heat was spreading, her flesh throbbing and fizzing in anticipation.

'It was, um, a bit short. Sorry.' Luke reached for his crumpled trousers. He tried to drag his underpants up.

'It was fine, Luke,' Sally breathed consolingly. 'It will be better next time,' she added.

Next time? Luke had been completely focussed, blind and deaf to the world around him. The last ten minutes had been spent seeing, hearing, tasting just the one thing that he had to do.

'You don't need to get dressed yet.' Sally pulled Luke close to her again. 'Come on, give me a cuddle.' She wrapped him in her arms, cushioning his frame against her softness. 'Do you like being close to me?'

'Yes.' Luke's voice was shaky. He wanted to say more, but the words did not come.

'I like having you close. It's comforting,' offered Sally.

'Yes.'

'Feeling our skin touching...'

'Um, yes.'

'Do you like that?' She was running her fingertips over his back and around his buttocks.

'Yes. It's nice.' The lightness of her touch tracked up and down his spine, tickling and tingling.

Sally relaxed her hold. 'You don't have to do anything you don't want to, you know.' She caught his eye before he could avoid it, drawing him in, capturing him with the stunning energy of her crystal blue gaze. 'I do what I want to. Not just sex, everything.' Sally spoke in a matter-of-fact way. 'If there's something that I want then I have it.'

'I wish I could do that.'

'You can do it if you want.' Sally's voice was firm and

confident.

'But it's easy for you. You've got a job.'

'That's true,' Sally acknowledged.

'And you've got somewhere of your own,' added Luke.

'Yes, I have.' Sally watched Luke. He did not have a way with words, but it hardly mattered. She could read so much more in his face. She had seen his apprehension, elation and satisfaction. Now she saw wistfulness.

'You're lucky,' stated Luke.

'Why?'

'You don't have someone watching you all the time, telling you what to do. You're free to do whatever you like. You've got money...'

'Doesn't that make me even sexier?' asked Sally, drilling into Luke's eyes with the sharp steel of her aquamarine gaze.

Luke swallowed.

Sally smiled, satisfied. 'So tell me,' she continued. 'What would you do? For a job, I mean.'

'Something in an office, with computers. It would have to be programming, I suppose. Technology is what I am best at.' Luke considered for a moment. 'Yes, that's about all I could do, really.'

'Really?'

'Yes.'

Sally's fingertips traced over his hair and down his neck. They followed the curve of his shoulder and tickled along his arm. 'I think you have other skills too, Luke.'

The line of palm trees rested, their tired star-burst heads sleeping against the rolled pillows of grey clouds. Abbey stood between two of them. Their rough trunks curved a little, textured and ringed by natural collars that marked the years. The fair-weather residents of summer were gone and Calle los Calamares, the street of squids, was silent. Brown-tipped fans hung from the trees, useless old leaves that just could not accept that their time was over. She turned to face the apartment. That was starting to look a little tired too, though it had some way to go before it caught up with the trees. The building needed minor repairs and major painting. There was no prospect of Lewis getting up a ladder with a pot of paint and a brush. Abbey loved painting, but not this kind. Anyway, she hated heights. Perhaps Alvaro could do it in the spring. Her gaze dropped to the shrubs that dotted the little garden. Unlike the palms, the shrubs were only too happy to shed their leaves. The remains of their efforts had been confiscated by the wind. Piles had accumulated in the corners on each side of the doorway. It was a blustery day but the air felt unnaturally warm, almost kind, as it lapped about her face. Masterful with her broom, she swept vigorously. She picked up a pile to carry to the bin. There was a pair of red shoes in her way, dramatic and unexpected intrusions into her rustic little world.

Jackie looked down the tree-lined road. It was deserted except for a gardener working at one of the apartments. The afternoon sky was darkening. Perhaps it would rain soon. Jackie noticed new things every day, things that she had spent years missing. Driving past in a car, even with the roof down, was not the same as walking. Her world was different now. It was slower, more measured. The scale was entirely different. Where she had seen just walls and hedges, now she saw the stones and leaves that made them. Most of the flowers of summer were gone but the birds still called. A wind rose from the Mediterranean, lifted over Castillo and played with the trees. A few leaves blew along the pavement, scattering in front of Jackie's new shoes as she walked. She paused to look over a solidly stuccoed wall, white-painted with long slivers of rock adorning its top. Rows of stroppy cordyline plants glared back, beetroot-purple with rage. They were prisoners, their long narrow leaves strapped to their spindly stems with string by some over-zealous and misguided owner. Crystal sun-charms hung in the windows, even though this side faced north. Definitely an empty holiday home, number forty-two was cruelly locked up and left on hold until next year.

Next door was much more appealing. It had a high wall that was inset with pierced concrete blocks. There was once a fashion for these in nineteen-seventies England. Each block had a circle of oval holes right through it, arranged like the petals of a flower. Through the holes it was easy to view the disorganised jumble that was bursting to escape from within the garden. Bougainvillea bushes and Valencia roses competed for space with overgrown rosemary and thyme. There were terracotta planters everywhere. Instead of crystal sun-catchers, this house featured a black dog in the window. It was real, it was alive and it had noticed Jackie. It leapt about and banged its nose on the window, barking and yelping at her. Jackie walked on. That gardener was still there, wearing a hopelessly unfashionable brown overcoat and making a great deal of noise with a broom. He was in Lewis' garden. Lewis was too mean to pay for a wall around his garden, so it collected all the debris that cared to enter it.

'Oh!' Jackie stopped dead.

'Jackie!' Abbey looked up from the bright footwear to examine its owner, all the while fighting to keep a good grip on her bundle of leaves. 'It's great to see you. Hang on a minute while I finish off.'

Jackie watched, Abbey swept. A second bundle was kidnapped and stuffed securely into the bin.

'Sorry, I just had to finish off. I couldn't leave it,' started Abbey apologetically.

'Oh, don't worry about it. I don't mind. It's done now?'

'Yes, it's done.' *What a hideous way of speaking.* Abbey did not care for the way that Jackie's voice turned up to express her questions. It was inexplicably irritating.

'Let's go in. I need to talk.' Jackie's voice was serious

now. 'And by the way, Abbey.' A grave announcement was imminent.

'Yes?'

'That coat is hideous.'

'Here you are.' Abbey pushed a hot drink across the worktop.

'Thanks.' Jackie slurped. 'It's good.'

'You sound surprised.'

'No, it really is good.'

'Ok.' Abbey accepted the praise. 'It is good. But not great. I just can't make coffee like Juan's, whatever I do.'

'Perhaps it's Lewis' machine.' Jackie nodded towards the tired contraption. 'It's time he got a new one. You should tell him.'

'It's up to him what he does in his apartment,' said Abbey, her voice edged with a bitterness that she could not disguise.

'Ooh!' teased Jackie. 'Listen to you!'

'Well, you know what I mean.'

'Yes. Lewis just does what he wants to do,' Jackie agreed. 'You can stare at my face, you know. Everyone else does.'

'I wasn't looking at your face.' Abbey was both defensive and truthful. She was looking at Jackie's hair. It was long and impossibly blonde but not quite perfect. 'Your roots need doing.'

'Roots?' Jackie frowned.

'Which hairdresser do you use?' Abbey continued, neatly illustrating her point.

'Ha ha ha!' Jackie laughed. It was a comfortable, easy sound. 'Yes, they do need doing. I use the peluquería near Maribel's shop. I think her sister runs it. Lewis told me about it.'

'Well, he would do, wouldn't he? I go there too.'

'So why is your hair...' Jackie's voice tailed off as she realised her mistake. She changed the subject crudely. 'It's winter now.'

'I bet it's snowing in England.'

'And cold and dark,' added Jackie. 'I'd rather be here. Wouldn't you?'

Abbey was slow to answer. 'Well, kind of.'

'Don't be so damn stupid. It's a thousand times better living here. What's wrong with it?'

Abbey was pensive. 'Lewis asked me too. About leaving England.' She sipped her coffee. *It really isn't very good.* 'I feel sad about moving, I don't know why. I should be happy, but I'm not. Are you?'

'Yes, of course I am. Anyway, I have to stay now. They can't find me here.'

It was hot. Beads of sweat prickled on Abbey's head and ran down her temples. She drew on the tiny green towel, adjusting it so that her crotch was covered more securely. Everyone could see her breasts, there was nothing she could do about that. The best that she could hope for was that no-one would notice how small they were in the dim yellow light. She was the only one in the sauna who seemed to be troubled by nudity. It did not seem to bother the others at all. Jackie was playing the game, tossing her mane every time she spoke. With each toss her two chocolate-brown jellies lifted, jiggled and settled back on her chest. There was no point in Abbey tossing her head about or shimmying her shoulders, the effect would be laughable. She sneaked another sly look at the man on the bench opposite. Phil was a big man. Big feet, thick thighs, a belly that had rather too much overhang. Above that, a smooth hairless chest. Abbey giggled silently. Phil's chest was well padded, with enough fat to compete with her own modest proposals. He had a round face and a domed, shaved head. *Why does he shave his head?* It was peppered with perspiration. Abbey caught herself staring and swept her eyes downwards. There was nothing to see. Whatever equipment Phil was endowed with was cleverly clenched between the pillows of his thighs.

'More steam?'

Abbey jumped.

Phil stood, angling his head under the low wooden ceiling. He walked the few paces across to the sauna heater and ladled water into it. A burst of wet heat erupted and hissed, the little cabin filled with its heavy energy.

'This is a great little place you found, Jackie.' Phil issued his compliment as he sauntered back to the bench. Abbey could not help looking at his humble manhood. She giggled silently again. There was no justification for Phil's nonchalance.

'Well, I couldn't use it when I was in. As a patient, I mean,' Jackie explained. 'They wouldn't let me come in here.'

'Odd, Isn't it?' Lewis spoke for the first time in a while. 'They have such fantastic facilities, they are open to the public, but they don't tell anyone.'

'Yes, we would probably never have known unless Jackie had discovered it.' Phil smiled his round, lardy smile. 'Thank you, Jackie.'

Jackie smiled back, tossed her hair and brandished her assets.

'Hola!' The cheery greeting was accompanied by two new people and an icy blast.

The heavy door closed again, cutting off the chill air. The young couple slipped off their robes as everyone else shuffled along to make space on the benches. Abbey looked the newcomers up and down, then turned and checked Jackie's expression. Disappointingly, it completely failed to reflect the surprise that Abbey felt. Best not say anything in here. It was such a cosy pack of bodies that even a whisper could not remain unheard.

The showers were every bit as good as the sauna. They were clean, new and lamentably under-used.

'Did you see those two that came in?' Abbey rushed to

ask Jackie.

'Yes. What about them?'

'Well, they had no hair... I mean, they had shaved. Everything.'

'So?'

'I was just, um, just commenting...' mumbled Abbey.

'Did you like it?'

'Like it?' *Why would I like it?* Abbey busied herself in front of the mirror.

'Abbey, you need to relax,' Jackie soothed. 'Everyone's different, you know.'

'They know how to charge, don't they?'

'Yes, they do,' responded Phil, his voice flat.

'I'm a writer.' Lewis forced a laugh. 'Well, I try to be one.' He sipped his straw-coloured beer and waited for Phil to reply in kind. The beer was very cold and extraordinarily devoid of flavour. Lewis changed tack. 'Ugh, this is awful. Like the sort of mass-produced stuff they sell back home. You know, overpriced and much too gassy. What do you think?'

'Overpriced and gassy. Yes.' Phil echoed Lewis, his words lacking any sense of conviction.

'I can't believe we haven't met before. There can't be that many English people in Castillo,' suggested Lewis.

'I suppose not,' Phil said indifferently.

'I live on Los Calamares,' offered Lewis. 'What about you?'

'I live with Jackie.'

'With Jackie?' It was a rare display of surprise from Lewis. Jackie never kept secrets from him. He was always the first to hear even the most trivial bits of gossip.

Phil nodded and slurped at his glass of tasteless fizzy liquid.

'Her apartment is fantastic,' said Lewis. Complimenting the man's new girlfriend should work. 'Plenty of room. Stylish too, just like Jackie.'

'Yes. Plenty of room.'

Lewis considering buying another round of beers. 'No,' he muttered. There was little hope of getting drunk no matter how many pints of yellow bilge water he swallowed.

Abbey followed Jackie through the swing doors, fresh from the shower and desperate for a long, cool drink. Jackie blocked her view with a waterfall of fluffy fibres that sprayed over her head and cascaded down her shoulders. Her hair looked fantastic, even after its battle with the hair-dryer. Bar stool legs scraped, Lewis leaped up. He flicked a smile at Jackie as he passed her.

'Oh!' Abbey was powerless, swept up against Lewis, her face pressed against the skin of his neck.

'You're back!' rasped Lewis.

Abbey could barely breathe, let alone speak. The overpowering pressure of Lewis' anaconda arms relaxed as he unwrapped his prey. She fell away, breathless. 'Did you miss me that much? It can't have been more than ten minutes!' she gasped.

'It's that man,' whispered Lewis conspiratorially. 'I can't stand another second of it. I mean, what's wrong with him?' Lewis shook his head. 'Where did she find him?'

'I don't know... yet. We'll talk about it later. Are you going to get me a drink?'

Gabriela was in exceptional form, swishing and mopping with energetic delight. She finished in the corner with quite a flourish, flicking the mop off the floor tiles and into the bucket. Abbey had never seen an old lady move with such agility. Her own mother was sloth-like by comparison. Rita acted out some kind of slow-motion pantomime whenever she thought that someone was watching. Gabriela took her cleaning tools outside, marched back in and grabbed Abbey, kissing her on both cheeks and giving her a gargantuan hug.

'Feliz cumpleaños!'

'Qué?' What? Abbey was momentarily stunned. 'Oh, muchas gracias, Gabriela.' Abbey thanked the cleaner very much for wishing her a happy birthday. 'How did you know?'

'Lewis told me. Jackie told me. Her man told me too. They all did. Everyone loves you, Abbey.'

Abbey felt herself blushing.

'How old are you?' asked Gabriela. It was a polite and well-intentioned inquiry.

'Um.' Abbey paused to translate the number into Spanish. 'Cuarenta años.' Forty years.

'Ah, you still look so young!' exclaimed Gabriela. 'I hope you have a lovely day.'

'Thank you, Gabriela.'

The door closed and Abbey was alone in the apartment. *A lovely day.* She pondered what it would take to fulfil that wish. She should do something that brought her joy. Perhaps she could start on a new picture. A sigh forced its way out and Abbey sank down into the chair in the corner. She had not picked up a brush for weeks. Everyone else got on with their lives whilst hers seemed to be on hold. She was just waiting, filling time. Life was passing her by. Lewis got on with his life. He came and went and sometimes he barely seemed to notice her. Jackie spent all her time with her new boyfriend, though it was difficult to see why. That just left Abbey. She was alone, she was forty. She felt it coming, a cold and merciless wave of sadness. It was too strong for her. She was crushed, smothered, gasping for air as the cruel tears engulfed her.

Chapter Thirteen

'Lewis said it's in the bedroom.' Alvaro was wearing his blue overalls and a cheeky smile.

'Yes, it is,' confirmed Abbey. Alvaro did not move. He waited at the door, his little folding ladder in one hand and a toolbox in the other.

'Do you want me to show you?' Surely Alvaro knew where the bedroom was. 'It's this way,' said Abbey coldly.

'Right up there?' Alvaro surveyed the holes in the wall and the collection of little wooden planks on the floor. He was hiding behind his moustache, pretending that he didn't know how the shelves got broken.

'Yes. Right up there.' Abbey held firm, refusing to say any more than she had to.

'But so high. Cómo?' How?

'I pulled on them.'

It was not enough for Alvaro. Today he was rich, endowed with a wealth of privileged information. He smoothed down his moustache and watched the English woman squirm. 'You pulled on them? You must have pulled hard.'

'I was drunk, Alvaro,' stated Abbey with uncharacteristic finality. 'Would you like coffee?'

'No gracias, señora.' No thank you, madam. Alvaro unfolded his step ladder and set it down firmly, making quite a drama of checking that it was stable enough to carry him safely to the extreme altitude of the holes in the wall.

Jackie was out of focus, a jumble of red lips, yellow hair and brown skin that was saying things from the other giant sofa. 'You see, it really works,' said Jackie's voice. 'It fixes everything for me...' The red lips drooped. '...almost everything.'

Abbey tried to understand Jackie but it was too hard. She gave up and carried out some simple tests on herself

138

instead. She tried to worry about her mother. Rita had forgotten Abbey's birthday. There was no card, no message, nothing at all from her. Jackie seemed to be right. 'I don't care about Mother,' Abbey announced. 'And I don't care that I am forty now.' As strong as brandy, the orujo was working.

'That's the spirit!' Jackie laughed. 'The spirit! Get it?'

'Ha ha ha!' The laughter seemed to come from somewhere outside Abbey's head. She swallowed and made a determined effort to sound coherent. 'So, where did you say Phil is?'

'I already told you. He's at the swimming pool.'

'The one in The Hotel. Yes, you did say.'

'He loves swimming,' continued Jackie. 'He likes to keep fit, you see.'

Abbey did not see at all. *Ugh, that belly.* Abbey had greasy memories of an overweight, balding man in a sauna. They were not suggestive of a keep-fit enthusiast. 'Yes, I see,' she lied.

Jackie was still talking about her boyfriend. 'He used to be a champion, you know. A champion swimmer.' She looked like she really believed it.

Maybe when he was younger, thought Abbey. 'Didn't you want to go with him?' she asked aloud.

'You know I don't like it. I can't swim very well and it spoils my hair.' She tossed her head to emphasise her point.

'Why didn't you tell me about him?' blurted Abbey.

'Phil? I did tell you.'

'You didn't say he was going to live with you.'

'Didn't I? Sorry, I thought I did. Where else could he live anyway? He can't sleep on the beach.'

'Beach?' Abbey's confusion grew. 'He could live in an apartment.'

The red lips saddened again. 'His business is not doing well. Anyway, it's done now.' said Jackie quietly.

'What is?'

'Nothing,' said Jackie with forced brightness. 'Nothing at all. Pass me that bottle would you?'

'Afuera?'

'Sí!' Lewis retrieved an impressively heavy-looking manuscript, a half-smoked cigar and a tiny white cup of coffee from the table and followed Juan. The suggestion to sit outside was a good one. There was little point living in such a wonderful place only to squander its benefits by sitting indoors. 'Don't bother with that, Juan. I don't need it.'

Juan gave up struggling to open the blue and white umbrella. 'Sí, señor.' He left it cloaking the pole, flapping in the wind that tripped along the boulevard. 'More coffee?'

'In a while, Juan. I've barely tasted this one.' Lewis sat down, scraping the chair around a bit to obtain the best view. 'Perfect.' He re-lit his cigar and took a couple of puffs, then picked up the manuscript. He put it down again and the pages fluttered under the slack umbrella. The sun was a yellow rosebud filled with promise, ascending through a milk blue sky. Lewis eased off his jumper and reached for his cigar and his coffee. This time he left the manuscript where it was, the pages turning over as if flicked by ghost fingers. He had to get this thing published now. Another few months and the money would run out and then where would he be? He would find himself selling the apartment, moving back to the dark misery of England and casting about to find a job. That would be a catastrophic defeat marking the loss of everything he had built up. Apart from money, things were pretty good now. Summer was on its way, he had good friends and he had a live-in lover who was both obliging and economical. That part of his life had been surprisingly easy to arrange. It would be a shame to lose it all, a wretched calamity if the coming season turned out to be his last one spent in the warm embrace of Castillo.

'Café, señor?' Juan was back for a second attempt at selling hot beverages.

'What time is it? Nearly two? I'd better have some food.'

Juan's face lit up. 'What would you like?'

'Um, I don't know, Juan. Whatever's easy for you.' Juan had never brought a bad dish to the table yet.

'And to drink?' asked Juan.

Lewis had a sudden rush of déjà vu that transported him back to long-forgotten package holidays in sweaty and crowded over-developed resorts. For a second he was a teenager again, trying to understand what the waiters were asking him as his parents waited impatiently. 'Oh. Cerveza, por favor.' Cold beer would be nice today.

Abbey sighed. 'I've tried watching him.'

'And what did you see?' enquired Jackie.

'Nothing, really.'

'Have you asked him?'

'No. Well, I did ask once but he ignored me.'

'Well just go ahead and ask him again then. What are you frightened of? He won't bite you.' Jackie giggled. 'Well, he might do... if you're lucky.'

'Jackie, you know I'm not into all that pervy stuff.' Abbey sipped from her glass. 'Not much of it, anyway.' She paused and the alcohol swirled around her head. 'Have you tried it?'

'Tried what?'

'You know. Something different.'

'Abbey!' Jackie was shocked, not by the question but by the person asking. 'Of course I have,' she announced. Her statement was bold, straightforward and matter-of-fact.

'I thought you might have. What is it like?'

'Which bit?'

'Any of it.'

'It's ok. To be honest it's over-rated. I don't bother any

more. These days the usual stuff is enough for me.'

Abbey nodded encouragingly but Jackie did not seem to be in the mood to reveal any further details of her exploits.

'How did we get onto the subject?' Jackie asked. 'What were we talking about?'

Abbey worked her way back through the rolling clouds of their conversation 'Love. Not sex.'

'Ah, yes, love. You were asking about Lewis and love, weren't you?' Jackie did not wait for confirmation. 'Why?'

'Why? It's obvious, isn't it?'

'Not to me it isn't.' Jackie wandered over to the enormous window. Like a perfect mural, the rooftops and trees of Castillo framed the distant panorama of glittering sea. 'What does it mean anyway? I can't see the point of it.'

'Abbey keeps watching me,' Lewis lamented.

'Why?' asked Juan.

'I think she's trying to trap me.'

'Trap you?'

'Yes, you know, Juan. Get me to commit myself,' Lewis explained.

'Ah, you mean she wants to marry you!' Juan sounded triumphant.

'If you insist on putting it like that, yes,' said Lewis grudgingly.

'She is beautiful and talented. And she wants you.' Juan was listing as many of Abbey's good points as he could think of, without crossing the line into indecency. 'She's better for you then that mandaparte. So what's your problem?'

'Mandaparte?' That was a new word for Lewis.

'Show-off,' translated Juan simply.

'Oh, you mean Jackie. Of course Abbey's not a show-off like Jackie if that's what you're saying.' Lewis took a sip of cerveza, cold and clean. His eyes tracked the cars as they passed each way along the sea-front boulevard. 'Those two women are such a contrast, I can't understand how they get along.' Lewis was thoughtful. 'But they do. In fact they seem quite close.'

Juan refused to be diverted from his cause. 'You could have a big wedding up at the castle.' Drawing up a chair, he nodded towards the proud relic that dominated Castillo.

'Don't be ridiculous. How much do you think that would cost? Listen, it's simple really. I don't want to get married. What if I changed my mind? Now that would cost me a fortune. It would ruin me. I'd lose my apartment... Anyway, I don't need the stress.'

Juan settled into his chair. 'Marriage is good, Lewis. Look at me and Reina.'

Lewis snorted. 'I've been looking at you and Reina for years. If it's supposed to make me want to get married then I must have missed the point somewhere.'

The men were sparring, indulging in a masculine mixture of competitive mocking, mutual ridicule and occasional compassion.

'But we have the perfect marriage,' insisted Juan.

'What about the shouting? That's not perfect.'

'So, sometimes we argue. Everyone does. You argue with Abbey, don't you?'

Lewis nodded.

'You have to have give and take, you know, Lewis. Accommodate each other.' The afternoon sunlight played through the last few strands of hair that decorated Juan's head. 'You can't just have the bits that you want. You have to take it all, good and bad.'

Lewis was momentarily stumped, trying to translate something like *I don't need you to lecture me* into suitable Spanish.

A look of concern wrinkled Juan's face. 'Are you listening to me?'

'Yes. I'm listening,' said Lewis pensively. He was hearing wise words from an older man, sound, rational and unwelcome.

'You don't want me telling you how to live your life, do you?' suggested Juan.

'You read my mind.'

'No, I saw that bad look you gave me.'

'Oh. Sorry, Juan.'

'It's alright.' Juan moved on. 'Did you enjoy your meal?'

'Yes, it was lovely. It tasted rather fishy. What was it?'

'Pulpo á feira,' declared Juan, lighting the fuse.

'That does not tell me anything. You haven't done that dish for me before. Come on, what's in it?'

'Paprika, potatoes and bread.' Juan dropped the bomb. 'With boiled octopus.'

'Octopus?'

'That's what I said. Octopus. I wanted to try something new from the Northwest. You're the first customer who ordered it.'

'But I didn't order it!' Lewis exploded.

'You said you enjoyed it, though.' Juan was unperturbed.

'That's because it was very good,' admitted Lewis.

Juan was satisfied with his first customer reaction to the new dish. 'I could add it to the Cafetería menu.'

'That's a good idea. I think you should, Juan.' Lewis was open to new ideas when he could see their merit.

'Juan! What are you doing?' A woman's piercing voice intruded. Like a barbed hook on a fishing line it reached out from behind them, threatening to snag its prey.

'I have to go. Reina is calling me.' Juan looked like a schoolboy caught truanting.

'Juan! Are you wasting time chatting again?' Reina was getting closer and angrier.

'You'd better go, Juan,' advised Lewis. 'And remember what you told me about marriage!'

'Jackie, why are you on the floor?' Phil marched into the apartment and stood over her, his arms folded and jaw set.

'I can't get up. Ish my legs,' bleated Jackie.

'It's not your legs, Jackie, it's your brain.'

'Brain? Wosh wrong wiv my brain?'

'It's had too much drink, that's what's wrong. It's not even dark yet and just look at you.'

Jackie looked but she did not see anything that merited reporting.

Phil turned to address the other woman. 'Abbey, I think it's time for you to go.'

Abbey jumped up, instantly on the defensive. It was Jackie's apartment and Jackie's alcohol. 'If she wants to get drunk then that's her decision.' Abbey listened to herself speak. She unexpectedly found herself fiercely defending her friend. She was surprised how assured and steady her voice sounded.

'I'm not blaming you, Abbey. She doesn't know when she's had enough. How long was I gone? Two hours?' Phil was intent on dominating the situation.

Jackie consulted her wrist. It was watch-less. 'Three,' slurred Jackie, allowing her arm to flop back onto the floor.

'How do you know?' Phil threw his words at Jackie, heartlessly casting them like crusty little rocks. 'You don't even know what day it is.'

'Yesh I do. It's...' Jackie squinted at Phil through the watery slits of her half-closed eyes. 'Miércoles.' Wednesday, she said. Everyone in the room was English.

Phil did not bother to tell her that it was actually Thursday. 'Come on, let's get you into bed. You can sleep it off.' He tugged crudely at Jackie, jerking her up into a crooked sitting position. She rested her forehead on her bent knees and mumbled incoherently.

'Are you up to walking home?' Phil asked Abbey.

'Yes, of course I am,' Abbey snapped.

Jackie peeped around her knees at Abbey, gave up quickly and resumed babbling.

Abbey glanced at Phil. 'I'll help you with Jackie,' she insisted.

After enjoying a cloudless day riding unchallenged through the translucent blue-white sky, the sun tiptoed away to hide timidly behind the hills. The evening slipped around the terrace, enveloping Lewis. He shrugged his jacket over his shoulders and stooped a little to light a cigar. He was alone with the night until someone fell over the wall and created an untidy heap at the side of the terrace.

'Abbey?'

'Humph,' replied the heap.

Lewis dropped his cigar and strode over to examine the wreckage. He found an elbow and pulled on it. Like a marionette, Abbey unfolded and stood shakily. She was floppy, hanging loosely as if suspended by strings at her joints. 'How much have you had?' accused Lewis.

'How much what?' slurred Abbey.

'Oh never mind. Come on, I'll get you into bed.'

'But I don't want to go to bed,' appealed Abbey, her childlike eyes wide and watery. 'I want to sit out here with you.'

'That might not be such a bad idea. Perhaps it will help you sober up a bit,' agreed Lewis. He picked up his cigar and drew air through it, bringing it back to life.

'I want one of those,' Abbey pleaded.

'Abbey, you don't smoke.'

'I do now.'

'If you say so. Here you are. Do you want me to light it for you?'

'I can light it myself,' insisted the little girl's voice. Her confidence was not matched by her competence. 'I said, I can do it myself!' Abbey knocked Lewis' hand out of the way and finally succeeded in applying a flame to the end of her cigar. The red circle glowed and faded as she drew on it. She coughed and drew again. 'I'm forty today, you know.'

'I know.' Lewis smiled at her.

Abbey caught the tail end of his gesture and returned it. She blew out a mouthful of smoke. 'Did you get me some flowers?' It seemed much easier to ask Lewis questions when she was drunk.

'Yes, I did.'

'I don't believe you!'

'Well, look inside then. They are in the bedroom.'

'I'll look later. Lewis?'

'Yes?' He watched her with kind green eyes.

'Lewis, I don't like being forty.'

'It's only a number, Abbey. Really, it isn't important. You're just as lovely today as you were yesterday.'

'But it makes me seem so old. Old and unsexy.'

'Is unsexy a word?'

'I don't think so. But you know what I mean.' Abbey dropped her cigar into the ashtray, half of it unsmoked. 'I don't like smoking,' she announced.

'You said that the last time you tried,' laughed Lewis.

'Did I? I forgot.'

'I expect you did.' Lewis wrapped an arm around her shoulders and she rested her head against him.

'Did you really get me flowers?' asked Abbey.

'Of course I did. It's your birthday,' Lewis said with reassuring warmth.

'And Lewis?'

'Yes?'

'Do you love me?'

Lewis tugged Abbey up. 'I'll show you the flowers.'

Abbey felt his hardness, deeper and deeper inside. Pleasure and pain played a sensual game, their sensations mixing and merging. Lewis gripped her hips in his hands. His body pressed up behind her and she felt the roughness of his cheek against the side of her face. His movements quickened, lifting her up onto her toes. She reached out for support and her fingertips found the reassuring firmness of a stout bookshelf. As she curled her hands over its rounded edge, Lewis shouted in her ear. It was a choking, wordless cry that checked the heat of his breath. Abbey felt the soles of her feet leave the floor. Lewis' fingers pressed into her, grasping at her flesh. The animal energy shattered and crumbled, the clawing hands relaxed, Abbey felt the floor under her feet once again. The wood came down as she fell, a cascade of planks and splinters and jumbled books that fragmented over her shoulders.

'Oh my God!' Abbey was part of the pile, a confusion of arms, legs, shelves and paperbacks. Amongst the mayhem stood a man, feet planted wide, a strong hand waiting to pull her up. Abbey laughed and the man laughed. Together they waded out of the splintered ocean of debris, then turned to look back. 'Oh Lewis, I'm sorry. What are we going to do?' asked Abbey.

'Nothing. And you don't need to be sorry.'

'But I just broke your shelves.'

'We broke them. It was a team activity.'

Laughter took over, fuelled by elation, release and relief.

'I need a shower,' announced Lewis hoarsely.

'I'll join you.'

'There isn't enough room for two,' Lewis cautioned.

'Yes there is. I'll show you!' Abbey skipped out of the bedroom, pulling her lover behind her.

Chapter Fourteen

The flowers hung their heads, ashamed of who they were and what they had become.

'I don't much like the look of you,' observed one of them.

'What are you talking about? You're not exactly a pretty sight yourself,' retorted its target in a high-pitched, squeaky voice.

'I'm taller than you.'

'So? You're just as dead. And you haven't got any petals left, either. At least I've got some petals.'

'I've got leaves. Who needs petals? You're too small.' The voice was dry and chafing. 'You were never any good. They just put you in the bunch to get rid of you.'

'Bully!' The victim's voice rose to a tremolo squeal.

'It's true,' continued the bully. 'No-one cares about you.'

'Yes they do.'

'Don't,' rattled the bully.

'Do!'

'Will you two stop arguing?' A brown chrysanthemum stepped in. 'It's bad enough standing here like this without you two going on and on. Can't a poor old stem get any peace?'

'Ooh, listen to her!' sang the bully. 'You'd thing she was queen of the bunch to hear her talk!'

'I am.'

'What?' challenged the bully.

'I said, I am. So leave Petunia alone.'

'I'm not a petunia,' squeaked the little stalk.

'What are you?' asked the queen.

'I'm a... a... I don't know.'

'See, it's like I said. She's only here to make up the numbers,' shrilled the bully triumphantly.

'No I'm not,' protested Petunia.

'I don't care if you are or not,' interrupted the queen.

'Shh,' she hissed. 'Someone's coming.'

Abbey stopped pretending to be dead flowers and their pathetic conversation ended. She picked up the vase and carried it outside. The brown stalks and wilted leaves tumbled onto the garden, splashed over by the stale water in which they had lived and died.

The cacti cast spiky shadows. There were tall ribbed ones and stubby fat round ones. Some of the largest and oldest cacti in the collection originally came from England, sneaked in by Lewis when he first succumbed to the warm hospitality of Spain. Abbey studied each in turn, grouped neatly in their terracotta pots on the terrace. She started to move the pots around, arranging them so that the tallest and mightiest plants were at the back and the little ones with woolly white coats were at the front. There were vicious spines under that harmless looking disguise, hiding and waiting to prick the careless skin of the unwary.

'There. That's right.' Abbey stood back a bit to assess her still-life subjects. 'Yes. Perfect. I just need all my stuff now.' She backed away further. One more step, just to check the proportions.

'Tiene cuidado!' Careful!

Abbey turned and saw the worn face and caring black eyes. 'Oh, Gabriela. You made me jump.'

The old lady laughed. 'I've been in the apartment for half an hour. I came out to shake the rug. Didn't you notice me?'

'No. Not at all. I thought you were coming at eleven.'

'Pero... es once y media.' But it's half past eleven, laughed the old lady.

'Half past. Yes...' echoed Abbey absent-mindedly. 'I was just going in to get my easel.'

'I thought so. You're going to paint the cacti,' stated Gabriela. She rested a hooked hand on Abbey's arm. 'He was lonely for a long time, you know.'

Abbey was dumbfounded.

'For years Lewis was on his own here,' continued Gabriela. 'I was worried about him.' She looked into the distance, as if she could see right through the trees and buildings to the waves breaking on the shore. 'I thought he would go back home in the end. But he stayed. And then...'

'And then?' Abbey was hanging onto every word.

'And then you came. So beautiful, like the first white rose after winter.'

'You flatter me, Gabriela.'

'No. It's true. You're good for him.'

'Oh, thank you.' Abbey did not know what else to say.

The housekeeper adopted a sombre tone. 'But you must be careful.'

'Careful? Why?' Abbey felt a knot of fear forming inside her stomach.

'At the fiesta, they snatch the pretty girls and make them join the dancing.'

'Dancing?' Abbey dared to breathe again. Those black eyes were laughing at her. 'Oh, you are naughty, Gabriela!' Abbey giggled.

The brush was alive, an animated stick with a wet, hairy tip. It dipped into the brown paint, then darted to the canvas. It hurried away for more paint, then in seconds it was back, dancing over yesterday's broad colour washes. It stroked the surface, outlining and defining. Without warning it was discarded, dropped into the pot in favour of a skinny cousin. Ridges and spines appeared on the painting, black and sharp.

'It's like magic,' said Lewis at last.

'Do you really think so?' asked Abbey.

'Yes, I do. Like a pianist at a concert, or someone dancing the tango, or...'

'Or an artist painting?'

Lewis laughed. 'Yes, an artist painting. But not just any artist.' He played with Abbey's hair, lifting it away from her face.

151

'It's drying quickly today,' observed Abbey.

Lewis watched Abbey, noticing how her eyes flickered from paint to picture and back. Her eyelashes were long, her lips were happy. 'I was going to suggest that we went sunbathing today,' he ventured.

'That sounds like a good idea,' replied Abbey, still focussed upon her artistic enterprise.

'It's going to be hot enough by midday,' Lewis explained.

The brush hovered, midway between paint and canvas. Then it jumped back into the pot. 'We'll go now, shall we?'

'There's no rush. This afternoon will be fine.' Lewis dropped his shoulders. He had inadvertently halted something special. It felt like he had slammed the piano lid down on that concert pianist's hands. 'I like watching you paint,' he added hurriedly. 'And I want to see the picture when it's finished.'

'Oh, I couldn't possibly complete it today anyway.' Abbey was wiping things on a damp cloth. 'It takes a lot longer than that.' She dragged her easel deeper into the shade. 'Come on, let's go to the beach.'

'You'll get tan lines.'

'I like tan lines.'

'Nobody likes tan lines. You'll look funny. White tits!' Lewis laughed at his own joke.

'So? It doesn't matter,' Abbey pouted. 'Jackie tried to make me go topless last year,' she added.

'Did you do it?' asked Lewis, hoping to explore any opportunity.

'No, of course I didn't.' Abbey sat on the beach towel and looked down her nose. She wriggled around, trying to settle her breasts in the cups of her bikini top. She did not remember having to do anything like that last summer. 'Lewis, do you think I'm getting bigger?'

'Bigger?' Lewis stalled. It was wise to tread carefully.

'Oh, it doesn't matter. Pass me my book, will you?'

Lewis rummaged through the bag. There were books and bottles and drinks, an assorted medley of accessories and necessities all thrown in together. 'Which one?'

'The blue one. Yes, that one. Thanks.' Abbey thumbed through the book, searching for the right page.

'It's rubbish. I don't know why you read that stuff,' grumbled Lewis. He brushed the sand off the edge of the towel and took stock. The season was just getting under way but the tourist beach was quite busy because the town end of it was closed. Couples paraded, chatting and swinging their arms as they sauntered. Their feet splashed through the Mediterranean sea where its salty lips made watery transparent shelves on the slopes of the soft yellow sand.

'What do you think?' Abbey enquired in a carefully framed, matter of fact voice. 'I had to take the top off, it was too tight.'

Lewis switched on again. He had to catch up quickly. 'Very nice,' he pronounced. It was a terribly banal, ordinary compliment. Having spent half an hour scanning everyone else in view, he found himself staring at the most shapely and appealing topless woman on the tourist beach of Castillo. Unlike the others, this one was sharing his towel and waiting for a proper reply.

'You look lovely, Abbey. Good enough to eat.'

Abbey giggled and Lewis relaxed. She did look good, and he could feast whenever he chose.

'It's Fiesta San Juan tonight,' announced Lewis.

'What's that? Is it important?'

'Important? They love it. Saint John is Castillo's patron, so it's the biggest fiesta of the year. Surely you saw all the posters around town?'

'I can't say I noticed any,' said Abbey blankly.

'Well, it's the big one. The fireworks at ten o'clock are unbelievable.' Lewis thought for a moment. 'You were here last time. Remember?'

'Um, no.' The blank look deepened.

'It was your first night here.'

'Oh yes!' Abbey's face lit up. We were on the terrace, weren't we?' She did not give Lewis an opportunity to confirm her recollection. 'I can't believe it,' she exclaimed. 'Was it really a whole year ago?'

The rich musk of Latin rhythms sweetened the night air, a tapestry of sound woven through with laughter. Shouts, whistles, snatches of song threaded the evening. The music overflowed, escaping from the streets of Castillo and spilling onto the town beach. Firelight orange flickered on the happy faces that thronged the sea-front boulevard. Great cones burned on the beach, a mountain range of junk piles set alight. Old chairs and bits of wood, cast-offs and rubbish were transformed. For the last hours of their existence they were no longer useless and ugly. Heaped together they made delightful, tangled hills that lived and crackled and shot sparkling streams into the black heavens. Joy exploded in a cacophony of cheering applause as the first float battled along the road. The old lorry travelled at walking pace. Its driver hung out of the window and in turn a cigarette hung on his lip. He waved, the crowd waved back and screamed. With horns sounding, more floats snaked behind. They proceeded as carefully as their distracted, intoxicated drivers could manage, each with its precious load teetering on the back.

'They're enormous!' yelled Abbey in delight.

'Yes. They are good this year,' Lewis shouted back. Every vehicle carried a painted ninot, a figure that satirised a politician or a star. Each one was as tall as five people, made of papier-mâché and wood. Boos erupted from the crowd, directed at an enormous effigy of the prime minister. A huge-breasted bikini-clad blonde model was on the next float, drawing hoots of derisive laughter.

'They are going to the square,' explained Lewis. 'They will unload the ninots there and burn them after the fireworks.'

'They didn't do all this last year,' said Abbey.

'They do it every year,' assured Lewis. 'But you had other things on your mind last time.'

'What?' Abbey was struggling to hear Lewis over the music and blaring horns.

'I said, we were too busy last year. Oh, I'll tell you later.'

'I don't want them to be burned,' shouted Abbey. 'It's cruel.'

A twenty-foot high model of the transport minister went by. 'Abbey, they are only models,' stated Lewis, 'and the Spaniards hate their politicians.' He stopped there, his voice drowned out by the first of the salsa bands. Like giant hearts beating, the conga drums and bongos pounded. One after another the bands came, each of them beating away at their percussion and striking their hand-bells with gusto. As each band passed, its twenty or so members competed to outdo the team in front. Mesmerising rhythmic waves drowned the onlookers' senses with sensual primeval beats that filled them and left no room for anything else. Within each band were the girls in red and yellow and orange, wiggling their hips with impossible flexibility, stepping forward on each beat with the agility and fluidity of flowing gold. Abbey had given up trying to speak to Lewis or listen to his hoarsely-shouted replies. Every sense was filled, sight with the dancing red and flickering orange, ears ringing with salsa, the taste and smell of smoke on the sea air.

The crowd followed the parade up into town. 'They call it Las Fallas,' said Lewis, guiding Abbey into a slot in the heaving throng that was building deeper around the plaza.

'Las Fallas, yes,' Abbey echoed, pretending that she knew all about it.

Lewis was not that easy to fool. 'It's an ancient phrase. It means The Fires,' he continued.

'I don't want to watch them burn the ninots,' whimpered Abbey.

Lewis looked into her eyes. 'Would you rather go back?'

'Yes.'

'Then that's what we'll do. We can watch the fireworks from the terrace, like last year.'

Arm in arm, they walked back to the apartment. Their hearing was muffled, deafened by the shouting, still ringing from the salsa music. Bing bing bong, bing-bing-bong, bing-bing. The cow-bells repeated in Abbey's head. In this simplest of melodies played endlessly with just two notes lived the heat and passion of Spain. It was a sound which would remain with her forever.

'I've had enough of this.'

'Had enough of what, Nan?'

'You really can't see it, can you?'

'See what, Nan?' Luke's voice carried surprise, even disbelief.

'All this... all this rubbish.' Rita took a couple of steps into Luke's room. 'Everything is covered with it. The table, the floor, the windowsill. Everything.' Her voice fragmented with age and anger. 'Haven't you heard of litter bins? You know, where you put empty things when you've finished with them.'

'Yes, Nan, of course I have.'

'Then why don't you use them? It's disgusting. I mean, look at all this.' Rita swept a feeble foot across the floor, where empty drink cans competed with stained cardboard take-away boxes, screwed-up tissues and assorted, formless litter. 'And look at the carpet!'

Luke looked. Stains, great overlapping ovals of dark stickiness, stared back accusingly. 'Oh, sorry Nan.'

'Sorry? You'll be sorry. I bet whatever you spilt has gone right through to the floorboards.' Rita retreated to the doorway.

'Listen, Nan, I said I was sorry,' pleaded Luke. 'I'll clear it all up. I'll do it now.' He stood up and stepped through the ocean of litter. Rita blocked his route. 'Let me out so I can get some bags.' For an instant he felt the urge to push his way past, then came to his senses.

'Luke, it's not just the state of your room,' explained Rita. 'It's your sleeping too.'

'Sleeping?'

'Well, you stay up all night playing games and then you sleep all day. I hardly ever see you.' Rita paused for breath, then continued with her theme. 'It's just not natural, is it?'

'But Nan, I don't stay up playing games. I'm designing things.'

'What, all night? What can you design that takes all night?'

'Well, I'm working on...' Luke struggled to find a way to explain himself, to cross the yawning gulf that separated two generations. 'I'm working on graphics,' he blurted.

'Graphics? What's graphics?' It was clear from Rita's reply that Luke had failed in his endeavour. 'Anyway, that's it. I'm not having any more of it,' Rita grated emphatically. 'You've got to leave.'

The door closed and Luke was alone again. He sat on his bed and drew his knees up. The bed was a boat, a rectangular vessel that sailed through a sea of empty pop cans and pizza boxes. The wind had changed and Luke was going to have to find a new harbour.

Abbey watched herself with innocent eyes. She was standing in the hallway, absent-minded and naked in front of the tall mirror. She flicked back her hair to reveal her face. There were lines and subtle creases, the little wrinkles that marked the passing of time. *Well, I've been here for over a year now.* Her shoulders were darker than she remembered, still smooth and sprinkled with freckles. She brushed her fingers over her arms, finding them leaner and more sculpted yet still feminine. *I have to be strong.* Her fingers curved over each breast, lifting their weight alternately. She let them fall gently again, softly dropping into natural pear-fruit shapes. The white mounds decorated with pink points, familiar since her teens, were gone. Now she sported tanned hillocks topped with near-invisible brown caps. *I am still a woman. I'm not finished yet.* She turned to one side and then the other, fascinated by the way that her body narrowed at the waist and rounded out over her hips. She planted her feet further apart, separating her thighs. *It's such a shame. Just when I was starting to get somewhere.* Abbey ran her fingers over the roughness of her neatly trimmed triangle, carefully cropped to hide neatly inside her bikinis. A banging noise set her heart racing. Someone was rattling at the door, only a few feet away from her. Who could it be? Lewis was not expected back. It might be Gabriela, but she was not supposed to be here today. Maybe it was Alvaro. Exposed and vulnerable, Abbey was panic-stricken. She rushed to find her bath-robe. The banging and rattling sounded loud even from the bedroom. Shrugging the robe on quickly, she marched back to deal with the unwelcome caller.

'Jackie! It's you!'

Jackie galloped in, pushing past Abbey. 'I've lost my key,' she announced breathlessly. She turned back towards Abbey, still frozen in the open doorway. 'You were ages answering the door. I thought there was something wrong,' observed Jackie.

'Yes, there is,' stated Abbey flatly. It was not surprising to hear that Jackie had lost her key, but in the circumstances the timing of her loss was far from perfect.

'I've seen a boat!' exclaimed Jackie.

'Me too. Several in fact.' Abbey allowed herself a little joke, not expecting her sarcasm to be noticed.

'Not like this one. It's amazing.'

'Oh, I expect I have,' replied Abbey. *I was right. She's not listening at all.*

'It's white and blue. And it's just had a new engine fitted. Abbey, are you listening?'

'Mother rang last night,' said Abbey.

Jackie's face fell, the grin left her cherry red lips. 'Is she alright?'

'Yes, she's fine.'

'That's good. Well, it's down at the marina-'

'Jackie, I have to go back,' interrupted Abbey. 'Mother has told Luke to leave.'

'Well, he should be able to look after himself now, shouldn't he? How old is he?'

'He's twenty-one now.'

'Twenty-one? He'll be ok. What's your problem?'

'Jackie, it's not like that. He's not like other young men. He's... he's vulnerable.'

'Why doesn't he come here? He could live in Spain for a while.'

'Oh,' said Abbey. 'I never thought of that.'

'It would be educational for him,' Jackie suggested.

'Yes, I suppose it would,' Abbey conceded. Her mind was racing. Problem after problem chased each other. 'No, it's hopeless. We don't have enough room. We can't afford to keep him. We-'

'Abbey, you are such a pessimist. Listen, I'm supposed to be at the marina by now. Will you come with me to look at the boat?'

'No, Jackie, I can't. I've got to sort Luke and Mother out.'

'Suit yourself, then. I'll take Phil instead.' The door slammed.

Abbey's thoughts rattled through her head, a parade of troubles and regrets populated with miserable-looking images of Luke and Rita. 'I should have visited them more often,' muttered Abbey to herself. She tried to sniff back the tears. 'I'm too selfish, that's what I am. It's all my fault.'

Chapter Fifteen

The wind was light, just enough to set slack ropes clinking against metal masts. Abbey and Lewis sat on a wall, looking out over the marina and listening to the soft slop of wavelets that played between the boats and ran aground on the stones below their feet. Oblivious fish shoals played along the rocky edges in the warmth of the glassy shallows, hunting for morsels amongst the grey crags. Abbey shaded her eyes to look beyond the marina. The sea sparkled, energised by a sun-whitened sky. Hundreds of years ago there was a little port near Castillo, serving the fishing community's modest fleet of simple wooden vessels. It cut a square out of the coastline, framed by stone walls and paved paths. The town grew until its streets reached the port and its buildings covered the hillside behind. The rectangle of moorings was extended out into the sea with new walls topped by walkways. Wooden jetties projected like fingers between the rows of white yachts. It was still called El Puerto Pequeño, the little port, but now the few remnants of the fishing fleet huddled with shame in one far corner. Everywhere else was filled with chrome and white, the playthings of a few wealthy residents and many summer visitors. Rich people and tourists have higher expectations than bearded fishermen do, so at El Puerto Pequeño the municipal council had lifted a paving stone here and there to plant palm trees at intervals along the old harbour paths. Lewis flicked his sunglasses up to scan the white rows of pleasure craft, then dropped them back onto his nose.

'Which yacht is it?' he asked.

'I don't know. She said it's blue and white.'

'There's a blue one over there.' Lewis pointed into the glare.

'Where? Oh yes. I didn't see that one. But it might be this one.' Abbey pointed into a different part of the blinding light.

'Why didn't you ask her? It could be any of them. There are hundreds of blue and white ones.'

'Don't exaggerate, Lewis.'

'Alright, half a dozen then.'

Abbey chortled. 'It's hard to see anything from here.'

'You need some sunglasses. I thought you had a pair.'

'I did but you sat on them. Remember?'

'Well, you shouldn't have left them in the beach bag. How could I know?'

'So, why did you sit on the bag? Oh, forget it.' Abbey reached around Lewis and pulled his mouth onto hers, smothering his protests and bringing the bickering to an end.

Lewis broke free to gasp for air and change the subject. 'What happened with Luke?' he enquired.

Abbey shaded her eyes again, gazing out level over the decks and ropes to the horizon. 'Oh yes, Luke.' Her heart sank. 'And Mother,' she added glumly.

'So it's not settled yet, then?' asked Lewis.

Abbey looked away to avoid his questioning scrutiny. 'No. I had to force myself to come here today, I was so worried. But I don't want to let Jackie down either.'

'Your family is more important that Jackie,' said Lewis softly.

Abbey turned to look at Lewis again. His eyes were hidden by his sunglasses, but she read true compassion in his voice. 'Thank you, Lewis. But you know me. I try to keep everyone happy.'

'You can't be responsible for all of us, Abbey.'

'No, I suppose not.'

'Especially Jackie,' continued Lewis. 'She's always the same.'

'You're right. I don't know why we bothered to rush down here for eleven,' grumbled Abbey. 'It's been over an hour now.'

'She'll be here soon, I can feel it.' Lewis sounded as if he was stating his prediction as a fact. 'And the Luke thing will soon be sorted out.'

Abbey threw him a questioning look. 'I can't see how.'

Lewis was adamant. 'It will, I can feel that too.'

Two dark figures tripped along a distant walkway, black creatures against the white sheet of the sky. They disappeared behind the massive shape of a boat as if sucked into its shadow by gravity, then popped out into the streaming sunlight on the other side. The leading figure skipped along, its feet on springs. Its companion dragged behind, weighed down by a heavy load and shoes of lead.

Abbey jumped up. 'That's them, right over there. I'm sure of it.'

Lewis joined her. 'Where? I can't see anyone.'

'They've gone behind another boat now. Watch. You'll see them come out from the other side.'

'Yes, there they are. You're right. It does look like Jackie and Phil. Funny how you can tell even from here. Jackie's in front, isn't she?'

'That's what I thought. Come on.'

'It's here.' Juan sounded the alarm.

'What's here?' Reina asked, pushing past him into the kitchen.

'The fish van from Barcelona.'

'So?'

'So I need help carrying everything.' Juan was exasperated.

'Then ask chef,' shouted Reina, hidden somewhere in the back of Cafetería de la Luz.

'I've already called him. He's not here yet.'

'Then you'll have to do it yourself.'

'Oh come on, mi querida.' Juan attempted to inject some sweetness into his pleas.

Reina appeared in the doorway, filling its frame with her stubborn bulk. 'If chef's not here then who's going to get everything ready for tonight? Me, that's who.'

'But dear, it's only a few boxes,' appealed Juan.

'Then you can bring them in yourself. This wouldn't happen if you actually bought all the fish locally, like you tell the customers you do. Our fishermen don't stop outside and sound the horn, they bring it all in.'

Juan spread out his hands in dismay. 'But it's half the price from Barcelona. They charge double here. It would ruin us.'

'Ruin us? Pah! It's always about the money with you. What do you know? El burro sabe mas que tu!'

The donkey knows more than you. It was an old insult, expertly delivered by Reina with absolute finality. Juan went out alone to the van.

'Fast, isn't she?'

The wind whipped Abbey's hair into her eyes. She looped her fingers around the tresses and held them back. Jackie stood proudly at the wheel, grinning. Abbey joined her in the relative calm of the cabin where her words would not be stolen by the salty blast. 'Yes, Jackie, she is fast. Very fast.' *I wonder why boats are female.*

'I could use the sails instead of the engine, but they are so much trouble,' continued Jackie.

Abbey searched for a polite way of agreeing with her. 'Yes, Jackie, it's probably easier just to use the engine.' *It's probably safer, too.*

Abbey returned to the stern of the boat. The rear of the cabin was open to the elements, though she expected that there must be some secret way of closing it should the need arise. The other occupants lounged about inside, chatting and drinking. Phil had taken over at the helm, pulling on the wheel and pretending to look like an accomplished sailor. Lewis stood near to him, dutifully making shallow conversation. His lips moved, Phil nodded. Abbey wondered whether the words mattered. She leaned over the stern a little, watching the foam as it streaked from its birthplace under the craft. The wake broadened and fanned out, weakening and fading until at last the sea forgot it. The thoughts raced through Abbey's mind, a powerful stream of unbidden fear that forced itself upon her. What should she do about Luke? Most young men of twenty-one had at least some life skills, some inkling of how to cook a meal, dress properly and take basic care of themselves. But Luke was different. Inside, he was still so young, so childlike. What about Mother? She used to be so confident, strong, almost too severe. She was always there, the only constant figure in Abbey's life. Now Rita was frail and with time her needs would only increase. Abbey watched the spray as it rose from the stern and arced in the sunlight, then dropped back into the froth, merging, softening, melting away. She felt a rush of unexpected envy, curiously jealous of the foam and the waves. If only her troubles were like them. She broke away from their hypnotic magnetism, ashamed that she had just wished away her son and her mother. It was time to go back inside but she could not face making small talk. In the cabin, Captain Phil was still at the wheel but Lewis had given up talking to him. From a safe distance, Abbey found herself staring at the shine on the top of Phil's head and wondering if he shaved it like that in an attempt to disguise his bald patch. He was older than she had first guessed, certainly less young than Jackie. The men moved around and it looked like Lewis was coming out to see Abbey. It would be so consoling if he simply asked her how she was doing, put an arm around her, offered a little comfort to soften the pain she felt. He reached the opening then turned, picked up a bottle and receded back into the shadows deep inside the cabin. Broken shards of reflected sky played tricks with the glass windows. Silhouetted figures shuffled, cards in a pack changing places. Pick a card, any card.

'Hey, Abbey.' It was Phil who slipped out of the pack. He moved closer so that they could talk without shouting. 'I can't stick any more of Jackie's yacking. Wow, are you ok?' The fake smile dropped from the roundness of his face, concern showed in its place.

'Yes, Phil, I'm fine, it's all good,' Abbey lied. Her eyes burned and she realised that she had failed miserably in her attempts to pretend that she was enjoying the trip. 'No, I'm not really,' she croaked.

'What is it? What's wrong?'

The world shrank until there was only Abbey and Phil and the rushing wind. She found herself examining him again. The smooth, shaved head caught the sunlight, the belly pushed his shirt out in a pregnant bulge.

'You can talk to me. I won't bite.' Phil spoke in terrible clichés but there was a ring of genuine concern in his voice, empathy in his posture.

'It's my son. You know I have a grown up son?'

'Yes, I do.' Phil was watching and waiting.

'Well, Mother wants him to leave. I just don't know what to do.'

'Oh yes, Jackie mentioned it. What does Lewis think? You have talked to Lewis about it, haven't you?'

Abbey glanced inside. Lewis had his back to them, taking another turn at the wheel. 'Yes, of course I have,' she said.

'So what did he say?'

'He said it will be alright... that's all.'

Phil shook his head, disappointed. Lewis could do better than that. 'I hope he's right.' For a second Phil touched Abbey's shoulder. 'Just remember, you can always talk to me if you need to. I have a family too, you know.'

Another searching look into her eyes, then Phil turned back into the cabin and re-joined the idle, shallow chit-chat. Abbey replayed the last few minutes in her mind, comparing the two men. Lewis was so many things. He was strong, fine-looking and sexually exhilarating but that was not enough. The conversation had shown Phil in a new light, revealing hidden qualities. He was back at the wheel now, expertly piloting the boat back into the harbour. There was a silly old saying, something that says you cannot judge a book by its cover. She had misjudged Phil, got it all wrong. He was a kind man, surprisingly accomplished, completely sincere and dependable. For a second she wondered if it would have been a bit like this if her father had lived as long as he should. The first harbour walls were coming alongside now. Childhood memories of Dad flooded in, reminders of a time when she always had someone to turn to, someone who would listen and advise. With Dad there was the security of a different kind of love that was unconditional, unlimited. Abbey turned back to face the open sea, the hazy horizon trickled and quivered through her tears.

Luke stood by the window, watching the traffic scurrying below. People walked, shop doors opened and closed, money changed hands. The urban activity did not trouble him anything like as much as he had expected. He could barely hear the cars through the double glazing. The litter-free pavements were bounded by black painted railings adorned with long planters filled with flowers. Their petals were broad and red, colour splashes that spread in the uncertain sunlight of an English summer. He turned back into the room and found the telephone at the other end, across the unbroken expanse of soft, biscuit-brown carpet.

'Mum?'

'Luke! How are you... where are you?'

'I'm fine, Mum. How are you?' asked Luke lightly.

'I'm worried about you, Luke. You and Nan.'

'Well, I'm fine, Mum. There's nothing to worry about.'

'Of course there is. Where are you? You didn't answer my question,' persisted Abbey. 'Are you still in Calborough with Nan?'

'No, I had to move out. Didn't she tell you?'

'Yes, she told me she was throwing you out, Luke. Because of the mess.'

'I'm not like that now, Mum.'

'What?' Abbey was incredulous.

'I said I'm not like that any more.'

'I can't believe...' Abbey stopped herself. 'So, where are you then?' She tried a third time.

'I live in town now.'

'Town? In some filthy rented room?'

'No, Mum. It's not like that at all.' Luke was relaxed and confident. 'It's clean and there's loads of space. You should see it.'

'Clean? There you go again,' warned Abbey.

'Spotless,' waved Luke dismissively. He dropped the bomb. 'Sally keeps it tidy.' The shell detonated explosively.

'Sally? Who's Sally?' squeaked Abbey, remote and bodiless in the telephone earpiece.

'She's my girlfriend.'

Abbey gasped. 'You never told me you had a girlfriend!'

'You never asked. Anyway, I thought you'd have realised.'

Abbey wondered what clues she must have missed. The name Sally seemed familiar, someone had mentioned her before. Who was it? Abbey was baffled. 'What is she like? Has she got a job? Does she look after you?' Her questions popped out like automatic gunfire.

'She's brilliant. Of course she's got a job. Yes, she takes care of me.' Luke's answers squeezed in between the questions. 'And Mum?'

'Yes?'

'I think she loves me,' Luke confided. He paused, waiting for a reaction that never came. 'Mum, listen. She's back now. I'll call you again later. Ok?'

'Yes Luke, ok,' agreed Abbey weakly. 'Bye.'

'Lewis, you were right.' Shafts of evening sunlight streamed through the terrace, linking the two people.

'Right about what?'

'About Luke. You said it would sort itself out and it

has.'

Lewis nodded without looking at Abbey. His gaze remained level and distant.

'Don't you want to know what he said?' Abbey prodded.

'I heard you on the telephone. It was easy to guess what he was saying.' Lewis chuckled. 'You should have seen your face,' he teased, 'it was a picture. Speaking of which, have you thought about painting this?'

'Painting the sea? Everyone does that, it's such a cliché,' protested Abbey.

'I didn't mean the sea, I meant all of it. The flowers, the rooftops, then the sea and the sky too.'

Abbey sat back and considered the suggestion. The scene was framed by the limits of the terrace roof and the first stands of trees that thrust upwards from the gardens and villas below. The proportions were good, the perspective was spectacular and it was all right here waiting for her to capture. She looked across at Lewis and his gaze connected with her. She felt a rush of something, a surge of feelings that was a curious blend of sadness and relief. She was still here in Spain, an actress playing out a charmed life in an exquisite setting. Green eyes were exploring her face. Could Lewis read her thoughts? *That's ridiculous.* Abbey berated herself for contemplating such a silly, childish notion. He knew that she had nearly run out of money, because she had told him. Conversely, Abbey knew that hardship was just around the corner for Lewis unless he found a publisher soon. These were facts, simple practical matters. They could even be expressed in hard, cold numbers like those she used to present at Infotext in tedious financial reports and forecasts. Abbey sighed and wished that mind-reading was not just a fantasy, because then she could know what Lewis really thought.

'Lewis?' she began.

'Yes?'

His eyes questioned and Abbey looked deep into them.

Close up, she could see that their green depths were not pure and uniform. The more she looked, the more detail she saw. They were like little round forests where myriad twigs and branches knitted and crossed, a screen with teasing gaps through which just enough could be seen to hint that there was much, much more to learn.

'What is it, Abbey?' Lewis broke the silence.

'Well...' *Go on, ask now.*

Lewis brushed the hair from Abbey's face.

'Um,' she said.

'Do you want to talk about Luke? Or us? Or something else?'

The door was open, the opportunity was offered. 'I don't know,' sighed Abbey weakly.

'I care about you, Abbey,' assured Lewis. 'You know that, don't you?'

'Yes, of course I do.'

'And I am pleased that Luke has found somewhere good to live. It's incredible, really.'

Abbey stared.

'Oh, I don't mean that in a bad way. I mean it's marvellous how he's got someone who cares for him.'

'But it should be me, shouldn't it?' blurted Abbey. 'I should be there to look after him instead of running away here and living it up. I got carried away with all this Spain stuff.'

'No,' interjected Lewis simply.

'Yes I did,' said Abbey emphatically. 'I've been selfish and only thought about myself. I left them all in England as if I didn't give a damn. But I do.'

'I know you do.'

Abbey ignored Lewis. 'If I'd stayed there then none of this would have happened.'

'But Luke is an adult now. And Rita is fine in her flat. You have your own life to live, Abbey. Just for once, you have to think of yourself.'

This time, Abbey did not stare, she nodded in

agreement. 'Yes, Lewis. I've always put other people first. No-one ever did that for me, it's always been one way since I was little. There are two types of people, you know.'

'You mean givers and takers?'

'Exactly. There are kind people, and then everyone else who takes advantage of them. Why are they like that?'

'I think it's just human nature,' pondered Lewis. 'You are a giver, of course. So you have to think of yourself sometimes, even if it does feel selfish.'

'Uhuh,' acknowledged Abbey.

'Well, now you have done it,' Lewis continued, his tone warm and heartening. 'You broke free and came here. You've done something for Abbey and it's going to be peachy.'

'Peachy? Ha ha!' Abbey and Lewis laughed together.

Lewis gestured at the vista laid out before them. 'Can you see where the sea meets the sky?' he asked.

Abbey leaned in closer towards him and her hair brushed against his cheek. 'No, it's too hazy,' she admitted.

'Exactly,' pronounced Lewis. 'It's hidden, like a mysterious bond between two contrasting things. Like us.' He pulled Abbey close and she let it happen, melting into his passion.

Rita was walking around her chair, circling it mindlessly. She broke free from her orbit and shuffled into the kitchen. 'What have I come in here for?' She shook her head as she looked around. There was nothing she needed to fetch, no jobs to be done. Everything in her flat in Calborough was precisely where she last left it, perfectly ordered and tidy. She wandered back into the lounge and did another circuit around the armchair, stopping by the telephone on the side table. 'I'll have to tell her,' she rasped.

'Hello? Abbey?'

A man's voice answered.

'Is that Lewis? Can you get Abbey for me?' asked Rita.

The reply was a stream of angry sounds made up of unfamiliar syllables. Rita could not make out a single word.

'I'm sorry,' she said. 'I must have dialled a wrong number.'

The deluge of foreign speech never paused for a second.

Rita gathered her strength. 'I said I'm sorry! Do you understand?' she shouted.

It was quite obvious that he did not. Rita slammed the phone down. She could feel her heart banging in her chest. She slumped into the armchair, perspiring and chilled at the same time. 'Even if Lewis had answered it wouldn't have made any difference. All he thinks about is himself,' she muttered breathlessly. She looked across at the telephone. 'Abbey never rings me. Luke is no better either.' The room seemed to be turning around her. 'It's no good, I'll have to try again.' She was reaching out for the telephone, leaning over the broad arm of her chair, when the blackness came.

Chapter Sixteen

Feet shuffled, the queue advanced a couple of steps. Someone at the front was arguing. More staff arrived, reinforcements for the beleaguered young girl behind the check-in desk. Voices rose above the background babble, piercing the permanent fog of noise that echoed and reverberated through the cavernous airport building. A tired-looking man in front of Abbey turned round to her and released an exasperated sigh which whistled through his pointed grey beard.

'Qué pasa?' Abbey asked what was happening.

'His case is too big, that's all.'

'Didn't he check it first?' puzzled Abbey.

The old man laughed knowingly. 'No, my dear, of course not.'

Abbey was anxious. 'We'll miss the flight.'

The aged traveller smiled wryly. 'No te preocupes.' Do not worry. 'The boss is here now.'

The shouting stopped, a thunder-faced man stamped away from the check-in desk.

'Bufón,' muttered Abbey's new friend. 'Stupid fool. They charge ninety to put it in the hold,' he observed with obvious satisfaction.

The queue started moving forward again. Abbey shouldered her bag and shambled along with it. The old man reached the counter and presented his documents. He was waved through in seconds.

'Adiós!' His unexpected goodbye was left hanging in the air as the crowd swallowed his short dark form.

Abbey had spent fifteen minutes engaged in a Spanish conversation and barely even noticed. She strode up to the desk. 'Hola,' she greeted the clerk.

'London Regional?'

'Sí.' Yes, confirmed Abbey.

'Bueno.' Right.

Abbey went through to Departures. *I hope I remember*

to speak English when I arrive.

'Where's Phil?' Lewis' deep voice spread lazily through the heavy afternoon air.

Jackie drew a cigarette from her lips. Crimson-banded with lipstick, she tapped it on the ashtray. 'He's at The Hotel again.'

'At the swimming pool?' asked Lewis nonchalantly, already knowing what the answer would be.

Jackie nodded and drew deeply on her cigarette. She blew a jet of smoke through pursed cherry lips. Liberated, the smoke danced around the tables and blue umbrellas of Cafetería de la Luz.

Lewis reached for his packet of cigars. 'I always smoke more when I'm with you,' he accused Jackie.

'No you don't.'

'Do.'

'Don't.' Jackie stubbed out her cigarette. 'This is childish. You can't blame me for making you smoke more. You do what you want. That's you all over, isn't it, Lewis? Stubborn.'

'No I'm not.'

'Don't start me off again.' Jackie wore sunglasses even in the umbrella's shade. She lifted them to look Lewis up and down. 'Your shoulders look bigger. Have you started weight-training again?'

'Yes I have,' admitted Lewis. 'A couple of times a week.'

'I though so. So why do you scoff at Phil's swimming?'

'Because he does rather a lot of it, I suppose,' answered Lewis. He saw the opportunity for one more dig. 'He must be a powerful swimmer by now. Is he going to swim the English Channel?'

'See, you just can't resist it, can you? Anyway, we must be a thousand miles away from the Channel. We're in Spain, remember?'

Lewis did not need reminding. He watched the cars

slipping past on the boulevard. Beyond, the Mediterranean Sea rolled lazily, each wide wave rising softly, peaking and falling over just in time to kiss the sand. Summer lasted for a long time in Castillo and almost every day was just like this one. 'There are a lot of holiday-makers here this year,' he observed. 'All pushing prams. Every one of them.'

'I bet you've never pushed one in your life, have you?'

'You know, Jackie, I think you're right. I've never even got close.' Lewis drew on his cigar. 'Not that I wanted to.'

'Well, Phil has. And so has Abbey. Have you heard from her yet?'

'Not a word.'

'It sounded like her mother is quite poorly,' said Jackie, voicing uncharacteristic concern. 'Aren't you worried about her?'

Forced into a defensive position, Lewis was quick to reply. 'Yes, of course I am.'

Jackie ignored him. She drained her little white cup. 'I need more coffee. Juan? Más café por favor!' More coffee please.

'Yes, please?'

The jarring address came as a shock to Abbey. She had forgotten how things were done in England. All too often here, service was delivered grudgingly, even rudely. She placed her order politely all the same. 'Lemon cheesecake please.' She pointed out her chosen dessert, an indulgent treat. 'And coffee, white, with sugar, please.' The girl behind the counter looked too young to be working there or indeed working at all. *She should still be at school, learning some manners.*

'Who's next? Yes, please?' The girl was already barking at the next customer.

Abbey picked up her paper cup and left in a cloud of despair. The café was no more than a section of the arrivals hall, its limits marked out by a different colour of brown flooring. She made to sit down, then hovered as an old instinct cut in. A quick check on the chair seat confirmed that she had just avoided smearing her jeans with some kind of unidentified stickiness. Disgusted, she moved across to another chair. People passed by, struggling into coats as they hurried out into the chill rain of an English summer. Answers awaited Abbey beyond those revolving glass doors. It would take her half an hour to get into town, then probably just as long again to solve the clues in Luke's sketchy instructions and find his city apartment. She raised the coffee cup to her lips. It was a large cup, cleverly made in layers with corrugated paper to keep the outside cool and the contents warm. Attractively printed with coffee bean shapes, it bore an impressive logo that promised a richly refreshing experience. She took a lip-scalding sip. *Instant coffee? At that price?*

Unveiled by the low tide, the sand was set into tiers of wavelets, ochre, yellow and brown. Lewis walked east, with each step kicking the marionette of his shadow ahead of him. The low sun cast a rubber-band caricature that stretched away from his padding feet, its elongated form hugging the rippled beach. It was like a comical puppet whose absurdly long legs rose and fell in turn as it loped along. Each knee formed preposterous angles as it bent to lift and drop a giant limb. Lewis tried a few experiments, pretending to pull on a string so that an arm extended from the beanstalk body, stretching and deforming as it reached towards the mannequin's slender head. On his left the boulevard traffic passed, hidden by the beach wall. Only muted residues of formless sound, breathless and exhausted, revealed its presence. To the right, the sea whispered and waited impatiently to reclaim its shell-strewn territory. Lewis wondered why Abbey had not rung him yet. Perhaps their worst fears were playing out and a catastrophe was unfolding, so dire and overwhelming that she was too harried to find a moment to make contact. The shadow puppet strode up the beach, heading for a gap in

175

the wall. It reached the exit, turned and folded up into nothingness.

'Cuidado!' Careful!

Lewis stopped dead. A round and greasy countenance filled his vision.

'Lewis, what's the hurry?' wheezed the face.

'Oh, Juan. Perdón!' Lewis apologised to his café owner friend. 'Never mind me, what are you doing? You look like you've just run a marathon.'

Juan hooked a heavy arm around Lewis and they set off towards the café together. 'I'm looking for chef,' Juan explained.

'Why isn't he at La Luz? It will be filling up soon, it's Friday night.'

'Sé,' rasped Juan. I know.

'What are you going to do?' asked Lewis.

Juan released his hold on Lewis and spread his hands in defeat. 'No sé.' I don't know.

The two men stood at the side of the boulevard, each troubled by his own predicament. The traffic passed unheeded. Across the road, customers in Cafetería de la Luz waited unfed.

'Juan, I'm sorry, I have to go,' said Lewis despondently. 'I've got to ring Abbey and find out what's happening in England.'

'Venga,' acknowledged Juan. He turned to cross the road. 'See you later.'

Lewis padded through the silent apartment, leaving the terrace doors open. He wandered aimlessly through the rooms, visiting each one in turn. The kitchen was immaculately clean. Everything was hidden in drawers or set out neatly on the worktops. The bedroom was the same. Gabriela had been today, sweeping through with practised proficiency, stacking and folding as she went. Flawlessly ordered, everything was just as Lewis liked it but the regularity no longer pleased him. Little eddies of wind crept in from the terrace and sneaked through the hallway, carrying a syrupy sweetness blended from the evening flowers. The apartment was his home, the place that he had chosen to be. He was a single man when he bought it, free to do as he pleased without seeking the permission or approval of anyone else. Now there was Abbey and with her came new experiences and distractions. To him she brought an intensity of passion and intimacy that he had never before known. She gave him a sense of purpose and direction, with the comfort that empathy and compassion bring. Lewis was already being drawn into her conflicts, reluctantly becoming mired in anxieties about her well-being and in turn that of her family. Things were changing for him, perhaps too quickly. There was a price to be paid for all this, a forfeit that he was reluctant to make. The price would be paid with his freedom. Would losing the precious privilege of a single man's lifestyle be worthwhile? It was impossible to know. Mindlessly, he found himself back in the bedroom. He opened a window and the curtains lifted. Honeyed night air, animated by the sounds of hundreds of cicadas, breathed life into the suffocating stillness of the room. A small grey teddy bear sat up on the pillow, watching him. It was the one that they had bought from Maribel's shop on that first shopping trip. Though little more than a walk through the old town of Castillo, everything on that bright morning had been new to Abbey. Lewis was filled with sentimental nostalgia as he remembered her face, that little girl look of surprise and wonder in her eyes. Disconsolate, he picked up the teddy and hugged it to him. In the desolate apartment there was no-one to see his tears.

'Hello Mum!' Luke pulled his mother into the hallway. 'Your hair is wet,' he declared. He kissed her on the cheek, then drew back to study her face. 'You look worried.'

'I haven't been to Nan's yet,' Abbey explained. 'I had to come through town anyway, so I called in here first.'

'She's upstairs,' stated Luke in businesslike tones. 'With Sally.'

'Upstairs?'

'Yes, Mum.'

'Here?'

'Yes, upstairs.' Luke pointed to the stairs that rose up behind him, closely flanked on both sides by plain white-painted walls. 'Everything is upstairs here,' he added wryly. 'Come on up, I'll show you.'

Abbey showed no sign of moving. 'But how does Nan get up there?'

'She walks up, like everyone else. What did you think she does?'

'It's just that... well, she's so sick now that I thought she couldn't run up and down stairs any more.'

'Well, Nan doesn't exactly run, obviously. But she's fine most of the time. She comes to visit every week. She gets on well with Sally.'

'She gets on with Sally,' echoed Abbey. 'That's good,' she added emptily. She followed Luke up the stairs.

Luke stopped at the top. 'Mum, you have to leave your shoes here because of the carpets.' He demonstrated the house rule by kicking off his trainers. 'You'll get used to it,' he chuckled, opening the door.

'Hello Abbey.'

'Mother,' Abbey said simply.

'Have you come to see me?' enquired Rita with crudely faked indifference. 'It's been a while. Why don't you come back more often?'

'It's expensive, Mum. I had to borrow the airfare from Lewis this time.'

'Why didn't you ask me? You know I'd pay for it.'

'I did ask you! You said you can't afford it on your pension.'

'Oh, did I?' Rita grated, then switched from ineffective deceit to trivial decoy. 'How was your journey?'

'Fine until I got to London. It's so dark and cold here.'

'It hasn't taken you long to forget what an English summer is like, has it?' Rita declared.

'No, I suppose I've been spoilt,' conceded Abbey. 'It's sunny all summer in Castillo. You look well, Mum. I was worried about you after you had that blackout.'

'I'm fit as a fiddle, nothing wrong with me,' insisted Rita stubbornly. 'Just a bit faint from time to time, that's all.' She changed tack again. 'Your hair's wet. Sally?' she called, turning towards the kitchen doorway, 'have you got a towel?'

Sally swept into the room, bearing the requested article. Abbey took the towel and inspected Sally's dress. It was long, black, needlessly ornate and remarkably antiquated. The waist was laced tight and the bodice above cupped Sally's breasts, presenting them in mounds of pearly, swollen display. Abbey was compelled to stare at the young woman, appraising her. Kohl-lined eyes of sapphire were set in a flawless ivory face. A chiffon veil of champagne hair cascaded over Sally's shoulders, falling as lacy curtains around her enviable bosom. Nothing about her was contemporary, nothing in vogue. Abbey struggled to categorise her son's girlfriend. Perhaps she was mock Gothic or something like that. *She could do with a bit of sunshine,* thought Abbey. The powder-blue eyes were waiting politely.

Abbey offered her hand. 'Sally, I'm Abbey,' she announced.

'Pleased to meet you, Miss Houndslow,' purred Sally.

'Días!' Lewis used the everyday, short version of the traditional Spanish greeting.

'Oh, Lewis.' Maribel hurried out from behind the worn old wooden counter of her shop. She strained up to kiss him on both cheeks.

'Maribel, qué tal?' How are things?

'So-so, Lewis. Business is much slacker this season. They come in and look around, but they don't buy anything,' bemoaned Maribel. 'I've not seen you for a while.' She was back behind the counter. 'Now then, what are you looking for today?' Her eyebrows lifted in anticipation.

'To be honest I just called in for a chat.'

Maribel's eyebrows fell again and the corners of her mouth sagged.

'Lo siento,' apologised Lewis, 'I'll buy something as well.' He scanned the shelves, searching for a suitable token purchase. He picked up a hank of useful-looking cord and checked the price tag. 'Ten?'

'That's the summer price, for tourists,' Maribel said hastily. 'It's just seven to you.'

Maribel's new double-pricing scheme was puzzling. Some other shops did the same thing, but they were ones which stocked gifts and luxury goods, not ironmongery and dishcloths. 'Do tourists buy rope?' Lewis spoke his thoughts aloud.

'No.'

Lewis opened his mouth, then shut it again. He was here to ask for advice, not give it. He reached into his pocket and brought out a handful of coins. 'Seven? Here you are. Maribel?'

'Yes?'

'I need to talk to you about Abbey.'

'Ooh, sí sí.' Yes, Maribel was expecting that it would be about Abbey.

'She's gone back to England to visit her family,' started Lewis.

'I know,' nodded Maribel.

Lewis ploughed on. 'Her mother is sick.'

'Yes, I know.'

'Her son has got a new girlfriend,' Lewis continued, pressing on through his list of worries.

'Uhuh, that's right.'

'Maribel, how do you know everything already?'

'Mi amigo.' My friend. 'How do you think I know? She

told me, of course. She was in here a couple of days ago, buying toiletries for her journey. She told me about her family.' Mischief played in Maribel's aged eyes. 'And about you.'

'I was going to ask you what I should do, but I expect there's no point now,' Lewis grumbled glumly.

'But Lewis, you don't need to ask me. I already told you last year.'

'Did you?'

'Sí.' Maribel leaned closer, her face set with pious sincerity. 'I'll tell you one more time. Marry the girl!'

The alarm sounded, an intensely high pitched warble that cut through the busy shopping street. Barely three steps out of the glass and chrome automatic doors, Abbey froze. *It can't be my fault, I paid for everything.* A heavy hand fell upon her shoulder and pulled, compelling her to turn back to face the department store façade and a wretched interrogation.

'Abbey?'

'Debbie! Oh, it's just you.'

'Yes, of course it is.' Abbey's half-forgotten friend brushed a dusting of pastry flakes from her lips. She was eating a hot sausage roll, a timeless example of British food that was impossibly high in both calories and gratification. 'Who did you think it was?'

'I expected a security guard. You know, big and hefty with a black uniform, a radio...'

'And a truncheon like a policeman? Ha ha ha. Poor Abbey.' Debbie hooked her arm through Abbey's. 'That alarm always goes off, it happens to me every time I shop there. I don't know why they bother with it. Come on, let's go and have a cup of tea somewhere.'

'Abbey's late,' Rita grumbled.

'She'll be back any minute,' Sally reassured.

'The shops will be closing. She should be back by now.

It will be dark soon. What if she gets lost?'

'She won't get lost, Rita. And it stays light until nine at this time of year. What did she need to get?' enquired Sally politely.

'I asked her to fetch me some underwear. I have a certain type, you know. Not those skimpy little modern ones that wouldn't cover a mouse's bits, proper ones that keep you warm. There's only one place in town that sells them now.'

'Oh, I see.' Sally swallowed and decided not to explore the subject further. 'Well, I expect she'll be here soon. Would you like another cup of tea?'

The buzz was unique to English restaurants, a complex recipe of assorted chatter, rattling crockery and unidentifiable music. 'So you're still at Infotext, then?' Abbey called across the little table to Debbie.

'Yes, Abbey, I am. It's much better now I'm out of Accounts.'

Abbey put her mug of tea down. 'You left Accounts? I thought you'd stay there forever.'

'What do you take me for, some kind of loser? I was just biding my time, Abbey, waiting for something better.'

'I can't believe there's anything at Infotext that's actually worth waiting for.'

'You spent too many years working for Vanessa. It's different in other departments. There's still the pressure to get things done of course, but at least your efforts are rewarded. Now that I'm in Marketing the time just flies by. The team is too small, you see, and everything's such a rush. It's great fun.'

'I see,' ventured Abbey, struggling to envisage the experience.

'Actually, Vanessa moved too,' Debbie remarked. 'She's doing recruitment now. That witch, dealing with people all day long. Can you imagine? I mean, you'd think she'd scare them all away.'

'Yes, you would,' agreed Abbey with a chuckle.

Debbie wrinkled her nose. 'Maybe that's why we're so short-staffed.' She skipped effortlessly onto another theme. 'They sell lovely cheesecake here. Having some?'

'Oh Debbie, no, not for me.'

'Why not? You're as thin as a rake. I'll get us one each.' Debbie nodded at the waitress. 'I'll get more tea as well. By the way, Abbey?'

'Yes?'

'I adore your suntan. It makes you look so, um, foreign here.'

'Thanks.' There was probably a compliment in there somewhere.

'So, tell me Abbey, how are you getting on with Lewis?'

'Fine.'

'That tells me a lot,' mocked Debbie.

'It's fine, Debbie. He's very kind and thoughtful. He even praises my painting. It would be better if he showed me some commitment, though.'

'You missed my point, Abbey. I asked how you're getting on. You know, between the sheets.'

'Oh!' Abbey had forgotten what it was like to have friends like Debbie, the sort that you can safely confide in. There was a time when a question like that, coming from Debbie, would be casually folded into a conversation without fuss. Jackie asked the same questions, but she was just prying. She was not quite interfering but keeping a watch on everyone and checking that their relationships suited her. Debbie had a different objective entirely. She wanted to know the nitty gritty, the intimate details. Abbey dragged her chair round so that she was right alongside Debbie. No-one else could possibly overhear her now.

'What? Really?' gasped Debbie.

Abbey nodded and grinned. She continued, conspiratorially shielding her mouth on one side with a cupped hand.

Debbie's eyes widened in disbelief. 'No!'

'Yes.'

'No-one has ever done that for me.'

'Have you asked?'

'No, but...'

'Hey.' Abbey was inspired. 'Have you ever tried-' She put her mouth right up to Debbie's ear and whispered.

Debbie gasped. 'You wicked harlot! I don't know how you dare.' She covered Abbey's hand with her own. 'I hope he was gentle,' she said, wide-eyed.

Abbey smiled serenely, satisfied that she hadn't lost her touch. 'He can cook beautifully, too. The food in Spain is fantastic, so fresh and healthy.'

'I can see that. How much weight have you lost?'

'A bit. Quite a lot, actually. Except on top, that is.'

Debbie forked up the last of her cheesecake. 'Do you think I could try to eat like you and lose some weight?' She popped the delayed morsel into her mouth.

'Do you want me to be honest?' asked Abbey.

Debbie nodded and swallowed.

'Then the answer is no.'

Chapter Seventeen

By eight o'clock Juan was already exhausted. It was the height of the summer season, the best time of the year. For a few weeks there was good money to be made. In Castillo, like much of Spain, diners ate late and La Luz was always busiest after nine. Juan raced around the kitchen from cupboard to oven, refrigerator to work bench. The plan was to get as many portions of popular dishes prepared as possible beforehand. After that, Reina would have to keep on cooking whilst he took orders, brought out meals and served drinks. Eggs, onions, potatoes, garlic. It was all a blur, with no time to think in words. His actions were automated by years of sweat and toil. Chopped, sliced or blended, then grilled, baked or boiled, Juan had done it all a thousand times before. The customers, regular locals and one-off tourists alike, would soon be enjoying their meals in blissful ignorance of the unseen labour that went on all night behind the swing door. Reina kept shouting out her ideas across the kitchen, describing her ever more implausible and unrealistic plans to replace chef. Juan rejected them all. Advertising the position was pointless. It was impossible to find a good cook in peak season and Juan could ill afford to waste time turning away a succession of inept incompetents. Dusk fell softly around Castillo, the streets filled with people and so did the café seats.

'Quiero dos gazpachos, Reina.' Juan burst into the kitchen after taking a round of orders.

'You want two soups?'

'Sí.'

'Well, tell the customers they can't have soup. It's all gone.'

'Impossible.'

'You made the soup today, Juan. How much did you do?'

'The same as ever. There's always some left over.'

'Not tonight. They'll have to start with something else.'

185

'Uff!' Juan departed to serve up the bad news.

'And tell them there's no charge for it!' Reina hurled the stones of her words after him.

With a white cloth draped over one arm, Juan stood at the table between two customers. Barely contained within his shirt, his belly hung apologetically over his black trousers. 'Señor, señorita, I'm so sorry,' he began, 'but we have no soup.'

'But Juan, you do have soup,' the man insisted.

'No, sir. I am sorry, we are very busy tonight and we have none left,' said Juan, attempting to reinforce his message. His customers did not seem to be taking his apology at all seriously. They were giggling like children and pointing at something. An old lady's arm reached around Juan and placed first one and then another soup bowl on the table.

'Gazpacho,' stated Reina pointedly. 'Enjoy your meal.'

'How did you-'

'Never mind how.' Reina's knife-sharp words cut Juan's enquiry short. 'It was chilling in the fridge,' she revealed, addressing the customers cordially. She turned back to Juan. 'Would you come back to the kitchen with me?' she enquired amiably.

'Why?' Juan knew when to be cautious.

'I've had a new idea.'

Juan's response was as automatic as peeling potatoes. He laughed.

All the corridors were identical, long square tubes whose low ceilings and walls converged to some point that was lost in distant perspective. Occasionally, the blank walls were punctuated by doors that led to unknown, mysterious lands. *Mother always finds something that needs doing at the last minute and makes me late. She does it every time.* Abbey's travel bag, bloated and lumpy from hurried packing, bounced on her shoulder as she ran. Abbey was travelling with just carry-on hand luggage,

186

enabling her to skip baggage check-in and go straight from the security area to the departure gates. A tight budget meant using one of the cheap airlines and they were the ones who boarded from the most distant gates in the airport. The sign for gate twenty-seven came into focus at the end of the corridor. *This is the one. It's due to leave in fifteen minutes. I hope I'm not too late.* She raced into the departure area, breathless, determined, buoyed with relief at reaching the right place. It was deserted. The rigid rows of fixed blue seats were devoid of passengers, no-one stood by the little desk at the glass door waiting to inspect her boarding card. Beyond the security cordon and through that door lay her only chance of travelling home. Rivulets of rain traced down the glass, Abbey's heart raced with anxiety and exertion. She slumped into the nearest chair and slung down her bag. Exhausted, she slipped off her shoes and contemplated her burning feet and lamentable situation. She lived in Castillo now, not Calborough or some dismal British suburb. Home had never seemed farther away.

'It's busy tonight,' observed Lewis.

'Mmf,' replied Jackie with a full mouth. 'Juan's taking a long time with our drinks. I need wine. I ordered red tonight.'

'I saw him a minute ago, talking to that couple over there.' Lewis nodded across the restaurant. 'I don't think he went to the tables outside, he seems to have vanished.'

'Men that size don't just vanish,' Jackie jested.

'Jackie, that wasn't a very nice thing to say.'

'It's true. He seems to be getting fatter.'

'Can we change the subject?'

'To?' prompted Jackie.

'To something else. Anything. Tell me about your chemistry,' Lewis suggested.

'My chemistry?'

'You know, the pharmaceuticals or whatever it was

that you studied.'

'Lewis, that was years ago, I've forgotten it all now. When you don't use something it slips away.'

'I expect it does,' conceded Lewis.

'Actually, I did go to la farmacia today to see el farmacéutico. I had to give him un soborno.'

Despite Jackie's quirky language concoction, the meaning was all too clear and Lewis was aghast. 'You gave the pharmacist a bribe? Whatever for?'

'Shh! I needed something,' hissed Jackie. 'Something special.'

Lewis leaned closer. 'Are you poorly? Can I help at all?' he asked solemnly.

'It's not for me, it's for Phil.'

'Is Phil unwell then? He seemed fine last time I saw him.'

'I can't talk about it. Look, Juan's back.' Jackie waved across the restaurant. 'I think he's bringing my vino tinto now.'

'Madam, may I help you?' The young man looked down upon the dishevelled woman. She was barefoot, red-faced and surprisingly pretty for her age. London Regional was a busy airport, a bewildering rabbit-warren of vast halls, interminable walkways and misleading signs. He happened upon its victims daily, the jaded hapless casualties that fell by the wayside. The comedy of their predicaments had ceased to be amusing long ago. Businesslike compassion replaced it, a mixture of human empathy and practical efficiency. 'Where are you heading to?'

'Spain. But it doesn't matter now, I've missed my flight,' said the woman despairingly.

The young man adjusted his black tie, setting it neatly against the blue of his shirt. 'Which airport?'

'Castillo,' she answered glumly.

He pulled a slim object from a holster on his belt and spoke into it. As he talked, he watched the woman. Where had he seen her before? It must have been right here, queueing for a Castillo flight. He slipped the device away again. 'May I see your boarding card, madam?'

'Yes, of course. Here.' She proffered the document and it was as creased and dejected as its owner.

'That's fine, madam. Follow me quickly, please.' He unhooked the thick blue rope that separated the waiting area from the exit and beckoned her through. A wave of his access card released the door lock, a press of his hand swung the door open. 'It's that plane over there. They said they will only hold it for two minutes more. Please use the front steps to board.' Cold, drizzle-laden air rushed in through the open doorway, the woman raced out. The airline official called after her in alarm. 'Madam, you forgot your shoes!'

Abbey took her seat and fastened the metal buckle, pulling the lap belt tight over her hips. The aeroplane was moving, imperceptibly at first. It glided away from the airport buildings. Air surged through the big engines, impelled by the irresistible energy of their spinning fans. Hiss became whistle, then shriek and roar. A hurricane jetted from under each wing. The world was a metal tube, carrying its precious cargo home. It speared up into the floss of clouds, penetrating them, piercing through to the clean azure. Abbey was travelling again and this time it felt good, it felt right. She was going back, returning to the warm bosom of her chosen country. Ahead lay a land filled with the fragrance of orange groves, the soulful strains of guitars, the romance and passion of songs and of her lover.

Juan was searching faces, seeking his target. There were hundreds of them to pick from, all moving and turning, disappearing behind obstacles and reappearing again in a different order. The males in the crowd were taller, they moved with a sense of hurried purpose. Almost every one of them bore a briefcase and a grim expression.

They must be businessmen, returning from London after yet another forgettable trip closing deals that made incomprehensible sums of money for their employers. One woman stood out from everyone else, though not because she was tall, brightly clothed or strikingly beautiful. She was none of those things. It was her demeanour that caught Juan's eye, the confident way in which she strode through the crowd, shoulders back, chin up. This must be the one he was after, but she was moving quickly. He stepped into the fray, anxious to ensnare her before she vanished, swallowed up and digested by the hungry battalion of air-weary travellers.

Abbey flew through the immigration customs check and then became ensnared in the packed jumble of new arrivals that barged and elbowed its ungainly way through the airport concourse. She was naturally an unselfish and forgiving person, but it was a matter of personal interest to get out of the hall and over to the taxi rank as quickly as possible. If she failed in this endeavour then there would surely be no vehicles remaining after the onslaught of the expense-account army. The alternative was not appealing. It would mean two bus rides which, together with the delays at the bus station, would take much longer than the flight from London itself. Even then, she would still face a long walk through the midnight streets of Castillo. *No, I am not doing that.* It seemed as if the foot-soldiers of every major company in the region had arrived at the airport together. United, they marched with seasoned, effortless aggression. Abbey thrust through them, meeting elbows and hard stares with raw determination and well-judged side swipes from her swinging shoulder bag. Someone short, fat and bothered was making for her, blundering across the turbulent river of bodies. He was a rumbling boulder in a raging river and the passengers milled about him, splashing, tumbling around and over him, separating and coming together again. The boulder reached her.

'Abbey! How are you?'

'Juan, what are you doing here?'

Juan pulled Abbey across to the shelter of a marbled pillar. 'I came to fetch you,' he explained. He leaned to kiss her on each cheek. 'Lewis told me which flight you were on.' He lifted the heavy bag from her shoulder and a weight from her mind.

'Is Lewis alright?' she asked. It was odd than he had not come himself.

'Sí. Follow me, my car is out here.'

Abbey pursued her rescuer out of the hall and into the reinvigorating heat of the Spanish summer evening. Juan moved his mass along quickly and Abbey found herself skipping to keep up. The ladies travelling bag crashed about comically on his mountainous back. Once or twice, his jovial round face turned back to check that she was still there. Under the yellow electric floodlights of the car-park his car looked even more decrepit than usual. In Abbey's eyes it was a wonderful sight, an unexpected reunion with a trusty old friend. She stopped at the battered passenger door, anticipating that its owner would come round and open it for her. Across the creased metal roof, Juan was leaning on the car and gasping for breath.

'I'll be better in a minute,' he wheezed apologetically.

'There's no hurry, Juan. I'm just so grateful to you for coming to get me.'

'You're welcome. It's nothing,' claimed Juan. He rested his chin on the edge of the roof and smiled sheepishly at her. Abbey grinned back politely.

'Do you like my café?' Juan enquired.

'Of course I do,' Abbey said reassuringly. 'It's wonderful,' she added with simple candour.

'That's good.' Juan eased himself upright. 'I want you to come and be my waitress.' He used her stunned silence to continue. 'The door's unlocked, you can get in.'

She pulled on the handle and the ageing hinges creaked.

'I'll show you how to make the best coffee in Castillo,'

Juan promised, taking his seat. He passed Abbey the end of a frayed seatbelt. His olive-oil face was begging for an answer. 'Will you do it?'

Abbey clicked the seatbelt into place. 'Por supuesto,' she said. Of course.

Lewis picked up a slim packet of cigarillos and his favourite lighter. The rush of the air conditioning unit faded as he opened the door to the terrace. He closed the door carefully behind him. Even after living in Spain for years, air conditioning was still the only way for him to get through the intense heat of mid-summer. He slipped the tip of a cigar between his lips, clicked and sucked. The first few draws were his favourite. It was like a promise, a contract between the smoker and the rich brown roll of dried leaves to spend a few intimate minutes together. The cicadas were busy, noisily going about their tiny lives with enormous vigour. Flying insects gathered under the terrace lamp, competing for its radiant attention. Some preferred fleshier hunting grounds and Lewis soon felt a few tiny needle-jabs on his forehead. Reclining in a chair, he brushed away the unwelcome mites and exhaled a cloud of smoke to discourage their accomplices. The orchestra of chirping cicadas was a backdrop. Upon this summer night canvas splashed hints of the last of the day's boulevard traffic and the muted tones of a distant ringing telephone. An occasional shout, coloured with laughter or lust, rose through the gardens below to paint bright streaks of sound. That telephone was still ringing.

'Blast!' Lewis balanced his half-burned cigar on the edge of an ashtray and went inside.

'Can I speak to Abbey?' said the telephone brusquely. No apologies, no explanations, not even a hint of politeness.

'I'm sorry, she's not here. Can I help?' offered Lewis.

'Why? When will she be back?' It was the voice of an old lady, one accustomed to issuing orders and expecting them to be carried out without question.

'It's Lewis speaking. Is that Rita?'

'Who did you think it was? Now, where is my daughter? I want to speak to her.'

'Rita, I'm sorry but she's not back yet. She's at work.'

'At work? In the evening?' Rita sounded incredulous. 'Anyway, Abbey hasn't got a job.'

Surely Rita must know. 'She works for Juan at Cafetería de la Luz. Perhaps she didn't tell you.' Lewis played the game a little longer.

'She never said a word,' retorted Rita crossly. 'I'm always the last to know about things.'

'Abbey's only been working there a couple of days. I'm sure she was going to tell you about it very soon,' explained Lewis in an attempt to smooth things over.

'Cafetería? That means café, doesn't it? She did say something about a waitress. Perhaps I misunderstood,' admitted Rita grudgingly. 'Why aren't you there with her? You've nothing else to do with your time.'

It was a broadside, a direct attack. 'Oh, I usually do go there,' Lewis assured the old crone. His statement was perfectly true, if only for other reasons. 'But tonight I had to stay here to get some work finished.' This was genuine too, despite him having achieved almost nothing all evening.

'I see.' Rita's tone was condescending.

Lewis remained silent, testing to see whether the skirmish was over. Even if it was, experience told him that it would not be the last.

'Tell me, Lewis, what time will Abbey be back tonight?'

'Let's see. I think it will be another hour or two.' Lewis detected some softening in his opponent and tried to exploit it with a saccharine, conciliatory tone. 'It's usually eleven or midnight on Fridays.'

'Midnight?' exploded Rita. Behind her anger welled frustration. There was a troubling disconnection between expectation and reality. 'But it's only nine o'clock.'

It took Lewis a moment to comprehend things. He was too slow.

'That's you all over, isn't it, Lewis? You don't even know what time of day it is.' Rita was a sniper, seeking out opportunities to fire off her deadly shots.

'There's a time difference, Rita. We're an hour ahead here.'

'Oh, yes, of course there is. I forgot.'

'No problem,' started Lewis.

'An hour ahead,' repeated Rita, interrupting him. 'I shall have to remember that when I visit.'

'Visit?'

'A week on Saturday. And I shall be watching you, Lewis Coleman.'

A million tiny eyes saw Lewis' terrace door open. They followed him as he stepped out into the foetid night, head bowed. The insect orchestra enveloped him with its monotonous symphony as he slumped into a chair and picked up the half-dead remains of his cigar. Smoke rose, leaves fluttered and turned, one by one the haze-softened stars were extinguished. A storm was coming to Castillo.

Abbey popped out from the bushes, hurdled the low terrace wall and rapped on the door. Lewis leapt up and pulled her inside.

'You're soaked to the skin,' he exclaimed.

'It doesn't matter, I like it,' Abbey replied lightly. 'It cooled me down.'

'Oh, that's good,' said Lewis doubtfully. 'But I think you should dry off.'

'Maybe you're right, Lewis.' Abbey wrapped herself around him, pressing the chill wet fabric of her black and white uniform onto his chest. She planted a noisy kiss on his lips. 'It's freezing in here.'

Lewis wrestled himself free. 'It's at the perfect temperature, in my opinion. But then I'm not wearing wet clothes.' He winked conspiratorially at his girlfriend. 'At least I wasn't until now.'

Abbey's eyes sparkled playfully. 'If I am going to get undressed then you have to do the same.' She wiggled her shoulders enticingly as she described her challenge.

Lewis was transfixed. Abbey's blouse, so fresh and snow-crisp at seven o'clock, was plastered over her body at midnight. It moulded perfectly, revealing soft round shapes punctuated by two sharp points. He ran his fingers over the thin wet cotton and began to pluck at the buttons that locked its erotic cargo within.

'No Lewis, not like that. Like this.' In seconds Abbey had flicked her top off. Her breasts hung like rain-drenched fruit, begging to be plucked and devoured. 'Now will you let me hug you?'

Chapter Eighteen

Crystal shards of diamond sunlight played like little children on the terrace, their carefree laughter almost audible. In and out they twisted, decorating everything on the terrace with their shimmering pattern. Finches and warblers visited, perching on the wall to drink from its pockets. Under their palm leaf umbrellas, the flowers offered their nectar in petal bowls of purple and yellow.

Abbey sighed. 'I love your garden. There's so much in it, always something new to see.'

'It's not really my garden. I don't think that those trees are mine. And beyond them, well, that part is definitely not mine.' Lewis stood up to look out through the palms and the shrubbery beyond, backed by the alternating gardens and roofs that descended towards the sea. 'I think the local council owns it. They take care of it, anyway.' He turned back and smiled wryly. 'When it suits them.'

'Move across, will you? You're blocking my view.' Abbey pulled her easel along a little way to reinforce her point.

Lewis drained the last of his coffee. 'You're doing a fine job of that picture,' he said, selecting his words with care. 'But there are lots of other places you could explore.' He put the cup down. 'What about the vineyards or the boulevard?'

Abbey dropped a slender brush into a pot. 'I prefer natural scenes when it's sunny. The vineyard is interesting, but it's really just straight rows of plants.' She picked up the brush again and dabbed at the canvas. 'I do like it in town,' she agreed, 'but roads and buildings are better at night or in the winter. It's the light, you see. You need the right quality of light for the subject.'

'Yes, I understand that,' Lewis replied boldly.

Abbey shot a glance of unspoken disbelief at him.

'I could drive you somewhere if you like,' Lewis continued.

196

'Yes, Lewis, I know you could.' Abbey's attention was absorbed by her painting. 'You took me into the mountain, remember?'

'I remember.' Lewis sounded pained. 'I'm only suggesting things. Trying to help.'

'Well, it's no help if you keep interrupting me, is it?' snapped Abbey.

'Sorry.' Lewis sat back in his chair and drew a red and gold coloured box from his pocket.

'I suppose you prefer cigars to women,' accused Abbey.

Lewis blew out a fine jet of smoke, an action which only served to confirm her allegation. He wondered if it was getting too dangerous to say anything else and concluded that silence was probably the safest thing right now. Eye contact might be best avoided too. He watched as a small bird hopped across the table, stealing crumbs. The visitor pecked its way over until it was almost at Abbey's elbow.

'That one is really tame,' ventured Lewis.

'Yes, he's sweet.' The bird took flight, arcing round Abbey's head and filling her ears with purring air. It swung right past Lewis and out of the terrace. 'Like you,' added Abbey.

'Huh?' Lewis was puzzled.

'I said like you. You're really sweet.'

'Oh.' Lewis risked a glance. 'Thank you.'

'Lewis, I'm sorry.'

Lewis studied his companion. She was haloed with sunlit hair. Sadness darkened her face against the golden background. 'You don't need to apologise to me,' he offered.

'Yes I do. It wasn't you I was angry with, it was Mother.' Abbey tossed her head and her hair flowed with the wind, settling again in feathery folds over her shoulders. 'It's not fair.' Three simple, childish words said it all.

'No, it's not,' agreed Lewis.

'She's invited herself over without any regard for me. For us, I mean.' Abbey was despondent. 'How will she manage the travelling? Where's she going to stay?'

'I don't know. I expected that she'd stay here with us.'

'Oh heavens no, I couldn't bear having her in the apartment all the time.'

'Neither could I, to be honest,' laughed Lewis emptily. 'She'll be on her way soon. What are we going to do?'

Abbey's hair lifted in the wind again. *I'll have to talk to her.*

Lewis inspected his coffee cup. It was still empty. 'I'll make another round,' he suggested.

'I'll do it,' insisted Abbey resolutely, rising from her seat. 'And I'm going to ring Mum now.'

'What's so special about it?'

'It's Italian leather.'

'Is that good then?'

'Of course it is,' Jackie pouted, 'and it was designed by Gabbini.' She lingered over the name, savouring its exquisite syllables.

'Gabbini? Yes, I think I've heard of her.'

'It's not a her, it's a him. Honestly, Phil, I would have thought that you would have known that.' She opened the handbag and peered into its gaping, toothless mouth. 'It's so soft inside. Feel it.'

Phil dutifully ran a fingertip over the patterned lining.

'See, it's worth it,' declared Jackie triumphantly. She lifted the luxury leather-ware to her ear and clicked the fastener closed. 'Oh, it even sounds perfect. And the smell! It's almost alive!'

'It was alive once, in a field somewhere,' muttered Phil.

'What?'

'Oh nothing. How much did you say it was?'

'I'm not sure.' Jackie caressed her extravagant

proposal as if it were a precious puppy, then clasped it to her chest. 'I think it's only a thousand. Phil, will you buy it for me?'

'A thousand?' Phil choked back a lavish selection of traditional British expletives. He was not dealing with wayward employees on the factory floor now. 'That's an unreasonable price,' he said, pacing his words with carefully studied diplomacy.

Jackie pressed on. 'It's a fantastic price for a Gabbini, Phil.' The handbag was almost hers. 'It might be less. I'll ask.'

'You don't need to ask, it will have the price on the label.'

'Label?' Jackie's eyes were wide with innocence. She made a show of searching for the price tag, delaying its discovery for as long as she could.

'What does it say?'

'One thousand, nine hundred and ninety five,' Jackie mumbled. 'I was nearly right.'

'Lewis, sit back a bit.'

Lewis sat back. Abbey placed his freshly-brewed drink on the terrace table in front of him.

'Mmm, that smells good,' proclaimed Lewis. 'What did she say?'

'Nothing.'

'No, I can't believe your mother said nothing.'

'Only because she didn't answer the phone.'

'Ah, I see. Now that does make sense. She must have set off already,' Lewis offered.

'That can't be right, she's still got hours to spare,' Abbey countered.

'Just because she makes you so late that you nearly get stranded doesn't mean that she'll do the same to herself.'

Abbey sat down next to Lewis and leaned against his shoulder. Soft hair caressed his cheek. 'You're right, Lewis.

That's what's so annoying about you. You're always right about everything. Why can't you be wrong, just for once?'

'Well, I...'

'Shh.' Abbey placed a forefinger over his lips. 'I love you anyway, Mr Right.'

The sky was cloudless, a radiant domed heaven ghosted through with the palest aquamarine. Surely it was too weak, too thin and fragile to support anything. Rita sat on a bench, accompanied by a collection of matching luggage. Enchanted, she gazed as silver darts cut upwards through the transparent film, magically streaking aloft on invisible threads spun by modern-day wizards. It was astonishing how much technological progress had been made in the fleeting decades of her lifetime.

'Madam, your wheelchair.'

Rita jumped, surprised out of her daydreaming. 'Oof.' She struggled up from her bench and plonked herself down into the wheelchair. 'My bags. What about my bags?'

'No problem, madam, they are coming with us too,' said the young man reassuringly. Sky and aircraft trails became ceiling tiles and air-conditioning ducts as the airport building closed around them.

'It said no entry on that door.' Rita gripped the wheelchair arms as the wheels hissed through a deserted passageway. 'And on that one.' They were through it in a second. 'Young man, are you sure you know where you're going?'

'Madam, of course I do. Relax, this is the best part of the journey.' Rita's chauffeur paced quickly yet smoothly through the corridors. 'I know this place like the back of my hand.' He pushed on the wheelchair handles with nonchalant ease, deftly steering his way as expertly as any airline pilot guides his mighty jet. They flew through a pair of doors. The narrow vista opened out into a departure lounge, a chaotic city whose streets were lined with blue chairs populated by agitated passengers and unruly holdalls.

Rita's magic-carpet ride had ended. 'Do I have to wait here now?' She viewed the scene with distaste.

'Certainly not, Mrs Houndslow. You have priority boarding, ahead of everyone else.'

'But I didn't pay for anything like that,' Rita blurted recklessly.

'Madam, we may be an inexpensive airline but we care about our passengers. There's no extra charge for it.'

The wheels clicked over concrete and carried Rita through a confusion of metal wings and oddly shaped little vehicles. Invisible zephyrs of air twisted around the waiting aircraft, sponging up their essence and delivering chemical smells to Rita as she passed through. The wind played with the airline employee's black tie, teasing it away from the front of his blue shirt so that it flapped whimsically over his shoulder.

'It's a lovely day,' remarked Rita.

'Yes.' The man was almost running now.

'Nice and warm,' Rita continued. 'Will it be hotter in Spain?' She had to raise her voice to be heard over the tangle of mechanical noise.

'It's usually a lot hotter,' came the shouted reply, 'but not today.' They reached the foot of a set of towering metal steps. 'It will be cool with storms when you arrive.'

Rita struggled out of the wheelchair. 'How could you possibly know that?'

'I am kept well informed.' The official patted his pocket. 'By radio. I am sorry that there are so many steps for you to climb,' he apologised.

'I'll be fine. You can leave me here.' Rita ascended the first step and faltered. 'Perhaps you could help me,' she gasped. Two dozen painfully slow lurches later and they reached the aircraft door.

'Enjoy your flight,' Rita's escort smiled. It was the kind of smile that betrays relief at a job well done and a task mercifully complete. It stayed on his lips as he turned and descended to greet the rest of his passengers.

The café was alive with laughter, buzzing with the convivial chatter of a thriving language. The ancient Latin roots of the vocabulary were still recognisable in its bright, vibrant verbs enriched by the rolling tongue of modern Spain. Voices rang out, competing for attention. Night-time came too quickly, crushing the last breaths from the fading daylight. Outside Cafetería de la Luz, raindrops spattered on the dusty pavement and ticked on the window glass. A tempestuous deluge tore from the black sky, bellowing in a dialect of thunderous vowels and lightning inflections. Safe under the soft yellow lights inside, the din rose to match the storm. Brash and feverish, the small-talk, banter and gossip continued unabated in an unscripted song accompanied by the percussion of clinking wine glasses and cutlery ringing upon plates. On the big table by the window, Lewis snorted and Jackie grimaced as Phil delivered another of his plays on words, a clever little pun which he considered to be an hilarious joke.

'Good evening everyone.' Juan beamed a porky greeting, ladling it over the guests like syrup. 'How are you tonight?'

'Great,' smiled Phil courteously.

'Absolutely wonderful, couldn't be better,' sneered Jackie, discourteously.

Lewis was last to reply. 'Good evening, Juan. How are you doing?'

'Estoy harto, Señor Lewis.'

'Fed up? Why?'

'Oh, the usual reason.' Juan nodded in the direction of the kitchen. 'Reina is in a bad mood.'

'Como siempre, Juan?' asked Lewis rhetorically.

Juan agreed bitterly. 'Sí, como siempre.' Yes, as always. Juan switched the smile back on. 'So, what would you like to drink?'

Abbey took her time in the kitchen, carefully setting out her ingredients on the worktop. She wanted to get the balance just right, aiming to produce something that would hint at Mediterranean cuisine yet remain familiar and British enough to please her visitor. She slipped out some plates from the homely wooden cupboards, then drifted from shelf to shelf searching for olives. How different things were at Cafetería de la Luz, where every imaginable foodstuff was lined up on the steel racks. *Unless Juan forgets to buy something.* Abbey allowed herself a little giggle as she turned to the simple gas hob. It was the sole cooking appliance in Lewis' apartment, unless you counted the electric kettle. *Just one little kettle.* How quickly things change. It was so easy to become accustomed to a different way of doing things, to the pressure of all that shouting and hurrying in the busy café kitchen. A night off, with only a couple of people to feed, was quite a contrast. The rain was drumming on the roof. It was even driving under the archway and hammering on the door. No, rain doesn't sound like that, even in the most vicious Spanish storm imaginable. Abbey dropped what she was doing and went to investigate. She yanked on the door handle and the storm fought back, twisting it from her grasp and forcing the door wide open. Under the arch stood a man, a very wet, decidedly agitated, uniformed man.

'Tome!' Take this!

Abbey grabbed a holdall and some kind of rigid cloth-covered carry-case from him.

'Y esto.' And this.

Abbey jumped back as the man propelled a wheeled suitcase over the threshold.

'Y su madre.' And your mother. The taxi driver shook his head. His tutting disapproval was drowned out by the storm that raged behind him.

'My mother?' Abbey countered. 'Where is she?'

The taxi driver jerked his chin over his shoulder. An unsteady shadow tottered up behind him. Boorish to the last, the driver thrust out his open hand.

Abbey looked from the upturned palm to the grimacing countenance of its vulgar owner. It was Abbey's turn to shake her head. If there was one thing in this country that she disliked intensely, it was tipping. For some unfathomable reason, it was considered to be a right rather than a privilege, an expectation not a reward. Abbey accepted tips in the café because she served her customers well and they wanted to acknowledge her efforts. True, her mother was not the most reasonable and appreciative kind, certainly not the sort who made a congenial passenger on a long taxi ride. She had probably spent the whole journey grumbling and chafing. That, though, was hardly the point. 'Mother!' Abbey reached around the glaring driver and pulled Rita inside. She slammed the door, shutting the detestable coachman out with the storm. 'Come through, the kettle's on.'

'That was lovely.' Lewis sat back contentedly and eased a pack of cigars from his pocket.

'Yes, it was.' Jackie toyed ostentatiously with her handbag, placing it squarely on the table in front of her and foraging within the shadows of its stomach. The solo performance was evidently a conjuring trick, concluding rather predictably with the appearance of a packet of cigarettes.

'You can't smoke inside,' cautioned Phil.

'Juan won't care tonight, Phil,' Jackie retorted. 'He's too busy to notice. Lewis, have you got a light?'

The door burst open and three or four little children exploded into Cafetería de la Luz. They raced around the tables, shouting and tripping. Perfectly unconcerned, their parents and grandparents leaned on the time-worn bar and ordered beer from Reina. Lewis and Jackie smoked and watched.

Phil fiddled about with his wine glass. 'He's coming to tell you now,' he warned.

'Lo siento,' I'm sorry. Perspiring apologetically, Juan reached the diners.

Lewis made as if to stub out his cigar.

'No, no, it's not the smoke. I think I'm going to need your table.'

'What time is it, Juan?'

'Nearly nine.'

'Mierda!' swore Lewis. 'I'm supposed to be back by nine for Rita.'

'Rita?' enquired Juan. 'Ah, the mother. Yes, Abbey told me about Rita. I think you'd better hurry, Lewis.'

Lewis turned to his companions. 'Shall I settle the bill?' he offered.

'We're going now as well,' said Jackie firmly. 'Don't worry, Phil will pay.'

'Shall we go halves, Phil?' Lewis had a strong sense of fair play.

'No, don't bother, Lewis. Not much point,' Phil lamented, 'I'm going to be bankrupted at this rate anyway.'

Jackie was bag-fishing again, then wasting time applying a fresh coat of lipstick. The men watched her ostentatious display with growing impatience.

Flamboyantly, Jackie clicked her handbag shut. 'It's a Gabbini, you know,' she announced.

'So there's all sorts of things for tea tonight,' Abbey explained brightly. She used the same name for the evening meal as her mother used to do at home, long ago. 'Fresh bread, cheese, olives. I got some cured meats too. This one is chorizo, it's been a tradition here for ages. Thousands of years, probably.' Abbey slid a large wooden chopping-board across the table, rather proud of the meaty display. Rubbery discs of pink, red and brown queued up in readiness, backed by a mountain range of crusty bread. 'Would you like to try some?'

'Thank you love. You shouldn't have gone to so much trouble for me.'

'It's only cold things, so it was no bother. I didn't cook because I wasn't sure what time you would get here.'

'I told you I'd be here by nine.'

'You said at nine, not by nine. You got here a bit early.'

'Early? What kind of a welcome is that? Am I wanted here or not?'

'Yes, Mother, of course you are.' It was only an hour or so into Rita's visit and Abbey was already resenting the whole thing. 'How was the travelling?' she asked, attempting to lighten the conversation.

'Fine. Do you know, it was sunny and warm at home.'

'Really?'

'Yes, and everything went so well.' Rita's face cracked into something resembling a smile. 'A nice young man helped me through the airport. He told me there was going to be some bad weather here.'

'He was right with that.'

'He was.'

'Did you get a good seat?' enquired Abbey.

'On the plane? Certainly.' Rita thought for a moment, chewing on bread and cheese. 'Well, I'm not sure. I mean, it's a long time since I've travelled like that. I was by the window, if that's good.'

'A window seat is always better,' Abbey affirmed.

'It was a very bumpy ride, I have to say. Especially near the end. Made me feel quite queasy, it did.' Rita stuffed a substantial medley of bread, cheese and sausage into her mouth.

Abbey tried not to watch, but failed. 'It looks like you've got over it,' she suggested.

Rita nodded. 'Aeroplanes haven't improved much over the years, have they?' she said, ejecting particles of chewed food with each syllable.

'Of course they have, Mum,' laughed Abbey. 'That was just turbulence. It's always rough flying in a thunderstorm!'

'I expect you're right, love. Now then, where's this

layabout man of yours?'

'He's on his way back now,' lied Abbey, hoping that she was right all the same. She offered a plate to Rita.

'What's this?'

'It's turrón.'

'Two Rons?'

'Ha ha!' Abbey choked with mirth.

'What's so funny?'

'Nothing, sorry. It's turrón, Mum, a traditional Spanish sweet. It's made with almonds and they say that it was invented somewhere near here.'

'Oh. That sounds nice, Abbey.'

'Mother, I do wish that you could find something kind to say about Lewis.'

'It's all true, though, isn't it? He hasn't got a job, he just sits about in the sunshine every day.' Rita snatched the plate from Abbey's hand. Thunder rolled. 'Well, maybe not today. But I expect that's what he does normally. It's usually hot and sunny here, isn't it?'

'Yes, it is. Sunny, I mean. But not the rest of what you said.' Abbey was walking a tightrope. 'He's a writer. A good one, too.'

'Pah. That's not work. I mean, even you've got a proper job now,' blasted Rita. 'He's late back from that meal.'

No, you're early. Much too early, thought Abbey.

Rita was enjoying her turrón, crunching her way through a second piece and candidly expressing her thoughts between mouthfuls. 'He'll be blind drunk, leering at all the women...'

'Hello, Mrs Houndslow!' A man's voice boomed out masterfully from right behind them. Mother and daughter both jumped in surprise.

'Lewis,' said Abbey, trembling with a mixture of shock and relief.

'Lewis,' echoed Rita, shivering with anger. She swivelled round to face her foe. Green eyes twinkled back with affable good humour. A welcoming smile softened the lines of Lewis' mouth, its timeless film-star appeal illuminating the power of his handsomely modelled face. A long-forgotten sensation stirred deep within Rita, the spirit of a maiden that had become buried ever more deeply as the pointless, banal decades passed.

'It's a pleasure to meet you, Mrs Houndslow. How was your journey?' Lewis asked politely.

'Perfect, thank you.' A different Rita was speaking, her voice singing a lyrical air. 'It's wonderful to meet you at last, after everything I've heard about you from Abbey.'

Lewis raised his eyebrows. 'You can't rely on second-hand information, Mrs Houndslow, especially if it's from her.' He winked slyly at Abbey. 'I think it's always much better to meet someone in person,' he continued, taking a seat alongside the visitor. The plate in front of her had already been cleared of food. If she had licked it then it could not have been cleaner.

'It looks like I've missed the best part of the evening, Mrs Houndslow,' suggested Lewis.

Rita extended a bony hand. 'Oh please Lewis, do call me Rita.'

Chapter Nineteen

Countless pairs of hands, young and old, clapped in unison. Every woman, girl, man and boy felt it, with body and soul united in the same heartbeat rhythm. The pulse of their palms echoed from the ancient walls of Castillo. As hot and sultry as the August night, dancers whirled through the square. Fans flicked seductively over the women's faces, lowered they shivered passionately by the gyrating hips of frilled red dresses. This was not stale, stereotyped choreography churned out for consumption by tourists. It was living, breathing history. The rhythms came from the Roma spirit that once roamed throughout southern Spain, the songs told of their troubled journeys. Proud, upstanding, the dancers projected their arms in curves above the roses in their hair. Men, black-shirted with their hair slicked back, shadowed the women. Their feet clicked over the ground, tapping out the contagious, stirring metre of the music. Together the fans, fingers and feet punctuated the dance, driving its urgency through crescendo after crescendo. Everyone was infected. The guitars grew louder, whoops of joy and cries of encouragement erupted from the ever-growing crowd. Flamenco had come to Castillo.

'It's quite old, isn't it?'

Lewis glanced at his passenger. 'That's what makes it a classic,' he replied, pulling heavily on the large, skinny steering wheel. 'And it means you have to manage without luxuries like power steering. It's a miracle that the air-conditioning still works most of the time. Comfortable?'

'Yes, thank you Lewis. Very comfortable. The seats are leather, aren't they? I like the colour. Burgundy, isn't it?'

Lewis squeezed a reply in. 'That's right.'

'Tom had a German car a bit like this,' Rita volunteered. 'Of course that was a few years ago.' Her voice tailed off sadly.

'I think I went in it once,' called Abbey from the back seat. 'When I was a little girl. He took me shopping and we had lunch somewhere posh in town. Speaking of which, Mum, what's it like at Hotel Gran Mar? Is your room ok?'

'It's not a room, Abbey, it's a suite and it's quite exquisite. Everything is provided. Everything. And the windows both look out over the sea.'

'Hotel Gran Mar? Isn't that the one that was in the paper?' asked Lewis. 'You know, the one that lost its five stars because someone wrote a bad review.'

'It got them back a week later,' explained Abbey, 'after all the fuss.' She glanced enviously at her mother. 'Hotel Gran Mar is famous, it's the only place here that some people will stay in.' *I wonder how Mother can afford it.*

'I don't think I can get any closer to the square.' Lewis drew up at the side of the road. 'It's taken fifteen minutes just to drive about a mile,' he lamented, 'but I suppose that's to be expected tonight.'

Rita looked around. They seemed to be on a shopping street where everything was closed and shuttered. Disenchanted, childlike, she turned to her driver. 'Is this it?' she piped.

'No, Rita, don't worry. The fiesta is in the middle, in the main square. It's only a few yards up this street. Abbey will show you. I'll park the car somewhere and walk back to join you.'

'Oh, that's alright then. Thank you for bringing us here, Lewis. And you do have a nice car. Yes, a very nice, comfortable car.'

Blue and white umbrellas flapped forlornly, a futile invitation to passers-by. The temptation of a leisurely evening of food, wine and convivial company at Cafetería de la Luz could not hope to compete with the rare delights promised by the fiesta in Castillo. Lengthening shadows flattered his shape as Juan gathered the dejected umbrellas and brought them inside.

'What a night,' Juan moaned. 'Not a single customer since we opened. Not one.' He pulled out a chair from under the big table by the window and sat down. Elbows planted on polished wood, chin resting on the broad palms of his stubby hands, he watched the last stragglers pass by the window as they made their way into town.

'It's like a graveyard in here.'

'Yes, dear.' Reina was at the bar, tidying things.

'Dead.'

'You're right, Juan.'

'No-one wants to eat tonight.'

'Perhaps later,' Reina suggested unconvincingly.

'I doubt it.'

'Look, Juan, you should expect a quiet night tonight. It happens every year. You know what it's like.'

Juan was not mollified. 'We might as well shut for the night. No point staying open, really, is there?'

The café was so extravagantly tidy that even Reina's unforgiving scrutiny was satisfied. The kitchen was shipshape, the bar was spotlessly clean. Every table was perfectly set, none had been disturbed since laying them ready at the end of the afternoon. 'You only want to shut so that you can follow your customers into town and see all those half-dressed women, don't you?' She examined the bottles of wine arrayed on the old shelves at the back, running her finger along them, turning a few to read their labels.

'What's wrong with that, even if it's true?' asked Juan. Reina was examining him with penetrating black eyes. 'Not that it is,' Juan added for safety. He turned back to the window. Behind him, a cork came out from a wine bottle with a wholesome report, a detonation that had Juan spinning round in alarm to see what had happened.

'Let's try this one.' Reina put two enormous wine glasses on the big table in front of her husband. She poured from the explosive bottle.

'What have you opened that for?' Juan was aghast.

'Try it,' she suggested.

Juan took hold of the glass, wrapping his chubby fingers expertly around its stem. He swirled and held the glass up against the light. Plum, violet, crimson, the wine traced around the polished vessel. He sniffed at the goblet, sipped from it and then sniffed again. 'Oh, this is a good one,' he stated simply.

'Yes, Juan, it is. I chose it for you.' Reina unwrapped her black headscarf and shook her hair free. 'It's the wine we drank on Saturday nights.'

'On Saturday nights?'

'I suppose you don't remember. We were much younger then, of course.' Reina smiled. 'So was the wine. But some things improve with age.' She pressed a bunch of keys into his hand. 'Lock the door, Juan.'

The boulevard was lined with cars along both sides, their bumpers almost touching each other. No matter that parking was forbidden along some stretches, such legal niceties as that were disregarded by drivers and police alike on fiestas. It was simply a practical matter. The ancient, narrow streets of Castillo old town had been full since late afternoon. The new roads that fed them were now crammed too. Every possible parking space was taken and Lewis cruised on, his search taking him steadily farther and farther away. Lewis loved his car. Once inside you were in a world of your own, floating along serenely in the tranquillity of a private cocoon. He had never seen another one quite the same and it matched his personality so intimately that he felt that it was almost part of him. Comfort, power and pleasure wrapped in a deceptively unassuming skin, the whole package was longer and wider than almost any other car in Castillo. He stopped alongside the first parking space that he thought he might squeeze into and began the shuffling process. First backwards, until the car behind shivered. Then forwards, pulling hard on the steering wheel to bring the front in. Once more rearwards, watching until that car twitched again. A final shimmy and the job was done. He jumped out, locked the door and took a moment to admire his accomplishment. From outside it looked like the impossible had been attained, as if he had simply moved the great rectangular block of his car in sideways.

'Better see where we are, so I can find it again,' Lewis thought aloud. 'Oh no, not the marina. I might as well have taken the car home instead.'

The yachts listened lazily and whispered back with ropes clinking on metal masts and water gurgling under hulls. Lewis wasted a few minutes more in a vain attempt to locate Jackie's boat. She had barely mentioned it since the first rush of enthusiasm that accompanied her grandiose acquisition. Lewis could not see it amongst the packed ranks of summer visitors. He turned and hurried towards town. He seemed to be the only person walking that way. He was a lone crusader, a solitary radical forging ahead on his chosen path. He had probably already missed the salsa girls and their barely-clothed gyrations. A shame, but hardly a catastrophe. If he hurried then he should catch the flamenco. That would still be a marvellous spectacle though it was considerably less risqué than the salsa. La Luz was about half way along Lewis' long march. If he hadn't wasted time looking for Jackie's ludicrous floating folly then he might have called in for a refreshing drink. In fact, he might as well do it anyway.

'Cerrado.' The umbrellas were gone, the sign in the café door said it was closed. Things were not going well. Lewis had missed his favourite part of the fiesta and he could not even enjoy a consoling chat with Juan.

'Oh, Lewis. Thank God you're here. How did you find us?' Abbey shouted over the music.

'All those fluorescent green jackets.' Lewis nodded towards the paramedics. 'And the crowd around you. What happened?'

'Mum just collapsed. I think it's the heat that did it.' Abbey brushed the back of her hand across her eyes, their blue contrasting with her dark summer tan. 'She's not used to it like we are.'

'Is there anything I can help with?' Lewis was watching the professionals attending to Rita.

'I don't think so, Lewis, thank you,' said Abbey. 'They seem to know what they are doing. Mother is sitting up now and they've called for an ambulance.'

'Doesn't she want you there with her?'

'Yes, of course she does but they told me to wait at the side.'

'What? That's ridiculous. It's your mother!' exploded Lewis. 'Just a minute.' He elbowed a wall of gaping spectators out of the way and engaged the attention of one of the emergency crew. After a short discussion reinforced with pointing and gesturing, he beckoned Abbey over to Rita's side.

'Abbey, did you tell them who you are?'

'Lewis, I'm not stupid,' retorted Abbey. 'Why do you always think I'm useless? I told them who I was and all about her fainting fits,' she continued. 'In Spanish, too.'

Lewis laughed.

'It's not funny,' scolded Abbey.

'Sorry, I'm not laughing at you,' apologised Lewis. 'They said that they didn't believe you were her daughter because she's English and you are, well...'

'I'm what?'

'Spanish.'

Lewis hurried past the shuttered shops and deserted bus-stops, wondering how difficult it was going to be to extricate his car. Yellow under the sickly street-lights, piles of refuse lay heaped by overflowing metal waste-bins. They languished in foul contemplation, brooding miserably as the last few hours of night died. There was just one car left by the marina. 'That was easy.' Lewis pressed the pedal and his mechanical companion responded, gliding away from the curb and along the deserted boulevard. 'If only everything else was so simple,' he muttered. He cruised through the silent streets, savouring the rare privilege of having it all to himself. There was no rush now, nothing left that needed organising. Rita was back in the luxurious embrace of Hotel Gran Mar. Abbey had accepted the hotel's gracious offer of accompanying her for one night. Traffic lights slipped by, green and red. What did it matter? Perhaps tomorrow would be better, but until then he was alone with his doubts, uneasily chewing over his qualms and misgivings. He cruised as far out of town as the vineyards and then turned back, confiding his secret fears to the glowing dials on the dashboard. In the morning the sun would come up, it would be hot and bright, Castillo would be teeming with life once again. Only that much was certain. What did the future hold? That was the trouble with life. You just could not know what lies in wait around the next corner.

'Where's your mother?' asked Jackie without looking up from her red handbag. She hooked out a thumb-sized plastic tube, ornately decorated with gold filigree swirls. Gripping with both hands, she broke the seal and twisted off the cap.

'She's gone shopping this morning.' Abbey sipped from her white cup and studied the sparkling horizon.

'Shopping?' The lipstick paused mid-air.

'Uhuh,' confirmed Abbey. 'In town.'

'She should be in hospital, under observation,' rebuked Jackie. The blue umbrellas fluttered, shadows rippled over the women.

Abbey turned to her friend. 'Do you think that would help?'

'If she has another fit then at least they would have a chance. They might be able to diagnose the problem. They are good at that sort of thing at The Hotel.'

'It might be weeks until it happens again,' Abbey ventured. 'Anyway, what do hotel staff know about medical things?'

A red-lipped Jackie laughed out loud. 'No, Abbey. Oh, you're such a card sometimes.' She slurped her drink without caring who noticed. 'That's why I like you. When I said The Hotel I didn't mean that over-priced hostel she's been staying at. It's just so pompous in there. Honestly, Gran Mar is worse than a cruise ship. I meant the clinic, Abbey. You know, the one that I was in after the crash. They were very good there and I thought they might be able to help your mother.'

'Rita is very stubborn, Jackie. She wanted to go shopping so Lewis kindly offered to take her. They are getting on very well, I must say.'

The sea view was blotted out by something dark and bulky. 'Are you ready to order, ladies?' Juan was hovering, a white cloth draped over one arm.

'Not yet.' Jackie waved their host away.

'You should be more kind to Juan, he's a good man,' said Abbey, trying not to sound too condescending.

'He's here to serve us,' Jackie retorted. She lit a cigarette. 'It's not poisoning,' she stated authoritatively.

'What are you talking about?'

'Your mother. I don't think it's drugs either. Not prescription ones, anyway.'

How can she know that? Abbey eyed Jackie questioningly. 'Does it have to have a cause? Isn't it just because she's getting old?'

'Getting old is not an illness. There's always an explanation, some reason for the pathology.'

Pathology? Abbey carefully seated her cup back on its saucer. 'Jackie, how much do you really know?'

'I don't know anything.' Jackie drew hard on her cigarette. 'I was only speculating. Sorry.' The rosy lips were clamped firmly shut, a sure sign that this chapter of the conversation had closed.

Abbey hunted for something innocuous to say, a mundane subject to break the awkward deadlock. Clothes were usually a safe bet. 'Aren't you using the Gabbini today?'

Jackie's mouth eased, but only enough to permit another long drag on her cigarette. She held the smoke in her lungs for an eternity, then allowed it to escape at last. 'I haven't got it any more,' she said coolly.

'That's a shame. It was a gorgeous bag.'

'Yes, it was. I gave it back.'

'You gave it back?' Abbey gasped. 'To Phil?'

'Yes. Well, I threw it at him in the street. He was annoying me.'

'Did you try to-'

'To find it? No point. The flamenco started and everyone rushed into the square. It was pandemonium. Like you said, it's a shame.' Jackie stubbed out her cigarette and dropped the crushed remains into the ashtray. 'Where's Juan? I'm hungry.'

Maribel stood in her shop. People passed by on the pavement, sometimes pausing to browse through her offerings. She could barely see out through the windows, they were packed with racks of t-shirts on hangers, purses dangling from stands, row after row of novelty key-rings and gaudy but useless souvenirs. During the summer it was always better to display all the cheap things right at the front, on stands that she carried out and arranged like a funnel that flared from the doorway. Maribel was careful to keep children's gifts low down where coveting eyes would see them and grasping little hands could pick them up. The season was coming to a close. Soon she would have to rely upon the sale of banal items, everyday household goods for cleaning and mending. Uninspiring as they were, at least such goods had genuine utility. Even a pack of dishcloths served a purpose and fulfilled a proper need. She left the counter and started yet another

217

methodical patrol of her empire, putting things back properly as she went. When holidaying families came in they spent the most money but left the greatest chaos in their wake. Sometimes it was mayhem by the end of the afternoon with countless articles picked from racks, examined and then thoughtlessly discarded somewhere else at the other side of the shop. Maribel spent a few minutes rearranging animal purses, cute little leather elephants and giraffes in green and purple with zips along their backs. High above them dangled a line of beer-bottle openers and corkscrews whose wooden handles were carved into perfectly accurate but unspeakably obscene shapes. The long ones were priced much higher than the short ones. Despite this, the biggest ones were by far the most popular. Perhaps they were lewd trophies, prize purchases made by shameless people to entertain their friends with.

'Buenas tardes, Maribel!' Good afternoon.

Maribel responded to Lewis' friendly greeting. 'Lewis, cómo estás?' How are you?

'Muy bien.' Very good. 'Maribel, I need a bottle opener,' Lewis continued.

'Oh, caramba! Good gracious, Lewis, are you sure?' gasped Maribel.

'Yes. Why? Have you run out?'

'Um, no, I've got plenty of them.' Maribel tilted her head towards the darkened cave of her shop where all the practical, sensible products were. 'Come with me, I'll show you.'

'Did you get everything?' Abbey pecked Lewis on the cheek as he came in through the apartment door.

'I think so. Wine, cheese, bread, olives and a corkscrew. I got a proper one like Juan's with all the tools on it,' Lewis announced proudly. 'Was there anything else?'

'Butter and eggs.'

'Dash it!'

218

'Lewis, I don't expect perfection,' cooed Abbey disarmingly. 'But if you'd written out a list like I suggested then you might have got it right.'

It was an expertly delivered rebuke and Lewis was crestfallen. He pushed past Abbey sullenly and busied himself putting things away in the kitchen.

Abbey followed him. 'It doesn't matter, there's enough butter left and I can borrow some eggs from next door when they get back. They've been out all day and that mangy dog of theirs hasn't stopped barking. It's been terrible.' She covered her ears to emphasise her point.

Lewis straightened up from a cupboard. 'I could hear it right up the street,' he confirmed. 'They don't look after it properly at all, do they? Poor thing, it would be better off dead.'

'Oh don't say that, Lewis, it's cruel.'

'Not as cruel as leaving it tied up outside all day.'

Abbey faced Lewis with a new challenge. 'Is there anything you can do? Mother will be back soon and she doesn't need all that noise.'

'I'll have a look.' Lewis turned and went out onto the terrace. The dog was in the garden alongside, tied up with rope or something. Lewis leaned over the terrace wall to get a better view. Man and dog stared at each other. Dog barked, man stepped back. The animal was tethered with a length of blue cord, the sort that Maribel sold in her shop. It was a miserable scene. The old dog was tired and desperately thirsty after hours alone in the garden with just the hot sun and a few chirping cicadas for company. Lewis was overcome with pity. Yes, he could do something about it.

Lewis went back inside and got what he needed from the kitchen drawer.

'Lewis, what's that for?'

'For the dog, like you said,' Lewis stated firmly.

'But, Lewis!'

He was already gone. Abbey ran outside after him. He

219

was in the neighbour's garden, the squareness of his muscled back turned to her. The dog cowered at his feet as he raised his arms up high. His hands were clasped together, the handle of the long knife secure in their grip.

Abbey's eyes widened in horror. 'No!'

The merciless steel blade flashed as it sliced down through the sunlight.

Chapter Twenty

They sat proudly in the opened box, three by three, teasing Abbey with their oval perfection. She reached for one, picked it out and let it roll into the cup of her palm. They were good eggs, large and heavy with tough brown shells. She giggled, imagining the scene when they were laid. 'Bwark, buck-buck-buck, bwark!' she cried. Hens were such wonderful creatures, strutting about all feathery and jerky, pecking at the ground searching for seeds and little creatures to eat. Then they sat on their hay, made a fuss and worked their magic. 'Cluck, cluck, cluck. Bwark!' Now it was time to smash their creations. Abbey crashed the first one on the edge of the glass bowl, twisted the shell open and tipped out its contents. A twinge of guilt pricked her. She repeated the process with the other five as quickly as she could, grabbed the whisk and beat everything into a shapeless sun-gold mass.

'Hello, my little chicken.'

'Lewis, I thought you were outside with Rita.' Abbey felt her cheeks colouring. 'You were listening, weren't you?'

Lewis winked at her. 'I might have been,' he teased.

'You know I don't like it.'

'Sorry.' Lewis felt obliged to utter a shallow apology so that Abbey could ignore it. 'I've just had a call from Juan,' he revealed.

'Oh yes? What's he ringing you for? He's my boss, not yours.'

'True, but he's my friend and he wanted me to know about the crown.'

'I haven't the foggiest idea what you're talking about, Lewis.' Abbey marched over to the fridge. 'I'm getting everything ready for tonight,' she explained, 'so that I don't have so much to do later.'

'You don't need to bother with all that work, it's not worth it.'

'Mother needs something special for her last evening here.' Abbey swept a pile of onions onto the chopping board. 'I thought I'd better use those eggs after all the trouble you went to.' She stopped chopping and looked directly at Lewis. 'I don't know how you got away with it after what you did.' She raised her eyebrows questioningly.

'Oh, it was nothing,' waved Lewis nonchalantly. 'They thanked me for looking after the dog, I asked if they had any eggs...'

'They *thanked* you?'

'Uhuh. They forgot they'd tied her up.'

'Ooh, the little liars,' chimed Abbey.

'Quite probably,' said Lewis coolly, 'and they'll have to knot the pieces of that rope back together if they want to forget her again.' He placed a reassuring arm around Abbey's shoulders. 'But I don't think they will.'

Reina jerked at the tablecloth and it slid towards her. Deftly she flicked it over a couple of times to fold it. Another twirl of the wrist and the cloth settled on top of its friends in the laundry bag. It would be a one way journey this time, though where they would end up was a mystery. There must be money to be made out of old linen because the laundry company was going to credit her with a discounted wash next time. That was good enough for Reina. She dragged the heavy bag through the restaurant and out into the hall at the back.

There was a painfully rusty noise outside. The café door burst open and a fat man with an enormous cardboard box stumbled in. 'I'm back, dear,' he announced.

Reina addressed her perspiring husband. 'So they were ready then? You'd better check that they got them right this time.'

'Yes, dear. When I've brought the food in.'

'Pass me that box, I'll do it myself.' Reina grabbed at the carton.

'Reina, it's heavy.'

The warning came too late. Like a scene from a silent comedy, the box tumbled onto the floor tiles and split open, scattering plastic-wrapped wads in every direction.

'Now look what you've done,' shouted Reina. 'Get back out there and fetch the food in before I clout you.'

Juan made several journeys between car and kitchen, taking care to avoid mishaps of any kind. He brought in the frozen things first. Reina was scrabbling about on the floor picking things up and muttering rude words. Next he brought in the chilled meat. Reina had piled the wads up on the big table by the window. She was quiet now, but Juan still hurried past avoiding eye contact. Finally he carried the crates of vegetables past. Reina was peeling open the plastic cover of one of the wads. Juan eased his load onto the floor and paused to watch.

'What are you staring at?' stabbed Reina.

'Nothing, dear.'

'Have you brought everything in?' Another jab.

'This is the last one.' Juan picked up a crate of onions and scrambled for the safety of the kitchen.

Reina drew a new tablecloth from its bag and unfolded it. The linen fell open, a sheet of dazzling white perfection. She ran appreciative fingers over its flawless surface, then spread it out to check the corner. It was all there, bold, blue and beautifully stitched.

'Juan, come and look at this,' called Reina, a rare thrill energising her voice.

'Yes, dear, in a minute.'

'No, now. Just come and look.'

Juan obeyed. Together the old couple spread the cloth out so that the crown monogram with the words Cafetería de la Luz in curly letters under it was proudly displayed.

'After all these years.' Juan looked up at his wife. 'And all that work.'

Reina's black eyes flashed. 'We've finally made it,' she smiled.

The mirror never lies. It is a soulless thing, a silver sheet of heartless, unfeeling glass that waits on the wall with timeless patience. Sally's bathroom mirror was large and heavy. It was framed with black wrought iron, each side adorned with whorls and Gothic shapes whose meanings were rooted in the distant past. It was a beautiful mirror, but it was still a perfectly honest one. The pale sky of Sally's blue eyes flicked up and down, examining her reflection. As straw-yellow as the harvest wheat in a rain-soaked English field, wet hair shelved over her bare white shoulders and cascaded around the mounds of her breasts. She smoothed a hand over her belly, turning sideways again to check just one more time. She could feel it, she could see it. There was no doubt now.

'Luke.'

'What?' Luke's voice echoed from the lounge.

'Luke, I want you to see something.'

'I'm busy. Can't you just tell me what it is?'

'Not really, Luke. It's important.'

'How important?' Luke appeared in the bathroom doorway. 'You're all wet. I expect you called me to fetch a towel,' he grumbled. 'Why didn't you just ask for one? It would have been much easier.'

Sally turned from the mirror and faced Luke. 'I don't want a towel. I want to tell you something.'

Luke made no effort to disguise his impatience. 'Yes?'

'Luke, the test was right. I'm pregnant.'

'Oh. That is important. I'll have to tell Mum. Hang on, I'll be right back.' Luke was gone.

'Luke!' Sally shouted after him. 'Don't tell her yet.' She followed him out of the bathroom, leaving a trail of soapy footprints behind.

'Here. You're shivering.' Luke wrapped his girlfriend carefully in the velvet softness of an enormous towel and threw his arms around her. 'Don't worry, we'll be alright,' he said.

Every table was proudly dressed with a brand new monogrammed tablecloth and a little vase of fresh roses. Just as satisfyingly, all but one were encircled with chattering Friday-night diners. The big table by the window had a neat little sign on it that said Reservado. Reserved. As usual, Juan and Reina's customers were a mixture of regular ones, occasional patrons and a few new faces. Three more people arrived, two women and a man. The man strode straight to the big table, pulled out a chair and sat down. He motioned at the others. The old lady joined him, the young one did not.

'Abbey, I'm disappointed in you,' Rita announced. 'You knew it was my last night, you wasted your time preparing all that food and now here you are in your little black skirt and your fancy white blouse ready to start an evening's waitressing.'

'Mother, I told you. Juan is going to be very busy tonight, he needs me to help.' Abbey took a second to look around her workplace. 'He was right, the café is already full. It's going to be hard work but I don't mind.'

'Well I do,' Rita grizzled.

'It will be interesting for you, Mum,' tried Abbey, 'to experience a proper little place with real character. It's not all pretentious and contrived like that restaurant at the Gran Mar, you know.'

Rita tutted and busied herself examining the rose vase.

'Lewis, have you heard from Jackie?' asked Abbey.

'Not a word.'

'She said she'd be here with Phil,' Abbey explained.

'What she says and what she does are rarely the same thing,' cautioned Lewis. 'You know what she's like with timekeeping. Always late!'

'Off you go, then, Abbey,' directed her mother. 'Don't mind us.' Rita picked up the menu and turned to Lewis. Like an abrupt cut between scenes in a badly-edited film, her demeanour switched instantly from churlish to charming. 'Now then Lewis, what do you recommend?'

'Señora?' A waiter was at the table and he was addressing Rita.

'Oh! He's speaking Spanish to me,' Rita appealed desperately to Lewis.

Lewis said something to the waiter.

'Ah, Mrs Houndslow,' he beamed. 'So good to meet you at last. I am called Juan.'

'That's better.' Rita could understand him now. 'I'd like... Lewis, what is it that I want?'

Lewis chuckled. 'It's ok, Rita, I'll order for you. I wonder if I should order something for Jackie and Phil as well. Better not, it will probably be ruined before they get here.' With exquisite timing the door opened, admitting a dapper couple and proving Lewis wrong.

'Jackie, Phil, come on,' said Lewis brightly, greeting the latecomers. He watched as the couple took their seats. Jackie was turned out as perfectly as ever, with everything brand-new and meticulously co-ordinated. Red shoes, red skirt, red handbag, red lips. Her expression was inscrutable and it was impossible to tell whether she was happy or sad, bitter or contented. Phil just looked grey and dejected. Neither of them had anything to say. 'Abbey is serving tonight,' announced Lewis simply.

Rita peered at her dinner plate with obvious distaste. 'What is this?' she asked Lewis.

'It's what you wanted, Rita.'

'It looks horrible. I'm going to ask the waiter to take it back. He's here now. Tell him for me, will you Lewis?'

Cafetería de la Luz was abuzz with a full complement of gossiping diners. Lewis spoke to Juan, his words masked by the hubbub.

'Señora, may I suggest that you try it? I think you will enjoy our food.' Juan puffed his chest up. 'We are a one-crown listed establishment,' he proclaimed loudly.

Rita understood his heavily accented English well

enough to pick out the parts that mattered to her. 'Only one?' she asked.

'Oh, thank you, señora,' replied Juan effusively. 'Thank you very much. Enjoy your meal.'

Rita watched him leave. 'Lewis,' she started, turning to her companion, 'why did he say that? And what's so funny?'

'I think Juan misunderstood you,' explained Lewis patiently. 'Not to worry. How's your supper?'

Rita paused, fork in hand. 'Smashing,' she said, 'Absolutely first class.'

'Lewis, it's strange,' Phil began.

'Uhuh.' Lewis raised a beer glass to his lips and took a hearty gulp.

Phil mirrored his friend's actions, then wiped his lips on the back of his hand and placed his trust in Lewis. 'Jackie is keeping me prisoner,' he confessed.

'Prisoner?' spat Lewis. He sat his glass down on the bar for safety.

'Well, not exactly prisoner, but I just can't seem to escape.'

Lewis moved closer to bolster Phil's confidence a little. 'What do you need to escape from?'

'It's as if I'm some kind of toy,' started Phil. He stopped again, silenced by a subtle signal from Lewis' hand.

Abbey rushed into the bar, smiled at the two men and hurried over to draw two large glasses of fizzy gold from a beer tap.

'Estrella?' she asked. Star beer, popular throughout the country. 'Aqui tiene, señor!' Here you are. With impressive brevity she succeeded in dispatching the drinks and their satisfied buyer. Another smile flashed and she was gone.

'All clear,' Lewis announced to Jackie's hostage.

'Yes. So, as I was saying.' Phil picked up his beer.

227

'Toy?' prompted Lewis.

Another wipe across the back of the hand. 'Or an accessory of some kind,' said Phil shamefully.

'Like a handbag?' offered Lewis.

'Just like that. Or even worse, shoes.' Both men laughed.

'So she wants to keep you to herself. I can't see much wrong with that,' said Lewis with brotherly compassion.

'That's not really the problem, Lewis. You know what Jackie's like.'

'Well, I suppose I do.' Lewis knew Jackie well as a friend, but Phil was a lot closer to her than that. 'Is she too, um, demanding?' Lewis ventured.

'Of course not,' blustered Phil. 'No woman is too demanding for me.'

'Hey, no-one's questioning your performance, Phil. It's just that she can be a bit over the top. She is with everything else that she does, anyway.'

'That's one way of putting it,' admitted Phil. 'But I can cope with her obsessions. All those fads eventually lose their appeal, sooner or later.'

'When she gets bored, you mean?'

'Exactly.' Phil drained his beer. 'And you know what she does when she's finished playing with one of her toys?' He stood his empty glass on the old wooden bar. 'She throws it away.'

Abbey brought out the sweets. Amongst the usual flans and marzipans there was a turrón for Rita. Nothing else came close to the magic of that dish and there could be no substitute for what Rita had come to believe was the definitive flavour of Spain. Two main courses arrived for the latecomers, too. Jackie pulled her plate close and set about consuming its spicy cargo. The other plate took its lonely place at Phil's vacant chair. There was no time for Abbey to ask about it. As she had already done a dozen times that evening, she rushed away from the table.

Halfway to the kitchen, Juan caught her by the elbow and thrust a wine bottle into her hand.

'Which table is this for?' she asked automatically.

'Abbey, sit down with your friends. Talk to them for a while,' commanded Juan.

'Oh, thank you Juan.' Abbey lifted the bottle. 'And the wine?'

'Regalo.' A gift.

Abbey did as she was told, slipping into Lewis' empty seat.

'Did we order more wine?' asked Rita. 'It's expensive here.'

'No, Mother, you didn't. It's a gift from Juan.' Abbey set to work with her corkscrew. 'It's not expensive, either. They charge double for the same one at Gran Mar.'

'What did you say, love?' shouted Rita over the heated babble of the packed restaurant.

'I said it's on the house.'

'Ooh, that's good.' Rita leaned close to Abbey. 'I must say I do like it here,' she confided giddily. 'Everyone is so friendly and the food is nice too. It hardly seems foreign at all.' Rita pushed her wine glass across to Abbey. 'I think you've picked a lovely man, Abbey. He'd make a smashing husband, you know.' Rita pointed a wizened hand at her wine glass without pausing. 'Fill it up, would you, love?'

Right at the bottom of the garden there was always shade from the blistering summer sun. When autumn swept in, the trees softened the wind. Even in winter, their canopy would diffuse the rain that fell. This was the perfect spot and that is where the wood was piled. It was a neat stack of panels, all planed smooth. The wind snatched at them, plundering the pine fragrance of new timber and running away with it amongst the apartments so that everyone could share in its uplifting vigour. Something moved. A canvas tool bag, faded and well-worn, plunked down onto the grass alongside the stack. It was followed in short order by a substantial terracotta bowl and a pair of workmen's boots. In the purposeful footwear stood a talented handyman, modest and unassuming as ever in his blue overalls. Alvaro sorted through the fragrant frames and picked out the base. His hammer and screwdriver were soon busy fitting and fastening, his moustache twisted as he whistled. The wind stole his tune too, spreading the joy of its news. Something new was being born, taking shape as the elements came together. The back and the sides went on, then the front with its specially-shaped doorway. Alvaro took his time assembling the roof, making sure that the two halves came together properly at the ridge. He packed his tools carefully in his bag, each one held in its own loop of cloth. There was just one more thing to do, then the job would be perfectly complete.

'Día, Alvaro.' Abbey called her greeting over the wall from the apartment next door.

'Abbey.' Alvaro looked startled. 'Good day to you.' He stood there holding the bowl.

'That looks good,' complimented Abbey, nodding towards the little house under the trees.

'Thank you,' said Alvaro, walking across to join Abbey at the wall. 'Smart, isn't it? Not bad for a few bits of old wood and some nails.'

'It's brilliant and you know it.'

Alvaro smiled sheepishly. 'How is your mother getting on? Does she like Spain?'

'She's been and gone, Alvaro. She loved it.' Abbey grimaced. 'Well, as far as I could tell. She's always been difficult,' she confided.

'She's from a different generation, Abbey,' Alvaro offered consolingly.

'Mmm, yes. But even though she's my mother I never know what she is really thinking. It's even worse on the phone.'

Alvaro looked puzzled.

'She rang me when she got back,' explained Abbey. 'She said that she had a bad journey and it made her poorly.'

'Oh dear,' Alvaro said compassionately.

'But like I said Alvaro, you just can't tell. She's said these things so many times that it's impossible to guess the truth.'

Alvaro coughed. 'Here, could you fill this for me?'

Abbey took the bowl inside, filled it and picked something up on her way back out. 'Here you are, Alvaro.' She handed the vessel back. 'I've got something else for you too.'

Alvaro unrolled the thick sheet of paper with hesitant fingers. He reflected for a long time on the pencil sketch that it bore. His eyes darted back and forth over the drawing, taking in the expertly rendered light and shade. There was a background of tropical trees, a middle-aged man in workmen's clothes, a half-finished wooden construction that was maybe waist-high. He cleared his throat. 'Were you watching me?'

Abbey nodded and smiled disarmingly.

'You must have been there for hours.' He rolled up the scroll and made to hand it back. 'I never noticed you.'

'You were too busy doing what you love.' Abbey held up a hand, not to receive the scroll but to block its return. 'It's for you, Alvaro,' she said. 'If you want it.'

The moustache lifted and Alvaro beamed. 'Yes, thank you. Very kind of you.' He picked up the old tool bag. 'It's none of my business but I hope your mother is well.' As he left he cast a glance back at the product of the morning's labours. Like Abbey said, it really was a super dog kennel, a snug retreat for its four-legged resident.

'It's for you.' Lewis offered the telephone to Abbey.

'Who is it?'

'I don't know.' Lewis was stumped. 'She just asked for you.' Abbey took the phone as Lewis tried to find some useful clues to add. 'She sounded quite young.'

'Hello, it's Abbey.'

Lewis kept close by, compelled by an odd combination of curiosity and compassion.

'Sally?' Abbey's eyes widened. 'Something personal? Yes, of course you can tell me.'

Lewis played with Abbey's hair as she talked, lifting it and bunching it up then letting it fall softly back. She was congratulating Sally about something, using the sort of language that is normally reserved for extraordinary occasions. 'What's the news?' he asked as the phone clicked.

Abbey became defensive. 'I'll tell you later.'

'No, tell me now.'

'Lewis, leave me alone. You wouldn't understand,' croaked Abbey. She pushed him out of the way.

'Where are you going?'

'I don't know. Anywhere.' Abbey rushed away through the hall and slammed the apartment door behind her.

Waves raced up onto the beach, fell hissing in great swathes of white foam and slunk away to rejoin the salty body that was their home. Abbey slipped off her shoes and stood at the edge, letting the cold water splash over her feet. She took a few more steps so that the soothing waves washed around her ankles. Was her mother really poorly again? What would happen to her? She was not Abbey's only worry, there was her son too. Luke was unemployed, he was going to be a father. What a fix. How would they cope? If Abbey had spent more time in England then all these things would not have happened. Perhaps she should go back now. *No, it's too late.* The sea was around her knees, a chilling wetness that rose and fell. Its depths were densely clouded, churning up sand to hide her feet from view. Shoving rudely, it pressed around her thighs, gripping and pulling. Abbey's dress was wet, clinging to her body. A brutish force took her around the hips, dragging her, snatching at her flailing arms. She was savagely engulfed as the waves rode over her. Salt burned the back of her throat and the sky was gone.

Chapter Twenty-One

Jackie stared at the gap, willing it to fill up once more. She tried walking around the boutique just in case she was mistaken. She circled all the stands draped with Italian leather, marched past the glass cabinets filled with twinkling gold from around the world. Perhaps Sarita had rearranged things, moving the collection to another spot. It wasn't behind the counter and it had not been promoted to grace the window display either. With only one exception, Sarita Suelo was set out exactly as it had been last time and each designer's range was still just where it should be. Jackie arrived back at the point where she had started and found herself staring at empty shelves again.

'Good morning, Jackie, how are you?' interrupted Sarita.

Jackie didn't bother returning the saccharine greeting. 'Where's the Gabbini collection?'

'I'm so sorry, no more Gabbini,' said Sarita.

'Never?'

'No, Jackie. Not here or anywhere else. They went bankrupt.'

Jackie's heart sank. 'Oh no. What went wrong?'

'They blamed it on exchange rates or something.' Sarita's tone turned bitter. 'It's an excuse, that's what it is. They took the money and didn't honour their commitments.' She shook her head. 'They owe me thousands. Still, that's my problem, not yours.'

Jackie eyed the void which used to be filled with so many beautiful temptations.

'I don't know what I'm going to do, Jackie.' Sarita's smooth sales pitch was gone. 'It's criminal what they did.' The shop owner looked distraught. 'I can't afford to re-stock. Perhaps I'll have to close.'

'That's preposterous,' exclaimed Jackie. 'There must be something you can fill the gap with.'

'No, not unless it's on sale or return,' Sarita lamented,

'and that stuff is all rubbish.'

'You need something colourful, different. A new range that looks good in the shop,' said Jackie as her face brightened. 'It doesn't have to be made of leather or gold, does it? As long as it's exquisite and expensive.'

'Jackie, like I said, it's over.'

'No, Sarita, you're not finished yet. I know exactly what you can put here.'

Abbey poured out her heart. 'Do you know, he's never once told me that he loves me. Not once.'

'Ah, that's a shame, Abbey. You are so beautiful, how could any man resist?'

Abbey's cheeks coloured. 'Gabriela, you're flattering me. I'm just an ordinary English girl.'

Gabriela sipped her drink. The black coals of her eyes were alive, lit by the staunch spirit of a lifetime spent caring for others. She smoothed her hand over the greying mass of her wiry hair and it sprang back resolutely. 'Men are all the same,' she advised. 'Big and strong on the outside, a lost child inside.'

'Oh, I don't think that's always true. Take Phil for instance, he's not like that at all.'

'Who's Phil?'

'Surely you've met him. You know, Jackie's emergency boyfriend.'

'I might have seen him once when he was visiting you. Is it the fat one?'

Abbey laughed. 'Gabriela, really!'

'Sorry, but that's about all I can remember about him. Did he have a bald head?'

'Yes, that's right. They all think he's useless. Jackie keeps him in order.'

'Does she?' asked Gabriela. She looked at the clock. 'I'll have to go soon, I've got another place to clean before I finish today.'

'That's a pity. What was I saying? Oh yes. Phil is

scared of Jackie, he's under her thumb.' Gabriela looked puzzled, Abbey giggled. 'Oh, perhaps you don't say that here. It means that he does whatever she tells him instead of speaking up for himself.'

'What does he do?'

'You mean his profession? He doesn't seem to do anything any more. He once mentioned something about owning a business in England. That's all I know. He spends a lot of time at The Hotel, using the pool and the gym. You'd never guess it by looking at him, though.'

'Very odd,' commented Gabriela, 'not like a Castillo man at all.'

'No, not at all. He and Lewis are like chalk and cheese.'

'What?'

'Chalk and cheese, things that are completely different to each other.'

'So Phil is weak and Lewis is strong, is that what you mean?' Gabriela stood up and brushed cake crumbs from her clothes.

Abbey got up too. 'No. I mean Lewis looks strong yet he's a softie.'

'That's what I said to start with,' stated Gabriela triumphantly as she turned to the door. 'So it was lucky that he saw you in the water yesterday and pulled you out.'

Abbey's mind cleared as she realised why the coffee-break with Gabriela had been such hard work. 'Oh, it wasn't Lewis that rescued me,' she explained. 'Fat, pathetic, shiny-headed Phil saved my life. That's what I've been trying to say. Inside him is a hero.'

'Do you like it?' Abbey asked with new-found confidence.

'Like it? Of course I do!'

Abbey pushed the bra upwards. Her body lifted with it, two rounds of flesh spilling impressively over the top. 'It's supposed to add two cup sizes. What do you think?' She thrust her chest under Lewis' nose.

He stared, spellbound. 'They're magnificent,' he announced, admiring the display.

'Yes, I thought I'd try one to see if it really worked,' Abbey said. She turned back to the mirror and admired her new outline. 'It's padded,' she explained as she faced him again, 'and under-wired too. It should look good in some of my dresses. Shall I try?'

'Um, no.' Lewis' shirt was off now. 'We can do that in a while.' His hand stroked over her shoulder and reached round the flattering underwear to find its fastener. He squeezed the strap expertly and the clip burst open. Abbey's latest lingerie addition fell away, revealing its pink-tipped cargo. 'It's a very good bra,' agreed Lewis, 'but you look even better now.'

'Oh, Lewis, you are naughty.'

'So?'

'So nothing.' Abbey watched in the mirror as her lover's hands stroked over her skin.

'Does that feel good?' Lewis whispered.

'Mmm.'

'And that?'

'Uhuh.' Abbey melted onto the bed, her eyes closed.

Jackie strode back from Sarita Suelo, each step springing jubilantly. By the time she reached the apartment she was struggling for breath. *It's no good, I'll have to get another car.* She hammered on the door enthusiastically and waited. Nothing happened. She knocked again and tried to turn the handle. Perhaps they were out. Jackie stepped back from under the arch and peered into the dark windows, searching for evidence of life within. There was no-one in the kitchen and the other window was obscured by curtains.

'Hola!' Hello.

Jackie hurried back to the doorway. 'Hi, I lost my key,' she replied casually, sizing up her friend. Abbey looked oddly agitated. There was something about her dress, too. It didn't look quite right. 'Oh, sorry Abbey. Are you busy?' asked Jackie.

'No, not at all.' Abbey coughed meaningfully. 'We've finished now. Are you coming in?'

Jackie followed her inside and noticed something else. 'Your label's sticking out,' she informed Abbey. 'Keep still, I'll tuck it in for you.'

'Oh, it's you,' Lewis greeted the visitor. 'I should have guessed.' He was shirtless, barefoot and unruffled.

'That's not a very nice welcome,' returned Jackie, feigning hurt. 'Come with me, I want to discuss something about Sarita's.'

'Sarita's?' Abbey made as if to follow them.

'Not you Abbey, I'll tell you later.' Jackie flashed a knowing grin at her. 'This is just between me and lover-boy.'

The wooden pews were cold and hard. Sturdily fashioned by some long-gone craftsman, they were uncomfortable relics from a bygone age. High in the chapel tower a lone bell fell quiet. Dusty silence filled the hall, touching all that lay within. It united the ancient oak rafters above with the stone floor below, enveloping everything in between with the musty chill of its joyless caress.

Luke shifted about uneasily in his new suit. 'There are only seven people here, Mum.'

'I know,' Abbey whispered back, 'I've already counted.'

Luke brushed at his cheek. 'It's so sad,' he said hoarsely, 'you'd think more people cared.'

'We're here Luke. That's what matters.' Abbey bowed her head and fumbled for the hymn book. She flicked through its dog-eared pages, barely seeing the verses of unfamiliar praise as they passed before her. Footsteps padded up the aisle behind her. It would probably be rude to look round. 'This might be the minister coming now,' she suggested. The sound stopped and its echoes died away. Abbey felt the archaic bench shiver.

'Lewis, you made it!'

'Hello Abbey. How are you doing?'

'I'm fine,' Abbey lied. 'How did you get here? All the flights were booked solid.'

'I waited at the airport. Eventually someone failed to show up, so I bought his seat.'

'That was clever. You're so resourceful-'

Lewis put a finger to his lips. 'Shh,' he said softly.

'We are gathered here today,' announced the minister with long-practised familiarity.

Abbey felt Lewis' hand fold around hers.

'To remember the life of Rita Violet Houndslow.'

Juan was holding a long metal pole. He poked about with it for a while, grumbling and cursing.

'Would you like me to do it, Juan? I'm taller than you,' Lewis offered.

'No, señor, I can reach.' Juan waved the pole about.

'I can do it,' piped up Abbey.

'Oh no, Abbey, you aren't strong enough,' asserted Juan.

'Yes I am,' returned Abbey with a hint of petulance. 'I've done it lots of times.'

'It's in now.' Creaking and squeaking sounds confirmed Juan's announcement. He cranked the handle on the bottom of the pole, the blue awning extended painfully and noisily. The fabric unfolded as the frame expanded, revealing the words Cafetería de la Luz in proud white letters.

'Ahah, su corona.' Your crown. Lewis pointed to the awning.

'It was Reina's idea to add that,' Juan explained, 'to attract more customers.'

'Yes, it might give you a boost at the end of the season,' Lewis agreed. He looked around for a suitable

table.

'Let's stay outside,' suggested Abbey, 'it's still warm enough.'

'Good idea.' Lewis chose one of the round tables under the shelter of the awning and took his seat.

Abbey pulled a chair around and joined him. 'It's better facing this way, you can watch everyone go by,' she declared.

Lewis dropped a tired-looking manuscript on the glass table top. 'Yes, though there aren't so many now. Just Spaniards and the odd expat.'

Abbey moved closer to Lewis. Across the boulevard, waves lapped innocently upon undisturbed sand. 'Everyone says buen día to me now,' she claimed.

Lewis grunted and turned a page.

'Are you listening to me, Lewis?'

'What?'

'I said that everyone says hello to me.'

'That's because you're so beautiful.'

Abbey studied Lewis carefully. It was quite impossible to tell if his words should be taken seriously.

Lewis tweaked his sunglasses up onto his forehead. 'They know you,' he added by way of explanation.

Deflated, Abbey turned back to people-watching. Juan brought coffee, Lewis rustled his papers, the minutes dawdled casually. The unmistakable smell of tobacco smoke caught Abbey's attention. She leaned forward to get a better view along the pavement. *Oh, of course. I should have known.* Something horrible bounced up to the café.

'I thought I'd find you here.' Jackie leaned over and dropped the remains of a cigarette into the ashtray. 'Well, what do you think?' she prompted.

The dress was garishly striped in pink, white and purple like some kind of children's confectionery. It was ghastly. 'It's, um, striking,' said Abbey with as much enthusiasm as she could muster.

Lewis glanced up from his work and did not hesitate to

offer his opinion. 'Jackie, it's an abomination,' he told her. 'Take it off.'

'Here Lewis, unzip me will you?' Jackie presented her back to him.

Lewis gave up trying to read. 'No, we can't have you sitting here in your knickers. Anyway, it's too cold for that. You can change into something else when you get home.' He pointedly slipped his sunglasses down over his eyes. 'We'll just have to avoid looking directly at you,' he taunted.

Luke was dreaming. He could see Sally and she was as big and fat as an elephant. Her belly was enormous and inside it was his son. He knew that it was a boy because things work like that in this kind of dream. Here the uncertainties of the real world are irrelevant and hidden knowledge is effortlessly revealed. There are never any explanations, there is no need for evidence. You simply feel an intuitive awareness, a fully-fledged perception implanted in your mind. That was how he already knew about the horrible bed-sits. Sally grew larger every day and felt sicker each morning. Her office rang and told her that she had to leave. It was a nightmare. Without money, they had to leave Sally's comfortable flat. The man at the council office found them somewhere to go, a decaying block of monstrous concrete and glass that towered over the shopping centre. Inside were scores of identical box-like rooms filled with hopeless young families. In Luke's dream there were babies crying, jobless youths playing loud music, doors banging. He was asleep but in this place there was no peace and no rest. A woman was groaning. Luke could hear her through the wall. Then he heard a toilet flush. A door opened and the woman walked into his bedroom. Luke was on the edge of terror, fighting to brush away the heavy curtains of sleep.

'You overslept again,' said the woman, 'but it doesn't matter. I'm not going to the office today.'

The voice belonged to Sally. She also owned a swollen belly and a pair of heavy, hanging breasts. Fear surged through Luke. 'Will we have to go to the Centre Flats?'

'What for?' asked Sally softly.

'To live there. You know, when we have to move.'

'Luke, I don't know what you are talking about.' Sally eased herself onto the edge of the bed and stroked his hair. 'You look terrible. What's wrong?'

'I don't know.' Luke desperately tried to hide his vulnerability. 'I must have been dreaming about something,' he blurted, 'but it's alright.' He had to be strong. 'I'll get up now. Would you like a mug of tea?'

Phil stumbled into Jackie's apartment. He dropped his sports bag onto the floor next to him and snorted in disgust. The afternoon was gone, three hours wasted with nothing to show for it. What a weak performance. He hated humiliation and was unaccustomed to defeat. Failing to complete a circuit of the gym was bad, barely managing a dozen lengths of the pool was even worse. He was overwhelmed by fatigue, an unfamiliar inertia that made every movement into a formidable challenge. He struggled to the cavernous kitchen and searched through the cupboards seeking some kind of remedy. After he had dragged his feet around the granite-topped island in the middle a couple of times he realised that he did not even know what he was looking for. He made for the lounge, tripping in slow motion over one of the room-wide steps that divided the apartment. He picked himself up and crossed to the panoramic window. The view over the trees and houses to the Mediterranean beyond was there waiting for him, set out magnificently in green, white and blue. Its beauty seemed distant and elusive, a remote and unreachable scene that his wandering mind could not grasp and hold on to. He gave up and heaved himself onto a sofa, sinking gratefully into its yielding mass. *I'll do better tomorrow.* Phil slipped away, claimed by sleep's casual embrace.

'It was my fault.' Abbey sipped from a tiny white cup. 'I should have gone back and taken care of her.'

'You're being too harsh on yourself,' Lewis said compassionately.

'It wouldn't have made any difference to your mother,' added Jackie.

'Don't you think so?' asked Abbey. Jackie's advice could be right, but it seemed rather harsh.

'No, of course not. Staying with your mother would have been such a pain and she'd have been just the same anyway.' Jackie lit another cigarette. 'You need to think of yourself, Abbey. You can't be held responsible for everyone else, you know.'

'Jackie,' cautioned Lewis.

'What?'

'Go easy on her. She's just lost her mother.' Lewis placed a reassuring hand on Abbey's shoulder.

Jackie spouted a defiant jet of smoke. 'Yes, and I'm trying to help her.' She ploughed on determinedly. 'Things will be easier now, you won't be worrying about her all the time.'

Abbey nodded, unconvinced that things were going to get better.

Jackie had not given up yet. 'I mean, you're free to do as you like now,' she blundered.

Abbey shifted about uncomfortably.

'I'm not doing this right, am I?' Jackie asked her companions.

'No, Jackie, you're not,' confirmed Lewis. 'So, what's Phil doing?'

'Oh, I don't know.' Jackie's cigarette waved about, then made its way back to her lips.

'I thought he might find the time to join us today,' pressed Lewis.

'Phil does what he wants,' said Jackie dismissively.

'Does he?' enquired Lewis cautiously.

'When I let him.' Jackie attempted to laugh but her efforts only produced a strangled snort.

Papers rustled. Lewis reached across the table to save his manuscript from the autumn breeze. Somewhere down by his feet, a once whole cup met its end. 'Damn, I must have caught it with the back of my hand.'

Abbey jumped up. 'I'll get the broom,' she announced.

Lewis motioned her back into the chair. 'You're not on duty until this evening. Leave it, Juan can sweep it up later. It's only a cup.'

'Something bad is going to happen,' Jackie observed.

'It already has,' stated Abbey.

Lewis pulled Abbey close, encircling her shoulders protectively.

'I wasn't referring to Mum,' Abbey said, 'I meant Jackie's dress.'

All three of them laughed.

Jackie stopped. 'You broke a cup, Lewis. It's a sign,' she said emphatically.

'Are you serious?' questioned Lewis, 'That's not like you at all.'

'Like I said,' insisted the woman in the candy-stripe dress, 'something bad is going to happen.'

Chapter Twenty-Two

The gold ones were a feeble deception. They were obviously fake, improbably yellow and just a little less lustrous than they ought to be. The silver coloured ones were really made of steel or something else that was coated with chrome. Alvaro picked up a pack of them. They looked good and strong, with flawless mirror-like surfaces. Still undecided, he put the hooks back and went in search of paint instead. The place was huge, a gargantuan warehouse filled with aisle after aisle of construction materials and tools of every conceivable kind. Despite the shameless claims of their endless advertising, the merchant did not stock everything. There was no Crystal Rose paint. At the long counter where the warehouse roof sloped down to meet the wall, a man in a red shirt was opening small brown cardboard boxes and taking things out of them.

Alvaro was running out of time. 'Discúlpeme.' Excuse me.

The man stopped emptying boxes.

'I need some hooks,' Alvaro told him.

'They're on aisle twenty one.' The uniformed assistant picked up another cube and tore it open.

'Yes, I know,' said Alvaro, 'but I need different hooks. Classy ones.'

'Wait here.'

Alvaro waited alone. Nothing happened for a while.

'Hola.' Hello. Something sweet, short and busty fluttered mascara-heavy eyelashes at the handyman.

Alvaro coughed nervously. It was obvious that the merchant supplied exactly the same red shirt to every employee with absolutely no regard for size or gender. 'Hola,' he replied timidly.

'He won't be long,' said the woman. The brightly coloured cloth stretched tightly over her chest.

Alvaro shuffled from foot to foot and tried to avoid eye

contact. He checked his watch and glanced anxiously in the direction of the car-park outside.

'How about these?' The man was back.

Alvaro turned the heavyweight iron hooks over in his hand. 'Too ornate.'

'Or these?' suggested the man stonily. He pushed some brass-ware at Alvaro.

The handyman's dejection evaporated. They were perfect. 'How much are they?'

'Thirty nine,' came the deadpan reply.

'For packs of two?' asked Alvaro cautiously.

'Oh, no señor, they are thirty nine each.'

Alvaro gulped but he had no choice. 'Seis, por favor.' Six, please.

The red shirt scanned the packets of smart brass hooks at a beeping till. 'Algo más, señor?' Anything else?

'Crystal Rose paint,' said Alvaro. 'There's none on the shelves,' he added as a precautionary defence against further rudeness.

'It's a special colour.'

Alvaro's exasperation grew. 'So can you mix some for me?'

'I don't mix paint, Selena does that,' said the monotonous voice flatly. 'Selena!'

Selena took instructions from her boss, Alvaro ogled her bulging crimson uniform, the musical till beeped joyously.

'So that's a total of two hundred and ninety three,' droned the warehouse supervisor vacantly as he tore off a slip of paper.

Alvaro was stunned. 'Bromeas?' Are you joking?

'That's enough for me, Jackie.' Abbey signalled when her glass of orujo reached half-full. 'I got plastered last time,' she pointed out. 'That stuff is really strong.'

Jackie stopped pouring. 'Don't be such a wimp, Abbey,' she chided, 'it won't hurt you.' With a flourish of the bottle she topped up her own glass instead. 'I'm going to the showroom tomorrow,' she announced.

Abbey looked around the enormous kitchen and wondered what Jackie could possibly find in a showroom that she did not already possess. Jackie's apartment seemed to have grown even larger than Abbey remembered. Perhaps Jackie wanted more furniture or some overpriced and tasteless sculptures to fill all those gaps and open spaces in the lounge.

Jackie stood at her panoramic window, gazing towards the distant horizon. 'It's really big, isn't it?'

'Yes. I wish Lewis' was like this.'

'Not the house, the sea,' laughed Jackie.

Abbey sipped her drink, coughed and joined her friend at the window. 'You can see for miles from here,' she admitted, 'but it's only the Mediterranean. The Atlantic Ocean is lots larger.'

'Well, you can't see that from here,' Jackie retorted petulantly. 'The Mediterranean is fine for me. You could still get lost in it for ever. No-one would ever find you.'

Abbey examined Jackie's face quizzically. Jackie gulped her orujo, faked a smile and changed the subject. 'I'm going to buy a new car. A fast one.'

Abbey gasped. 'Are you sure?'

'Course I am or I wouldn't say it, would I?' Jackie marched across to a sofa and sat down. She patted the seat next to her.

Abbey cautiously joined her prickly friend. 'Will you be safe in it?' she ventured.

'Oh, don't worry about that. I'm going to buy a German one this time. German cars are very safe.' Jackie's voice swelled with enthusiasm. 'Would you like to come to the showroom with me?'

'Why don't you take Phil?' suggested Abbey. 'He'd know what to look out for. Sales staff respect men more, you know. If they think Phil is in charge then you'll get a better price.'

'Phil?' spluttered Jackie. 'In charge? He's not even in charge of his own body.'

'Oh, Jackie,' Abbey remonstrated gently, 'you know that's not true. He does all he can to take care of himself.'

'At any rate, I don't need him. What does the price matter? I'll soon find the money.' Jackie's red lips parted, revealing her teeth and forging a synthetic white grin. 'Hey, I'm going to get another drink,' she said abruptly. 'Want one?'

'Not for me, thank you.'

'Suit yourself then.' Jackie bounded down the broad step. Clinking sounds echoed from the kitchen, accompanied by indistinct muttering. 'I don't know what he's doing in Spain at all. Should never have come here, if you ask me.'

'Were you speaking to me?' asked Abbey.

Jackie stood at Abbey's feet. 'What did I say?'

Abbey was torn between loyalty to her woozy host and concern for an isolated, friendless man. The humanity within her won. 'I think you were saying something about Phil,' she started carefully.

'Was I? Oh yes. He never wanted to come to Spain, Abbey. Did he ever tell you?'

'No, Jackie, he never said anything about that,' Abbey answered. 'He doesn't talk a lot. Perhaps that's why he's misunderstood so much.'

'Is he? Oh.' Jackie brushed the suggestion aside. 'Well, anyway, he wishes he had stayed in England instead of selling up. He had to sack dozens of people when he finished. Really hurt him, or so he says.' Jackie's face brightened. 'I had lunch at La Luz again,' she announced. 'Reina was serving. I thought you might be working there today.'

'I haven't done afternoons there since the summer peak,' explained Abbey, 'and I won't be there at all after this week.'

'Have you been sacked too?' Jackie prodded

mischievously. 'Well, it wasn't much of a job, was it?'

The insults were flowing as quickly as Jackie's orujo bottle was emptying. Abbey wondered if it was time to leave. She counted to ten in her head, the feelings subsided. 'I love working at the café, Jackie. I'll be back there next season.'

'Fine, if that's what you want.'

'I think I'd better go now, Lewis will be waiting for me,' said Abbey, keeping her tone neutral. 'Thanks for the orujo.'

'No problem.' Jackie was sparing with her words. 'Love to Lewis.'

'Thanks, I'll pass it on.'

'Oh, Abbey.' Jackie called her back from the door. 'I nearly forgot to tell you.'

'Yes?'

'Sarita wants to see you.'

Juan slammed the car door shut. It made a horrible noise and bounced back. He gripped the handle and shoved the reluctant door closed once more. This time it stayed where it should. Tutting and grumbling, he walked around his ailing vehicle. At the back he bent down to inspect a tyre. Worn rubber glowered back. The tyre was like an old man and he was mostly bald with a pudgy and bulging waist. This geriatric would have to last for a little while longer. Juan knelt down and looked underneath. Soft shadows from an overcast sky masked the cobweb of pipes and springs that crossed the curved metal floor. Wheezing, he pulled himself upright and leaned against the car. The lights needed checking next. Winter was on its way, mild and almost perfectly unobjectionable. With it would come the darkness of long nights where moisture-laden wind waltzed down from the hills and danced through the streets.

'Juan! Where have you been all morning?'

Juan was taken by surprise. 'Oh, mi querida!' My dear.

249

'Never mind that.' The old lady planted her hands on her hips and awaited his explanation.

'I went to the building supplies merchant.'

'But that's thirty kilometres away.' She nodded towards the road. 'I'm surprised you managed to get there and back without a piece dropping off.'

'But, dear.'

Reina ignored her husband's flustered objections. 'We're not building anything,' she said.

'No. I took Alvaro. He needed some bits.'

'Alvaro? What did you take him for?' challenged Reina. 'He never eats in the café.'

'He has a beer here from time to time,' Juan reminded her.

'A few beers don't merit sixty kilometres, do they? I needed you here doing something useful, not driving your friends around in that rust-heap.' Reina blocked the doorway resolutely.

Juan attempted to edge past his wife.

'You needn't bother, I've finished the accounts now,' Reina responded.

'Accounts?'

'Yes, business accounts. The tax office needs figures every year.'

'Oh, those,' nodded Juan.

'Aha, so you remember them now that I've done all the work.'

Juan's face fell. Earning his pardon was proving more arduous than usual. 'Sorry, dear.'

Reina let her hands drop from her hips. 'It's a lot better that I expected,' she announced. 'They are refunding some tax because we took Abbey on for the summer.'

'That's good!' Juan made another attempt to go inside.

'You're too late now. Go on, get back to your rust-heap and check the headlamps.'

It was over. Delighted to have earned his liberty, Juan set off back to the roadside.

'Don't spend too long on it,' Reina called after him, 'it's not worth it.'

'But, Reina.' Juan stopped and once again prepared to defend his faithful jalopy.

Reina rolled her eyes. 'You're like a child sometimes. Do I have to spell it out to you?'

'Uh?'

'I'm buying you a new one.' The café door slammed, leaving Juan to ponder his wife's words.

The letter box slapped shut letting something heavy and papery flop onto the hallway floor. Lewis raised an eyebrow as he bent down to pick up the envelopes. He didn't get many letters and on the infrequent occasions when the letter box rattled in the door it was usually just a banal document from the council or a leaflet advertising an impossibly cheap Spanish supermarket located miles out of town. He had little inclination to read about the council's plans for painting lines on the roads and even less desire to spend half a day in a remote and soulless shopping centre. He leafed through the wad. There were three identical sheets of gaudy red and yellow, emblazoned with the word Rebajas and far too many exclamation marks. Yet another fake sale at the supermarket then. The flyers fluttered into the waste-paper basket as Lewis passed it on his way to the terrace. He sat down to examine the two letters that remained. Both were fat and full of something. Whether their substance turned out to be thrill or threat remained to be discovered. One was white with a menacing blue imprint on it that said Bower and Salt, Solicitors. Fortunately it was for Abbey. The other one was in a brown envelope with a British stamp on it. There were no other clues at all but it was friendly-looking and heavy with promise. He tore it open and slipped out its tightly folded payload.

'Oh. Bloody hell. I don't believe it.' Lewis read the cream-coloured page again to make sure. 'Yes!' He leaped up and punched the air. 'I don't believe it! Yes! Yes! Oh yes!'

That was just the covering letter, an invitation to explore the ream of ivory paper bundled with it. His fingers trembled with excitement. There was a lot to check through, fine print packed with archaically fashioned legal terms. Right at the foot was a blank space and a plain black line. He reached into his pocket and drew out a plastic ball point pen. All it needed was an extravagant flourish to draw out a swirling corkscrew of ink that bore a resemblance to the name Lewis Coleman. He spread out the document on the wooden table and uncapped the pen. *Wait, this is too important to sign with a biro. I need a proper pen.*

'Abbey. I though you were still asleep.'

Abbey stood in the doorway, blinking. Autumn wind played disrespectfully with her morning hair, whipping it across her cheeks and tangling it around her neck. 'I heard some shouting. It sounded like a man, I think.' She brushed in vain at her chaotic mane.

'That's odd,' said Lewis, coolly evasive.

'Didn't you hear him?' asked Abbey. She caught sight of the paper-strewn table. 'What's all that?'

'Oh, it's...' Lewis stalled. Now was not the time. 'It's something I've been working on. There's a letter for you, too.'

'Great.'

Lewis set about tidying Abbey's hair as she tore open the seal. 'Bower and Salt,' she exclaimed with dismay. 'No.'

'What's up?' enquired Lewis.

'It's Mother.' Abbey shook herself free from Lewis. 'Why did she have to use them, of all people? It's not fair. Even when she's dead she still does it.' Abbey choked on her words, her shoulders shook. 'It's from the people who messed up my divorce. They want me go to back to sort out Mother's will. I expect they have already bungled that too. You can have it back. I don't want it.' She crumpled her papers into a rough ball and thrust it at her boyfriend.

Lewis calmly took the spiky mass. He placed a steadying hand on Abbey's shoulder.

'Leave me alone.' Abbey shrugged his hand away. 'No-one cares about me.'

'Like I said before, there are givers and takers, Abbey. You need to be kind to yourself.'

Abbey sniffed. 'Why should I?'

Lewis changed tack. 'I care about you, Abbey.'

'No you don't.'

'I do.'

'Then why don't you show it? You never do anything unless it pleases you,' spluttered Abbey forlornly.

Lewis studied Abbey's tear-streaked cheeks. He noticed the way that the little lines around the corners of her eyes crinkled, how her mouth sagged miserably at the corners under the weight of her troublesome news. He wrapped his arms around her and pulled her close. An unfamiliar sensation grew within him. It seemed to begin in his chest, radiating out into his arms, his fingers, his head. Fleetingly, Lewis wondered if that was what love felt like. He draped himself around Abbey, comforting and warming her like a soft cape. 'I do care,' he whispered.

Shop-fitting for Sarita Suelo was always a challenge. She was the finicky kind, a perfectionist who could find the subtlest flaws and insist on having them put right. Wise to this, Alvaro had gone to a great deal of trouble to be sure that everything was perfect. The wall was as flat as a sheet of glass and beautifully painted to match the rest of the shop exactly. Columns of smart brass hooks, arranged like buttons on a military tunic, marched up the expanse of subtle pink.

'How did you get Crystal Rose?' asked Sarita. 'I thought they'd stopped making it.'

Finding a match for that paint had been unexpectedly bothersome and costly. Alvaro eyed his client, wondering how much to tell her. It was best not to grumble too much, especially to a regular customer. 'That's correct,' he explained. 'It's not in the paint catalogues any more. It was difficult but I managed to find some.'

'It's a shame that it will soon be half-covered with pictures, then, isn't it?' Sarita marched about, inspecting the hooks and checking that they lined up properly.

'Have you tried the lights yet?' Alvaro's simple query resulted in perplexed silence. Incredibly, Sarita had missed something. Ever patient, Alvaro merely smiled politely. 'There's a new switch in the back room,' he revealed. The ends of his moustache twitched again. 'I've labelled it Gallery. I hope that's alright.'

'Gallery? That's a good word.' Sarita smiled sheepishly. 'Do you know, I've been so distracted that I never even thought about a name. Flick the switch for me, will you? I want to see the lights come on.' Sarita stationed herself in the middle of her new gallery and waited. A blade of pure white light washed down, smooth and uniform. Sarita clapped her hands together. 'Oh, que estupendo!' How wonderful, she exclaimed.

'Thank you, señora.' Alvaro pulled a slip of paper out from a breast pocket on his overalls. 'Perhaps you could take care of this?'

'Your bill?' Sarita Suelo inhaled deeply, marshalling the remnants of her shattered dignity. 'Leave it on the counter would you, Alvaro? I'll pay you next month.'

Abbey knitted her brow. The strident voice on the phone was instantly recognisable and entirely unwelcome. Each word was venom, a little packet of acid spite that travelled a thousand miles in an instant and lost none of its poison on the way.

'Hello Vanessa. Yes, it's Abbey.' *What have I done? Surely they can't blame me for anything after all this time.* 'I'm fine, thank you.' Abbey responded automatically. It did not really matter whether what she said was true, Vanessa would not care either way and almost any answer would do. The witch was talking again, saying how Infotext had gone from strength to strength. Abbey wandered over to her easel and started spreading a fresh sheet of vellum over it. 'Sales have gone through the roof? That's great, Vanessa.' Abbey pretended to be impressed.

Lewis appeared. He trailed about after Abbey and made no attempt to disguise his curiosity. Abbey ignored him. She opened the clips on her easel and slipped the edges of the sheet under them. 'In the marketing department? I see,' she said, trying to open a new pack of brushes. It was quite impossible with one hand so they would have to wait until Vanessa finished. 'No, Vanessa, he hasn't got a job, at least he didn't seem to be doing anything when I last spoke to him.' The voice on the phone was sugared with courtesy yet its tone was rigidly hostile. Abbey answered Vanessa's questions but kept her thoughts to herself. *What a vile woman. She's still horrid even when she says nice things.* 'It all sounds rather glamorous. Yes, he could do that,' Abbey confirmed. 'Of course he's very reliable, too,' she added for good measure.

Lewis pressed closer, desperate to share in the drama. He strained to hear the other side of the conversation. Irritated, Abbey waved him away. 'Smart and professional appearance?' Abbey grimaced. Lewis was loitering outside and his cigar smoke drifted into the apartment. 'Well, I haven't seen him lately but he always looks presentable,' she fibbed as she strode over to the door and pushed it closed. 'Yes, I'm sure next week will be fine, Vanessa. Thank you so much. Bye.'

'Yes!' Abbey shouted. The irony of it all was quite exquisite. For the first time in years she laughed heartily. 'I don't believe it. Oh, yes!'

Two men sat behind a long oak desk. One of them leaned forward stiffly and offered Lewis a dry handshake.

'Mr Coleman?'

'Yes.' Lewis acknowledged his name and took his seat.

'I'm Mr Salt, one of the partners,' announced the man stonily. Abbey stared at the solicitor's thick, old-fashioned spectacles. *No one wears glasses like that any more.* 'Please take a seat, Miss Houndslow,' Mr Salt instructed.

Abbey sat and shuffled nervously. The heavy chairs were ornate works that looked like they dated from Empire times.

'We are very sorry to hear of your sad loss,' said Mr Salt without feeling. His junior accomplice nodded obediently and ran his fingers down an unforgivably gaudy tie. 'Excuse me a moment.' The veteran lawyer shuffled through his papers.

'This is ridiculous,' Abbey whispered to Lewis. 'It's not like Mother owned much. Just how many overpaid solicitors does it take to read out a list of tatty old knick-knacks?'

Mr Salt coughed drily. 'First we have to go through a few formalities.' He pulled out a document and placed it squarely on the desk in front of him. 'Miss Houndslow, I trust that you'll be taking advantage of our investment advisor.' It was more of a statement than a question.

Abbey stole a glance at the young man with the horrible tie. He smiled back expectantly. Abbey realised that she was supposed to agree to the suggestion without questioning it. 'No thank you, Mr Salt. I don't think I shall be doing that,' she said firmly.

'Miss Houndslow.' Mr Salt leaned forward and scrutinised Abbey over the top of those terrible black spectacles. His stare skewered Abbey to the sturdy wooden members of her chair-back. He spoke deliberately and slowly, framing each word with rigorous precision. 'Miss Houndslow, five and three quarter million is a lot of money. It's not the sort of sum that you can just put in an ordinary savings account.' He paused to draw breath. 'You will be needing advice.'

Chapter Twenty-Three

There were windows everywhere, together making a belt of glass that completely encircled the office. Each pane was half-covered with some kind of frosted coating. All but the very tallest giraffes there had to stand up if they wanted to see what was going on outside the world of Infotext. The company valued its image immensely. Ever boastful, it favoured tall buildings that towered over the neighbourhood. Luke stood at his desk and watched. Far below him, narrow boats snaked along a canal and passed under the ancient stone bridge whose sturdy span bound together the two halves of a chaotic English town. He smoothed down his suit, worn only once before. He would be wearing smart clothes five days a week from now on.

'Luke Houndslow?' A man with a big nose and a small beard wanted to know. 'I'm Stephen Green.'

'Ah, good morning Mr Green,' said Luke politely.

'It's usually just Steve,' said the manager. He tugged at his beard thoughtfully. 'Though they call me some other names too,' he added wryly.

Luke chuckled, establishing an easy connection with the first boss of his career.

'I'll leave you to find your bearings,' said the bearded one. 'I'll be back in a while to discuss your first campaign.'

'Sounds fun,' Luke suggested.

'Oh, it is. We need a new brochure designing for the European team.' Steve's eyes twinkled mischievously. 'They were expecting it last week.'

Luke's eyebrows soared. 'Last week?'

'Don't worry, everything happens like that here. I thought it would be a nice little task to get you started on.' Steve tilted his head. 'The coffee machine is over there. Help yourself.'

'Thank you.'

'No problem. You'll probably be drinking quite a lot of it,' Steve laughed.

Luke pulled up his brand new swivel chair and made himself comfortable in it. Diffuse light bathed him. He leaned forward and pressed a button. The screen in front of him brightened. 'Welcome to Infotext,' it said. Just one click and Luke was on board. He was sailing into a new chapter of his life, embarking upon an enthralling journey packed with just the right kind of interesting artistic and technical challenges. Ahead lay the rewards of a good job with security, a sense of purpose and of course a salary paid every month. It was everything a family man could hope for.

Jackie pulled hard on the wheel. The boat swung through the harbour entrance at El Puerto Pequeño, the little port. It slewed across the smooth water within. She pulled back on the wheel, aiming for the gap she left two hours earlier. It was easy enough to spot, the summer season was long closed and no-one else had taken their craft out. Jackie's yacht turned back on itself like a puppy trying to catch its own tail. A couple more twists would do it now. The bow lined up, Jackie focussed on the berth ahead of her and opened the engine's throttle. The propeller burbled powerfully at the stern, projecting the boat forward like a blue and white dart. Masts and jetties and ropes flashed past, tantalising the very edges of Jackie's vision. As her craft shot in between its neighbours, Jackie sensed that she had done something wrong. In a desperate panic she threw the control into reverse. Water foamed up, kicking back vainly as the terrible noises started. Jackie thought that she counted three collisions. First the bow hit the stout wooden moorings, then everything twisted and port and starboard sides struck each of the adjacent yachts in turn. When the din stopped she threw a rope ashore, clambered off and took stock. It looked bad, but nothing like as nasty as she expected. It was fortunate that Abbey and Lewis were away. There might be enough time to get the damage fixed before they saw it and asked awkward questions. Of course Phil would not have crashed the boat like that. He took it out to sea like an old salt and he would have brought it back home just as expertly, slipping it elegantly into the berth and bringing it to rest in just the right position. *Well, it's done now.* She had to bring her craft back alone because there was no-one else to do it now. That was the whole point of the journey. Turning her back on the harbour, Jackie laughed bitterly. It was a hollow, desolate sound.

The sign on the door bore the name Mr N Holden. Its owner pushed down on a tarnished brass handle and breezed through into the room beyond. A distasteful, stale aroma greeted Abbey and Lewis as they followed him into a tight, darkly panelled little box. Abbey tried to avoid inhaling any more deeply than was absolutely necessary.

'I'm Nigel Holden,' announced the young man with the offensive tie. 'Do take a seat.' His guests stepped reluctantly closer to a pair of tired-looking chairs that faced the solitary desk. 'Not too fresh in here is it?' Mr Holden suggested, though he seemed quite untroubled by it.

Abbey looked from her host to the tiny window and back again. *It stinks of sweat.* 'Perhaps you don't use this room very much,' she offered.

'Oh, I'm in here all day,' said Mr Holden proudly. 'It's my office.'

Abbey glanced at the window again. 'Could you, um...'

'Let some fresh air in? Certainly.' Mr Holden busied himself with the creaking window-stay. After a good deal of pushing and grumbling he succeeded in propping the rusty porthole open. Cool, fresh oxygen swirled in.

'Thank you,' said Abbey, the relief plainly evident in her voice.

'Yes, thank you Nigel,' echoed Lewis.

'It's Mr Holden,' the advisor sniffed. He took his seat behind the desk. 'Now then, the estate of Mrs Rita

Houndslow. It's quite a tricky one, you know.'

'Is it?' Abbey interjected.

'Share holdings, property investments, gilts, bonds.' The man who must not be addressed as Nigel looked up from his paperwork. 'I've made a start on it already, Miss Houndslow.'

'You have? That's news to me, Mr Holden.' No-one had gone to the trouble of consulting Abbey first.

'Excellent. We thought that you would approve.' Mr Holden ploughed on obliviously. 'It seems that a lot of the assets were written in the name of Hart. Mr Thomas Hart.'

'Oh my God!' gasped Abbey, covering her open mouth with the flat of her hand. 'That's Tom.'

'You know of the gentleman?'

'Yes, of course I do. He was Mother's boyfriend.'

The advisor shot a quizzical look.

'That's not what she called him,' explained Abbey. 'She always said that Tom was her companion.'

'I see. So, this Mr Hart appears to have been a most fortunate man. Wise too, by the look of it.'

Lewis coughed noisily and fidgeted about, allowing his elbow to nudge against Abbey's arm.

Questions needed to be asked and Abbey took the cue perfectly. 'What makes you say that, Mr Holden?'

'Mr Hart was careful to assign his assets to benefit you after your mother's death. Naturally the tax-man would like to take a rather generous slice of the pie too.'

'Oh.' Abbey's heart sank.

'Don't worry, we know what we're doing. We're not like that lot over there in the Matrimony department.' Mr Holden nodded in their direction. 'We understand our clients and respect their wishes. Mrs Houndslow and Mr Hart can rest peacefully.' He looked genuinely sad for a second, then smiled conspiratorially. 'You'll get what's due to you, Miss Houndslow. Every penny of it.'

Two men stood at the bar. Convivial chatter rose and

fell behind them, peppering them with women's voices that bubbled and shrieked. The door to Cafetería de la Luz was propped open, jammed in position by a hand-sized wedge of wood. The ancient timber chock was bruised and beaten. Every edge and corner of it had been rounded off by the daily battering that was its only reward for a life of lowly service. Chirping cicadas hid amongst the tired remains of summer leaves out on the boulevard, each still calling forlornly for a mate. Their rasping tones, the ever-present sound of the Mediterranean night, stole uninvited into La Luz. Lewis drew on a cigar and the tip of the leaf-brown stick glowed orange. The smoke curled away, escaping to join the noisy insects under the warm blanket of another southern night. The café owner had endured life-long punishment, buffeted by the conflicts and demands of his business and his wife. Like the door wedge, he had taken the knocks in good humour and carried on undaunted. He continued to serve his customers with simple Spanish food and amiable conversation.

'Más bebidas, señores?' More drinks, gentlemen?

'Yes, Juan,' Lewis replied. He turned to the other customer. 'Another Estrella, Alvaro?'

'Sí,' Alvaro confirmed without a moment's pause, 'but let me pay for the beer this evening. I owe Juan a favour.'

'No, I'll get them. I'm expecting some money soon,' insisted Lewis.

'You mean from your prometida?' Alvaro suggested.

'No, from my publisher,' Lewis retorted, 'and Abbey is not my fiancée, Alvaro. Just my girlfriend.'

'That's not what everyone is saying,' said Alvaro, fumbling in his pocket for money.

'Everyone?' Lewis asked.

'Well, so Juan says.'

'Juan?' Lewis challenged their host.

The overweight proprietor chuckled heartily, producing a confession of guilt from the depths of his belly. He drew two large glasses of cool blonde beverage and set them on the counter-top. 'Put that cash away, my friends. These are gifts from La Luz.'

Lewis picked up a glass and tasted the nectar. 'Very kind of you, Juan. Thank you.'

'Yes, very kind,' agreed Alvaro.

'But don't let Reina find out,' Lewis winked at Juan, 'or she'll sack you.'

Abbey needed to organise her thoughts. This meant writing lists of things to do, shepherding vague notions and inspired ideas into purposeful order. The first list was meant to be all the things that she must do right away, mostly tedious and joyless tasks to tidy up loose ends. After that came an inventory of little treats to spread out over the next few weeks. Finally, on a page all to itself she set out a hand-drawn table and drew horizontal lines to split it into twelve sections. This was how she would manage the first full year of her new life, scheduling her dreams into a month by month programme.

'This is how my boobs are going to look,' announced a fruity voice.

Abbey looked up from her notepad and found herself staring at a straining bodice.

'Oh no, Jackie,' exclaimed Abbey, 'surely you're not going to.'

'You know me,' Jackie assured her friend. 'I'm booked in for next month.' She giggled like a teenage school-girl as she fished for a cigarette packet in her handbag. 'I'll be enormous. The men won't be able to resist me,' she claimed confidently, depositing herself in a chair and poking a cigarette between her cherry lips. 'You look busy. What are you writing?'

'I'm planning what I'm going to do,' said Abbey.

'Whatever for?'

'So I don't forget anything.'

'I wouldn't waste your time, Abbey. Just do whatever you feel like.' As she spoke, Jackie signalled across the café to Juan.

'I can't do that, Jackie. It's just not my style,' replied Abbey.

'It's high time you changed, then,' Jackie counselled. 'Live your life as it comes. That's what I do,' she declared blithely. 'Buenas tardes, Juan.'

Juan chuckled at Jackie's hopelessly British accent. She looked very pleased with herself, all lipstick and smiles. 'Buenas tardes,' he returned her greeting. 'Two glasses of wine?'

'Can we have two bottles of Rioja Castillo please, Juan?'

'Two bottles?' Juan quickly covered his surprise. 'Of course, señora.'

Jackie turned back to her compatriot. 'They're delivering my new car on Monday,' she announced.

'That's fantastic, Jackie,' returned Abbey, surprised at finding herself completely immune to Jackie's boasting. *It will be even more vulgar than her previous one.* 'I bet it's red.'

Jackie gasped. 'How did you know that?' she exclaimed.

'Oh, I just knew,' said Abbey flippantly.

'It's coming at eleven. I expect you already knew that as well,' Jackie snorted.

Abbey shook her head. 'No, I didn't.'

'Why don't you come round?' Jackie suggested. 'We could drive out somewhere.'

'Um.' None of Abbey's lists included a danger-filled car ride with Jackie.

'Ladies!' Juan leaned over the two women, straining to glean details of their conversation. He filled their glasses expertly, all the while gawking at the compelling sight of Jackie's padded bosom.

'Thank you Juan,' said Jackie pointedly.

'You're welcome, señora,' Juan boomed. He hovered around the table, clearing plates and waiting for the gossip to resume. 'Can I get you anything else?' he asked.

'No, that's all.' Jackie folded her arms across her chest.

'Thank you Juan, the wine's lovely,' said Abbey sweetly.

'Don't encourage him,' hissed Jackie. She watched as Juan's oily bulk made its way back to the bar. She picked up her glass and swirled it around before taking a graceless gulp of its contents. 'This one's always good. You can't go wrong with Rioja Castillo,' she stated with conviction. 'Try to keep up with me this time,' she added.

'Sorry, I didn't know it was a race.' Abbey took her first sip.

Jackie pressed on. 'You could have your boobs done too, sweetie,' she said, perfectly straight-faced.

Abbey shuddered at the ridiculous term of endearment, then threw one right back. 'Oh, I don't think so, darling,' she said lightly. 'It's just not me.'

Jackie slurped at the plum-coloured wine as she studied Abbey's petite form. 'Hmm, maybe you're right,' she conceded. 'Anyway, two thousand isn't anything like enough.'

Abbey's glass paused mid-air. 'Two thousand?'

'That's what I said. Sarita sold two of your paintings this morning.'

'She's got away with it,' Juan announced. 'Look at her. Not a care in the world.'

Lewis nodded sagely, Alvaro looked blank.

Juan was polishing glasses and arranging them on a shelf behind the bar. 'I wonder who will be next,' he pondered aloud.

'It won't be me,' said Lewis.

Hushed by ignorance, Alvaro shuffled about uncomfortably.

'Alvaro, you're supposed to be the one who spreads all the rumours,' Lewis goaded. 'If you came in here more

264

often then you'd know what was going on, amigo.' He addressed Alvaro as a friend.

Juan leant on the bar. 'He's right,' he assured Alvaro, 'you hear it all here. Speaking of which,' he said as he turned to Lewis, 'what's all this about you and Abbey? Have you booked the castle for your wedding?'

'Juan, we're not even engaged. The castle would be fun, though, wouldn't it? I expect we could afford it now.' Lewis threw a quick glance over his shoulder. Satisfied that the women were well out of earshot, he continued in a conspiratorial tone. 'Just imagine how different it could have been. If I hadn't been careful I might have ended up with Jackie.'

Juan grinned. 'Why do you think she'd have you anyway? Engreído!' Big-head!

They all laughed, guffawing like a bunch of carefree youths. Three grown men – a café owner, a handyman and a writer – were united by the universal bond that ties friends together the world over.

The moon was in a cheeky mood. Round and full and very white, it watched as Abbey and Lewis walked home. It lost sight of them from time to time as they disappeared under trees or roofs that momentarily cloaked them in deep shadows where the moon's cool gaze could not reach. The game of hide and seek continued all the way from Cafetería de la Luz to Lewis' apartment. From time to time the figures on the pavement paused and melded into one for a moment or so. Then they separated again, though not by very much, and continued along. In the gardens below the apartment, moonbeams and street lights cast a web of light and dark, falling upon the ground like a lacy net. Abbey and Lewis hid amongst the trees for a long time. Cicadas chirped, warm night air moved gently through the gardens and the moon crept higher. Serene, untroubled, it lingered patiently over the roof-tops. At last the figures reappeared. Like amusing little animals they hopped over

265

the low wall onto the terrace and back into the silvery caress of the moon's silken light.

'Oh, it's so lovely out here tonight,' sighed Abbey as she pulled back from Lewis' embrace. Her eyes glittered, diamonds that twinkled clear and silver in the moonlight. She felt Lewis brush away a drift of hair from her cheek. The cicadas in the garden fell silent.

'Abbey?' started Lewis.

'Yes?'

'I...'

'Umm? What is it, Lewis?' Abbey prompted gently. She felt his arms tighten around her shoulders.

'Abbey, I love you.' Lewis pulled her close and pressed his lips against hers.

Abbey felt herself melting into his world, becoming part of everything that defined him. This land of warmth and love and light would be hers too. There was just one thing that she had to do. For once impetuous and impulsive, she abandoned her habitual caution. The time was now. This was the moment to re-schedule her dream programme and bring one item forward. She wriggled free. 'Lewis?'

'Uhuh?' intoned Lewis deeply. The exquisite green of his eyes reflected the mysteries of the evening's shadows.

Abbey's honeyed voice did not waver. 'Will you marry me?'

'Yes, Abbey,' breathed Lewis. 'Yes!'

Abbey felt those strong arms around her again and this time she allowed herself to surrender, fully and completely.

Printed in Great Britain
by Amazon